PENGUIN BOOKS

SWEET BRAISED DUCK

Chew Ngee Tan was born and raised in Singapore with a love for reading and writing. She graduated from the National University of Singapore, majoring in Sociology. She completed a Master's degree in Liberal Studies at Rice University in Texas, USA, after working as an English Language and Social Studies educator in Singapore for a few years. Always intrigued by her own and others' experiences, historical events, and nature, she is now a writer who creates stories to capture the beauty of being human and the interconnectedness of life. *Sweet Braised Duck* is her first novel.

Sweet Braised Duck

Chew Ngee Tan

PENGUIN BOOKS

An imprint of Penguin Random House

PENGUIN BOOKS

USA | Canada | UK | Ireland | Australia
New Zealand | India | South Africa | China | Southeast Asia

Penguin Books is part of the Penguin Random House group of companies
whose addresses can be found at global.penguinrandomhouse.com

Published by Penguin Random House SEA Pte Ltd
9, Changi South Street 3, Level 08-01,
Singapore 486361

Penguin
Random House
SEA

First published in Penguin Books by Penguin Random House SEA 2023

Copyright © Chew Ngee Tan 2023

ISBN 9789815058864

Typeset in Adobe Caslon Pro by MAP Systems, Bangalore, India

www.penguin.sg

For Papa and Mama, with all my love and gratitude.
And for those, whose stories are lost to history.

Contents

Author's Note

Traditionally, Chinese people demonstrate respect by how they address one another. The Chinese maintain the use of titles when addressing one another in a family. It is common to hear people addressing each other using terms that describe their relationship instead of names. It is important to know how to correctly address a family member.

In this book, you will notice that the protagonist uses 'Ah Beh' instead of the usual 'Ah Ba' that Teochew community use to address the father. The protagonist also addresses his mother using 'Ah Mm' instead of 'Ah Ai'. 'Ah Beh' refers to the father's older brother and 'Ah Mm' refers to the father's older brother's wife in Teochew. In the past, some Chinese families were careful about the way children address their parents. There was a belief that children would one day be taken away or separated from their parents if they addressed their parents as 'Ah Ba' and 'Ah Ai'. Such kinship titles were considered intimate. Intimacy between children and parents might bring about separation or disharmony within the family. Therefore, children were taught to address their parents by titles used to refer to relatives.

Introduction

My father has been a traditional Teochew braised duck rice hawker in Singapore for many years. He rented an old-styled *kopitiam* for his business in the initial years and later moved to a stall in a market. It is a family business and my mother has been his greatest help. My parents work hard at the stall to keep the business going. They raised their four children with the money earned, always planning and saving for us. We are grateful we never have to go hungry. In fact, we always have more than enough.

For the past thirty-five years of my life, my parents would occasionally bring home leftover rice, braised duck meat and different parts of duck such as head, neck, gizzard, liver, intestine, feet and wings for our dinner. They are amazing. After eating my father's ducks for many years, I am still very much in love with this dish. All of us are.

One day my father told me he would be closing his business, perhaps in the next few years' time. I knew all along my parents are getting on in years and will not be able to manage the family business eventually. But when I first heard about my father's decision, I was filled with a lot of emotions. I felt a certain sorrow that only departures could bring. I could not imagine not having any more of my father's braised ducks to eat.

Braised ducks are a big part of my childhood. It has helped to strengthen our family bonds when we sit down to eat them together while sharing our lives with one another. Braised ducks are my father's pride. When he talks about his ducks, his eyes gleam with joy and satisfaction even now. I learned a lot about mastering an art to perfection from my father's attitude towards braising ducks. When my father's business was on the verge of collapsing after he moved his stall to the market a few years ago, all of us came together and strategized. Memories, like these, are precious. I will keep them forever in me.

I asked myself how I could continue my father's duck rice business. Many thoughts came to me. I could continue the business or change the business concept. But I may not be able to retain the original flavour of my father's duck rice. The duck rice I, or anyone else, will make will be different from the one my father makes. So, what is it I hope to keep?

I began to recall my father's stories. Those snippets of his younger days shared with me over dinner when we were staying together. My father's spirit of never giving up and continuous learning is admirable. He is a tough man, both inside and out. I hope his stories would continue to inspire others. I hope my children would know their grandfather's greatness. And most importantly, I want to celebrate him, the father whom I respect and a typical hawker we meet every day at the markets or hawker centres in Singapore whom we may not pay much attention to.

So, I started interviewing my father. I flipped through old albums at home, did a lot of research about Singapore's early days, and crafted open-ended questions for our discussion. Through a series of interviews with him, I was able to spin a whole new narrative and create a hero who has some traits of my father. I had a very fun time talking with my father. He is an exemplary storyteller who can describe scenes and people in fine detail. His descriptions often took me to the past, enabling me to write as if I were in the same room with my characters, living with them.

Besides allowing me to understand my father on a deeper level, this project also gave me a chance to find out more about the history of Singapore's unique and ever-changing food scene. Every dish has its own story and hawker food has always been central to life in Singapore. When I was abroad, I deeply craved Singapore food. I realized I do not just eat hawker food back home. Hawker food connects me to others, shapes my culture, and has provided me with a broad range of gastronomic choices while growing up. It is something I am very grateful for. Our hawker culture thrives not just because of the wide array of finger-licking food, but also the people who create them. Their stories matter. They are a big part of our Singaporean identity. Thus, I wish to honour them, as well as preserve the hawker culture by sharing a slice of life in this book.

At the same time, I want to sing praises of women of the past and present through this project, particularly women whose voices are suppressed due to repression and intimidation. I want to give voice to those women. They helped to build our nation in significant ways that were untold. Without them, perhaps Singapore would be different from what it is now. I also want to applaud women who work tirelessly behind-the-scenes in families and at workplaces. I share traits of my mother in this story. She is a woman of great love and strong conviction. This book exemplifies women's strengths. Women help to secure families and bring up children. As Singapore works towards our shared vision of a fairer and more inclusive society where men and women partner each other as equals, I hope women's hard work and sacrifices in our everyday life would be noticed and applauded.

This book is inspired by the experiences of my own family and those around me. Some of the events are real. This book tells how a boy lived through difficult times after arriving in Singapore with his mother in 1957. Through his lens, we understand the uncertainty and danger in early Singapore. This story is also about the process of growing up. The protagonist in the story had fun, faced challenges, struggled with decision-making, had regrets, and made mistakes. These are all natural. Youth is a time of problems, pain, and confusion. While he was grappling with them, he also learned to look forward and advance. I hope this story offers you hope and inspiration to face whatever challenges may come your way in your life.

Part One

Courage

One

'Kuang! Here!' Uncle Tham's eyes gleamed and touched mine. His palm waved in the air as I ran ecstatically to his stall. Then using his rough fingers, he carefully picked a few golden-brown *galy poks* from the small table in front of him and put them in a brown paper bag.

He looked up and waited. His wide grin remained unchanged.

'Ey, Uncle Tham!' I cried in exhilaration as I finally arrived. Salty drops flowed down my face and went into my mouth. Both my bowl-cut hair and dirtied uniform were saturated. They clung onto my skin, refusing to let go.

'Here you go, Kuang!' Uncle Tham swung the bag of buttery pockets of curry to my face. I bounced and seized it with my hands.

The delightful aroma of potatoes, onions, chicken, some special herbs and spices enveloped me. It seemed to have wafted out of the savoury crust, and crept into my nose, tickling those tiny hairs in my nostrils.

Galy pok was my favourite snack. It was love at first bite. Years ago, when I first ate Uncle Tham's galy pok, I was impressed by the thick aromatic spicy fillings that oozed out from the insanely thin crusts. It felt like a gentle stream of thick molten lava flowing in my mouth. Simple yet heartwarming. The mix of its viscous fillings and crispy flakey skin won me over instantaneously. It grew dangerously addictive with each bite, making me crave more and more.

So, I patronized Uncle Tham's stall once every month. It took me about twenty-eight days to accumulate ten golden cents. I had to scrimp to submit to my insane yearning. With ten cents, I could delight in two pouches of heaven.

It was all worth it.

As much as I craved for the puffs themselves, I also craved for the moment I exchanged a few coins for them. The feeling of holding some coins in my hand was blissful.

Uncle Tham's galy poks were beyond finger-licking good. They were mouth-watering. Succulent. Rich. Simply divine. How did he derive a recipe that was so unique?

In secret, I envied him for earning a living while eating these toothsome puffs. A way for him to survive would always be available thanks to his cooking skills.

I liked this hopeful feeling.

Sometimes I would imagine myself wearing Uncle Tham's clothes, making amazing food, and feeling gratified spotting long queues in front of my stall.

I let this idea stay in my vague dreams, at the back of my mind, collecting dust but never discarded.

But today, Uncle Tham did not seem to enjoy his puffs the way he always did. He was munching the sturdy flaky exterior off without catching any glimpse of it while kneading the dough for the next batch. He constantly lifted his head up to browse the surroundings, and then lowered it to focus back on his puffs. His brows stayed a little wrinkled while his hands were busy with the dough.

His expression was familiar. Stony but a little nervy. It echoed mine at dinner every evening.

* * *

Mue, kah na cai, cai pou neng.

Every single evening. The dishes on our dining table never changed.

It was depressing gathering at the table with ten people with two pathetic plates of food to share. I stared at the food vacantly, wishing for some changes that would never take place.

Not in this lifetime.

How about a plate of steamed yellow-roe crabs? Or fermented bean chicken? I smiled wistfully, running my finger along the edge of our table, as saliva kept accumulating in my mouth.

'Kuang,' a voice called out to me. I tuned out of my desires and returned to reality.

'Save for your brothers and sister, Kuang,' Ah Mm nudged me. Her tone was soft and careful. Like a gentle whisper murmured into my ears.

Of course, I did. I always listened to Ah Mm. I knew she had the kindest intention.

I could not ask for more porridge even though I really wished to. *I know. Just half a bowl.* An extra scoop of porridge would invite glares from those judging eyes lurking around. So, I held on to my half-a-bowl, saving myself from unnecessary guilt.

My eyes caught a glimpse of my siblings around me. Some were staring at the food, ready to begin. Some were playing with their chopsticks. One of them stabbed chopsticks into the fried egg and was immediately scowled at.

'Bad luck!' A voice yelled out. The chopsticks were grabbed away and thrown onto the floor.

No one moved. Not even our heads.

I pursed my lips.

Slowly, I scanned the table. After making sure everyone had enough in their bowls, I then lowered my head and focused back on my bowl of watery white grains.

Stony but a little nervy.

A dozen spiralled-patterned flattened pastry doughs sat before me like half-moons. Mesmerized, my thoughts drifted back to Uncle Tham. He was an amazing man. Not only because he made amazing galy poks. It was thanks to his help that Ah Mm and I managed to come to Singapore, after all.

Two

My family lived in Feng Mei village in Shantou, China, before moving to Singapore.

Ah Mm said Shantou was a special place. It lay at the mouth of the powerful Han River and gazed out at the sparkling South China Sea. It was a beautiful harbour city, home to many great mountains. Its winters were short and mild whereas summers were long, dry, and dreary.

The people living in Shantou mostly spoke the Teochew dialect and lived the Teochew's way of life. We were alike. Renowned for our love of drinking tea, for us, it was better to be without rice for three days, than without tea for a day.

Ah Mm made a huge pot of oolong tea every afternoon. She placed a little spoonful of tea leaves into the pot and added a lot of boiling water to it. It was not as rich as what people would have at inns and restaurants but still, I delighted in this simple ritual of tea drinking with my family after dinner.

At my village, everyone lived in old courtyard houses set out in neat squares and rows alongside the fields. The houses were made up of sturdy wooden structures and delicately engulfed bricked roofs.

Most people in my village were related in one way or another by blood or marriage. The entire Feng Mei village was inhabited by one surname-clan. When I was residing in Feng Mei village, a stranger walking along the streets could easily be my distant relative. The Teochew people regarded one another as *gaginang*, my own people. I grew to enjoy being in a tight-knit community. Almost everyone showed thoughtfulness towards one another, especially the young and old.

I could not quite recall my childhood in Shantou. My memories of those days felt like blurred rusty pages. I remembered my skin was bad. Terrible. Reddish-tanned brown, sunburnt most of the time. I scurried around half-naked every day during the long summers, with only a pair of shorts to preserve my dignity.

Blisters and clumps formed easily when little insects bit me. They occupied my body and made me scratch like a monkey. When those bumps broke open, pus oozed out like runny yolk escaping a poached egg. I had a terrible time bearing the itch and pain.

Children in my village were scattered around like dispersed seeds. We scampered out of our houses early in the morning after we had finished what we ought to do in the fields.

I followed the big brothers and sisters who lived in my neighbourhood, going in and out of their houses. To us, every object was a toy. We climbed onto heaps of rubble, made bamboo shoots into spears, and rolled in the mud when the rain fell.

We loved running in rivers and swimming in the open air.

I also watched them play pranks on adults and learn tricks from their friends. I could not remember how many times I broke into loud laughter when I was with them. We enjoyed watching the reactions of our unsuspecting victims, pronouncing victory the moment our little pranks landed others in momentary dismay. It was entertaining!

Such fun days left the deepest impression on me. I cherished those days as a child.

Since I was always out playing, I did not see my parents much.

Our dilapidated house could not contain my will for freedom. While nothing much in the house could make me stay, I had no choice but to return home for dinner. Ah Mm's plain dishes did not surprise my taste buds, but at the very least, they assured me that life could go on.

Mue, kah na cai, cai pou neng.

Every day, needless to check out what was laid on the table, I nipped a piece of something with my wooden chopsticks, tossed it into my mouth, and slurped a big mouthful of porridge. Loud and wild. I could hoover down a vast trough of porridge in five minutes, just like Ah Beh. The louder it was, the better.

Feng Mei village was my entire world. Rarely had I taken a step out of it. I had not had any thought of leaving it, or should I say, I did not know what existed outside of this old town.

* * *

Life was hard for my parents. They were always covered in sweat, and they always looked tired.

Ah Beh was a tall brawny man, with a large-boned torso and over used muscles. He had dark glowing skin just like me. Trained to carry heavy weights since a young age, Ah Beh could walk briskly even when he was lugging two big full pails of water on his shoulders.

Ah Mm always asked me to listen to Ah Beh. His words were very important. There was a good chance I would suffer a bad outcome if I ignored them. So, I listened to Ah Beh a lot. Ah Mm said that was the right thing to do.

I had mixed feelings towards Ah Beh. I respected him, yet at the same time, I was fearful of him. I often did not know what to say to him when we sat together. A mountain of words on my mind just collapsed into a few before I discharged them out of my mouth.

Ah Beh's deep powerful voice could easily scare me out of my wits whenever he yelled at me. He always said I was born with a pointed buttock, one that could not stay still on the ground. When I first heard Ah Beh saying that, I was worried. He did not sound like he was joking. Was I abnormal? I went around the town, eyeing buttocks of all sizes and fretting about my own, making myself a laughing stock.

Ah Beh worked at our tiny rice farm all the time. He worked like a dog to make ends meet. Together with my Ah Ma and two Ah Gou, they levelled, rolled, and prepared the fields. They also planted seedlings, weeded, and harvested the grains all by themselves.

Sixteen hours a day. Seven days a week.

It was no wonder Ah Ma and two Ah Guo were all skinny and brown as well. Their fingers were a bunch of old ginger strapped together.

I remember squatting in the fields with Ah Beh standing right in front of me, pulling out weeds. I lifted my head and gazed at him. His shadowy face ate into the blazing sun. Beads of his perspiration rained on me. For every decent Teochew man in my village, nothing was more important than fulfilling his duties as son, husband, and father. Ah Beh's firm determination to secure our livelihood was beyond my understanding at the age of five. Nevertheless, endless gratitude flowed within me whenever I thought of him working his fingers to the bone for the family.

Life was simple in Feng Mei village. We were pinching pennies, but we had enough to live on.

* * *

Our rural life revolved around the seasons. Mother Nature, however, did not make our life easy at times. The powdery soil in our field and the occasional extreme weather conditions made rice cultivation tedious and labour-consuming. Whenever harvests were bad, I could feel my parents' spirits being devoured by lack.

My parents' silence would reverberate throughout the house if they were unable to provide enough food. When there were no accompanying dishes on our table, Ah Mm would sprinkle some soy sauce into my porridge. She then stirred them, turning my white grains into thick brown goo. Sometimes, when we could not even afford to have grains, Ah Mm's eyes would shun mine when she scooped just rice water into my bowl.

'Even heavens want to forsake us,' Ah Mm tended to murmur to herself at times like these. Sometimes, she blamed the heavens for our plight. At other times, she lowered her head and apologized to the heavens.

Ah Mm was a fine-looking Teochew lady. A heart-shaped face, a small mouth with full but down-turned lips, and a pair of almond-shaped eyes below those full and natural-looking eyebrows. Though dull, her eyes could be striking at times when she was telling stories.

Ah Mm was also a virtuous wife and a caring mother, overseeing all domestic matters with diligence and thrift. She also showed great respect to Ah Beh by providing a listening ear for his woes. She loved embroidery and enjoyed making Teochew *kueh* whenever we had more money to spare. She married Ah Beh at a young age, entrusting her whole life to him. I had never heard her complain about anything at all, even though she had to survive all household chores on her own. She strongly believed in the working of deities, that they certainly would protect those who were sincere and tried their best.

When days were tough, she would pay a visit to the nearby temple and pray to Tor Ti Gong for security and luck.

Once, I caught Ah Mm kneeling with a stooped posture and blinking hard, refusing to let tears circle in her eyes as she prayed at the temple. Thighs tightened, her eyes were fixed on the godly figurine and her clamped-shut palms were shaking rhythmically. This image was engraved upon my heart for a very long time.

The sight of Ah Mm being overwhelmed told me something was not right. I watched her with a pained gaze, taking deep breaths to calm myself. The thought of swallowing brown goo or sipping cloudy water made me breathless, and I wished we would not have to do so for as long as possible. Since the age of five, I knew I did not want to be poor. A life without enough food meant a hard one.

I also prayed silently in my heart for Ah Mm to be happy.

* * *

I had never seen Ah Gong. He was absent since 1948. Nonetheless, I was curious about him. I began asking about Ah Gong when I turned older, and Ah Mm would share with me about him in secret. I got to learn more about my family history from Ah Mm's storytelling every evening when we were alone at home.

Ah Mm shared that Ah Gong had travelled to Singapore to seek fortune because he did not like to work hard at our farm. *How does one seek fortune? Can fortune really be sought after?*

'The heavens reward diligent people. Working hard is the noblest virtue, Kuang,' Ah Mm emphasized in a gentle tone after she spoke about Ah Gong's decision to travel overseas, as if hinting to me not to follow Ah Gong's footsteps. She certainly did not believe in money dropping from the skies.

According to Ah Mm, people in the village had always tittle-tattled how great Singapore was.

'Get a new life in Nanyang! Go for that golden land of opportunities! Those who went over to Singapore had grown rich and gained significant wealth within a short while!'

Rumours spread like wildfire. Such words tempted the hearts of those who craved easy success. Ah Gong was one of them.

He was bold. An indolent man with guts but lacked directions in life. He craved pleasure more than anything else. When he was living at Feng Mei village, he hollered at the family day and night. He would complain how hard he worked, but in truth, he always left the heavy chores to the women and his son while he skived at the backyard, puffing on his hand-rolled cigarettes.

No one in the family stopped Ah Gong from leaving for Singapore. No one wanted to. In fact, no one could because for the Teochew family, the grandfather was always the leader. Everyone respected him just because he was the grandfather.

Ah Ma and my parents fell silent when Ah Gong revealed his decision to venture southward. Even though his decision made them worry, it allowed them to hope for a better future.

Perhaps this time, he could achieve something.

Hope fortified their hearts and brought a glimpse of dawn in the deepest of darkness within them. Silently, the family wished him luck. And Ah Gong left without a word a few weeks later.

The migratory wave swept Ah Gong across the South China Sea in August 1948. He travelled by sea and managed to reach Singapore after some weeks. Unlike other Teochew migrants who remitted a part of their wages to their family at their homelands, Ah Gong's departure for a greener pasture made him a missing man. There was no news about him for the next three years.

* * *

A cloud of gloom hovered over my family for a very long time after Ah Gong was gone.

Amid the chaos brought about by the economic and social reformation in China, Ah Ma's concern for Ah Gong had never once ceased. In fact, everyone in the family yearned to know Ah Gong's whereabouts. They asked around the village and their fellow villagers helped to spread news about his disappearance. Month after month, hopes for his return began to vanish until one day, Ah Ma's nephew brought them a message.

His friend, also a Teochew from Shantou, was residing in Singapore and he managed to trace Ah Gong after a long time.

'Tieng has remarried.' Words in the letter stabbed my family like a piercing sword.

Clarity was harder to swallow than imagined fears.

Ah Mm told me it was the first time Ah Beh felt both disbelief and blame stirring into a massive ball in his heart. Ah Gong's long absence from home seemed to have hardened Ah Ma's heart. Her eyes had become a dry well since the arrival of the message and never did she mention a single word about the man who had betrayed her.

She kept that letter in her wooden chest. She also kept mum about her sorrow, which could be felt deeply but could not be seen.

Three

It was the year 1952. One morning when the wintry sun was the brightest, I was born. Ah Mm said the birth of me brought solace and fresh hopes to my family.

Nearing the end of winter, trees were getting ready to show their lofty arms. The air still bore the coldness and the river opposite our village appeared still. Sunrays fell upon my delicate skin as Ah Mm rocked me in her arms in the gentlest rhythm, hymning a melodious Teochew lullaby. The hint of my newborn smile also lifted every part of her being.

Ah Mm finally became a mother after so many years of waiting. She thought hardship had left her barren, like the parched earth that could not produce plants. Women who could not bear children were wasted lands.

Becoming a mother gave her a new purpose to live on. Life was no longer just about household chores and farming. It was also about providing enough for a new life. The whole family worked hard together to raise me up.

A Chinese proverb says, 'The pine stays green in winter, wisdom in hardship.' My family had forged closer relationships amidst the past years of adversity. Everyone also seemed to have grown in his or her role, especially Ah Beh.

The absence of a male leading figure in the family required Ah Beh to mature overnight. Ah Mm believed Ah Beh had already assumed this role a long time ago when Ah Gong was living with them. But now when heads were turned to him for decision-making, Ah Beh could not bite his lips anymore. He needed to say and act like he knew it best. That was a difficult thing to do.

* * *

Ah Mm knew Ah Beh's struggles. For the next five years, she fervently prayed for a better life for the family.

One of our gaginang from the village visited my family one day. I had never met him before. I recalled that morning Ah Beh said he was travelling to the market to hook up an ox to work in the fields. Ah Mm and I were surprised when he returned home with a guest in the afternoon.

Soon after the guest sat down and had his first sip of the *ganggu-te* Ah Mm brought him, he opened up to my parents about a possible route to a better life.

I ran to Ah Mm and curled myself up on her lap, watching tiny droplets of saliva travelling in the air as the two men talked loudly with each other.

'Opportunity knocks but once, Wak,' the guest tried his best to sell Ah Beh on going to Singapore with him. He claimed that fate had brought Ah Gong and him together in Singapore. A big mouthful of saliva droplets splashed into the air as he spoke. He explained non-stop, not giving Ah Beh a chance to say anything.

He also said Ah Gong wanted Ah Beh to go to Singapore. Good future. Many Teochew men from Shantou dreamt to go to Singapore. And he even mentioned Ah Gong's second wife. She could converse in the Malay language! That would make things easy.

The guest finally paused and stared at Ah Beh, waiting for his agreement. He then took another sip of the tea to clear his throat, as if getting ready for another round of persuasion.

I grew tired of staring at the two men with my side-lying posture. I rolled to the floor, and lay my body straight. Ah Mm moved my head and placed it on her lap.

'I am returning to Singapore next month. Come with me,' the guest added on. His voice was filled with so much enthusiasm.

An odd expression passed over Ah Beh's face, one that I did not understand at all. He gazed vacantly into the distance as he continued to listen to the guest. I turned my head on Ah Mm's lap to look at Ah Beh. Somehow, I knew some changes were going to take place. I could also feel a lot of strange emotions waiting to seep into Ah Beh's life if he made his decision.

The air in the room was heavy. It blanketed us and restricted Ah Beh's and Ah Mm's movements. Ah Beh stayed still for a long time. His head, lips and eyes were all stuck. Only his stomach bulged out and caved in. He remained silent for a long time before saying he would think about it.

Ah Mm sat in a corner, caressing my head in a repeated motion. On the contrary, Ah Mm's stomach did not bulge and cave as smoothly as Ah Beh's. Its movements were irregular. I could somehow hear noise within her too. The noise, however, did not just come from her stomach. It was a kind of messy noise that had consumed her whole being. Her frowns arched and almost touched each other. Then, released.

'Ah Mm,' I called. Her lips parted and she looked down. I could see her reddened eyes in the gaps of her thin eyelashes. Ah Mm looked into my eyes and hesitantly stretched her lips. She then slowly looked up again. Her lips moved slightly, mumbling something to herself. I could roughly make out the words. *Don't go, Wak.* After a while, Ah Mm moved her lips again. *Just go, Wak.* This string of words made up that messy noise and that messy noise made Ah Mm very sad.

* * *

Ah Beh was usually quiet. It was rare for him to open his mouth to speak. If he were to do so, it meant he really had something important to share. And when he spoke firmly and with some emotions, it meant that important something was an urgent thing.

One evening, Ah Beh spoke with a lot of crazy emotions over dinner.

Ah Beh said something about our farm. In the past, we could make a living with our harvests but now, the authority wanted to confiscate our land. We had to join some collective farming associations. Some people said this would make farming more efficient.

Ah Beh, however, doubted this proposal. He hissed and swore that great threats would befall the family if that happened. We might not have enough food to eat if we had to depend on the labor performed by all other farmers in the collective. What if there were people who decided to free-ride on the efforts of others?

I did not really understand Ah Beh's words. He was talking in gibberish. But in his mouthful of difficult words, I caught one sentence. Not enough food to eat. *What does this mean? More brown goo?* I gasped and widened my eyes. I hated brown goo. I did not want to eat it.

I shook my head vigorously.

Ah Beh said he did not want the family to go through another round of extreme deprivation and fear. Ah Ma nodded. My two Ah Gou also nodded.

They continued talking in gibberish. Ah Ma said, better to go than die together. Then, Ah Beh nodded.

The only person whose head did not move at all was Ah Mm. She sat at a corner of the house with her eyes blinking and blinking.

* * *

After many days of pondering, Ah Beh decided to heed his friend's advice and was set on travelling to Singapore. Ah Mm told me he was prepared for hardships. Ah Beh told Ah Mm he would come back rich, lead his family to betterment, to die here in Shantou and be buried where his ancestors were.

'Wak ah, come back soon. Next time, bring us with you. I want to follow you,' Ah Mm said as she pressed into Ah Beh's arms a few packets of *png* kueh and a soft blanket before he left for Singapore a month later. Her voice was trembling.

I stood beside Ah Mm, watching tears stream down her cheeks. She wiped them away with the back of her fingers. *Don't go, Wak.* Again, I could hear the same loud messy noise pounding within her. *Just go, Wak.* It reverberated into my being and I felt a void in my heart.

'Mui.' Ah Beh replied calmly. '*Mai kao.* Our future is shrouded by so much uncertainty. I don't know what would happen. Wait for my letter,' Ah Beh replied, looking firmly into her swollen eyes.

'It's time for me to go.'

The sun began to set. Ah Beh left without turning back to look at us. Ah Mm stood still, wiping her runny nose with her sleeves, many times, and then corrected her posture before dragging her feet back into the house.

I stood still in the long shadow of our courtyard house.

That day, I had so much to tell Ah Beh. But the words all remained unsaid.

* * *

Ah Beh sent Ah Mm a very long letter a few weeks after he set off for Singapore. A few pieces of brown coarse papers with words inked vertically. While reading the letter, Ah Mm wept. I could not help but plead Ah Mm to read the letter out to me. I wanted very much to know what had happened to Ah Beh.

Ah Mm did. As she read, her tears pitter-pattered on my feet.

Ah Beh was confined to a very tight space in a small ship on the route to Singapore. The people were packed like a herd of cattle. It was impossible to move even an inch.

Many people fell sick and vomited on the journey. The foul-smelling vomit odour was awfully unbearable. One middle-aged man passed away on the fourth day and had to be overthrown into the seas. Witnessing those painful moments, Ah Beh cringed. A sudden sensation of dread overcame him.

But Ah Beh did not forget about his promise to his family. As Ah Mm read the letter, I noticed Ah Beh's repeated usage of the phrases 'rest assured' and 'I will be alright'. *Would Ah Beh be fine?* The journey to Singapore seemed so tough.

Nevertheless, Ah Beh was fiercely determined to rise up against all odds despite being tangled in his own knots of insecurity. The letter did not mention Ah Beh's desire to return home, at all. Ah Beh indeed was a man who devoted his life to his family and would fulfil his promises no matter what.

After journeying on the sea, all the immigrants onboard were led to a station at Saint John's Island, one of the Southern Islands in Singapore. All immigrants needed to be screened for many diseases before they could enter the main island.

Ah Beh said days spent at Saint John's Island were a relief as compared to the terrible conditions inside the ship. He was at least given wholesome food and clean water to drink. However, it was a long wait. Besides the checks, one could do nothing except wait for permission to leave.

* * *

Ah Beh waited patiently. The long-awaited arrival day finally came after one week.

He reached Singapore on a bright day. When the ship docked at the bay, he was immediately overwhelmed by the complexity of the bustling port city. Ah Beh said Singapore was an interesting place. Unfamiliar tropical smells, strange-coloured people, and loud incomprehensible gibbering. Coming from a homogeneous village with a very close-knit community, at first Ah Beh felt extremely uneasy just thinking about his new reality. He did not know where to put himself in a foreign multicultural setting. But Ah Beh moved on to say that he was alright after some time. *Was he really fine?* Singapore seemed like a weird place to live in.

Following his friend, Ah Beh was introduced to a *towkay*. Without much money on hand, experience, and legal protection, Ah Beh ended up as a contracted *kuli*, manual labourer, for the mining industry.

Because of his well-muscled build, Ah Beh shared that his towkay made him carry five times the weight of what a normal kuli could endure in order to gain more profits.

Ah Mm gagged in tears when she read this part out to me. She thought the new life for Ah Beh in Singapore was not much better than the life he had fled. In fact, it was worse. It was true that Ah Beh was making more money. But he was definitely coping with an aching heart and a bruised body.

*　*　*

Ah Beh talked about the reunion with his long-lost father and new stepmother too.

He said Ah Gong had changed for the worse. He had failed to accomplish anything at all. He had been living off his wife who earned a meager sum as an illegal street hawker.

Ah Beh also wrote that Ah Gong and new Ah Ma had been asking him for money. It dawned on him that Ah Gong had suggested he come to Singapore not for the sake of his future, but instead for Ah Gong's own easy access to more money. Nonetheless, Ah Beh said he would be filial to them, regardless.

In his letter, Ah Beh also shared that he yearned longingly for Ah Mm and me. He was confronted with a strong sense of emptiness and boredom every now and then and he had no one to turn to.

Even though Ah Beh was immediately absorbed into a Teochew enclave at Boat Quay, and he met many gaginang from Shantou at his new home, he felt distant from them. He kept to himself all the time until he encountered Uncle Tham, the galy pok hawker whom Ah Beh bought his quick snack from during his break time at work.

In his letter, Ah Beh sang many praises of Uncle Tham. He said Uncle Tham was the kindest soul he had ever met.

Uncle Tham had been a travelling hawker in Singapore since 1950. He was an innovative man who tried to infuse his hometown spices with elements of Indian snacks and English puff pastries and sell them in crispy buttery pockets. His puffs were famous amongst residents and labourers at the Singapore River.

Ah Beh could not be more thankful towards Uncle Tham for his generosity. He would always give Ah Beh an extra puff for the standard price of two, knowing that Ah Beh had laboured so hard. Ah Beh would squat alongside Uncle Tham's stall by the Singapore River, chomping his galy poks while nattering non-stop with him.

Straightforward, and without pretense, Uncle Tham's heartfelt words allowed Ah Beh to be vulnerable in his sharing of feelings and experiences. Ah Beh revealed his desire to bring Ah Mm and me over to Singapore.

And, in Ah Beh's own words, penned resolutely in his letter, he told us how Uncle Tham had gently urged him to bring us over soon. 'Don't wait. Don't worry about all the paperwork. I can help you. My English not so good but I can still write and understand. *Bang sim*. I won't make the mistake of telling the officers you're bringing three wives over from China,' Uncle Tham had said while patting Ah Beh's shoulders assuredly.

To be understood is probably the first step to move forward. Thanks to Uncle Tham's encouraging words, Ah Beh dared to take his first step amidst the uncertainty.

So, that was how Ah Mm and I landed in Singapore. We came to Singapore a few months after Ah Beh, with the help of Uncle Tham.

Four

Never-ending summer. A madhouse. Extreme liveliness. A melting pot. I loved Singapore the moment I arrived.

From all the letters Ah Beh had sent us, I imagined Singapore as a place filled with many fun things to play and people of all colours. Dynamic and vibrant, it was a grand fishing port developing into a busy city. It must be totally different from our tiny Feng Mei village. If following those big brothers and sisters around to play tricks on others was this exciting, coming to Singapore was ten times more thrilling.

I had many sleepless nights before Ah Mm and I boarded the boat to Singapore. As much as I wanted to travel out of my village to see the world, my heart shrank into a meat ball, bouncing off my internal walls at times when I thought about leaving.

Ah Mm asked if I was sad leaving Feng Mei village.

I was.

I could not bear to leave Ah Ma and Ah Gou, as well as those big brothers and sisters whom I played with. Ah Ma was touching my head and face with her wrinkled hands a lot more. My two Ah Gou bought two packs of my favourite creamy milk candies and passed them to me before we set off. They kept telling me to be careful. And when they said it, they sniffed and sniffed. My nose too, stung and watered.

I guessed I would miss our farm and courtyard house a lot. Ah Beh said he was living in an apartment at a shophouse now. Just four walls and that was all. I could not imagine it. *What is an apartment? How big is it? How does a shophouse look like?* I could not wait to see it for myself.

Before I left the village, I turned around to have one last look at the rows of enclosed dwellings. The slanted brick roofs, the sturdy wooden structures, the fields and the ever-flowing river made a beautiful picture that was etched deeply in my heart. Goodbye, my hometown. *Will I be back soon? Or will I not?* The beautiful image blurred as my eyelids turned hot.

Nonetheless, those flashy images of Singapore formed in my head as we read Ah Beh's letters gave me the courage to wave to everyone, to even overcome the long and dull boat ride across the sea. I got to go through all that Ah Beh had experienced travelling to Singapore. It was insanely suffocating to be in a boat with so many people. But at the very least, I had Ah Mm next to me, assuring me that everything would be alright.

I sucked on the creamy candies, blotting out discomfort by focusing on my sweetened mouth.

* * *

I could still remember the moment Ah Mm and I walked across the long uneven plank connecting our miserable boat to the port of Singapore. I loved the fresh air. Breathing it made me feel invigorated. There were stars twinkling in my legs, making them wobbly. I guessed I bent my legs for too long in the boat. As we walked, Mm wrapped her hands around my armpits.

The plank shook. I was oscillating right and left.

'Candy!' I yelled out loud after dropping my last creamy candy into the sea. 'My candy!'

Flustered, I struggled to break free from Ah Mm's hold.

'Forget it, Kuang! *Gia!* Walk! Walk on!' Ah Mm shouted, squeezing my armpits even tighter and moving me forward.

Looking at the point where my candy hit the surface of the water, I shook my head. My last candy was gone.

Soon, sweetness was also gone from my mouth.

We jolted through the crowd to finally see Ah Beh and another man standing at the far end, their faces strained with worry and anticipation. Ah Beh was half-naked, with a towel hanging on his neck. I could tell that his tanned skin had turned duller and coarse. There were marks and discolourations here and there on his chest.

I called out to Ah Beh straightaway, this time without reservation.

'AH BEH! AH BEH! HERE!' I raised my voice and shrieked, waving my little hand in the air as I bounced my feet on the ground. I could not contain my excitement. My heart became a squashed tomato spurting a lot of juice.

Ah Beh spotted us. The worried look on his face transformed into a blooming flower, exuding joy. Even though Ah Beh was happy to see us, he did not run to us or even smile at us. He was the same old Ah Beh who stood reservedly and still like a soldier waiting to receive command. The only expression of his joy was perhaps the releasing of his folded arms to the sides.

Ah Mm was ambling slowly behind me. After catching sight of Ah Beh, she walked even slower, falling far behind. I turned my head around to look at her. Her eyes turned red as she placed her hand over her mouth, eyeing straight ahead. I could feel all the raucous noise within her dissipate into the air when her eyes met Ah Beh's. I knew Ah Mm was finally free of her sadness despite her crying.

I saw a middle-aged man with a baby face standing next to Ah Beh. He had deep dimples on both sides of his cheeks, and fine features on his face, almost looking like a beautiful lady. I knew almost instantly that the man must be Uncle Tham. As he spoke, I noticed his eloquence in different languages. He spoke to us in fluent Teochew, introducing himself and welcoming us warmly with his words. In order to get us some local street snacks, he ran to two street vendors ahead of us and spoke to them separately in strange languages. I was stunned by his ability to communicate with different people. He was absolutely impressive.

'Here, Kuang, have this! It's heavenly.' Uncle Tham exclaimed while shoving a little bag of long golden-yellow fritters to me. On closer look, I saw little white sesame seeds scattered everywhere on the crispy skin.

'What . . . What's this?' I asked, raising my brows and frowning at the same time.

'Haha! Smell it!' Uncle Tham replied, looking at me with his gently smiling eyes.

I bent my head a little and moved my nose closer. The fritters smelled like something I knew! I had tasted this before. My memories tracked back to the day I walked the streets of our town with Ah Mm last year. Locals were tending to their rice, sweet potato, vegetables of all kinds, and soybean on the lower banks of the river. I remembered there was also . . . Yes! Banana! Ah Mm bought one for me to try and it tasted so sweet. I would never forget the smell and taste of it.

'Is this banana?' I asked, my eyes glossed with a layer of curious glaze.

'Wa! *Jin kiang* ah Kuang! So smart! You're right! It's fried banana! In Singapore, we call it *goreng pisang*. See those people over there? Their skin colour is different from us and they speak a different language. Even though they're different, their food is amazing! So much spices and flavour. Uncle Tham makes galy poks. I learnt so much from them. Next time, you shall have a taste!'

My mouth stayed open as I listened to Uncle Tham. Saliva leaked non-stop from everywhere within it.

'Taste it! Taste it!' Uncle Tham said, hurrying me to have my first bite.

I nodded and bit into it. The banana within the crispy, chunky wrap oozed out straightaway. It was moistened by the fragrant oil that sprang out from the flattened golden-brown skin. But I did not just taste banana and oil. I could taste nuts, rice, and something else. Like a kind of fried fish. They all combined into a sweet and salty sticky batter as I continued to chew it in my mouth. It was one of the best things I had ever tasted thus far.

'Kuang, Singapore is a great place! There is so much more for you to experience. You're going to have fun.' Uncle Tham continued, pinching my cheek with his oily fingers, and laughing.

I was five, turning six. An age of exploration and discovery. I could not wait to start my life anew in this foreign land.

* * *

Well, let me be honest.

Coming to Singapore was not all roses. Dread settled in my stomach once I met my long-lost grandfather and new step-grandmother.

The first time we met, there was an awkward silence blanketing us, making me feel suffocated. Ah Gong's vile and black-toothed smirk excavated feelings of loathing buried deep in my heart. His jaws were sharply squarish and his big eyes bulged under those bushy brows as he glared at me. As he spoke, his upper lip curled into a snarl.

I was certain he was a spinetingling zombie in disguise. I could feel a strong desire in me to either escape or go on the defensive. My mind cycled through possible responses I could give him when he talked to me, and my body shrank in on itself. Perhaps Ah Gong did not like my sagging posture and stammering very much.

Ah Gong loathed me the first moment we met. I knew it. I did not like him, either.

I took a deep breath and huddled close to Ah Mm, eyes darting from Ah Beh to Ah Gong to my new Ah Ma. Ah Mm's body was very stiff. Like a stone-carved sculpture leaning forwards, her posture so stooped. Her facial muscles all tensed up and she kept clearing her throat as she smiled.

Ah Beh's eyes were different from what they were at the port. Curious yet nervy. He nodded slightly at Ah Gong and began moving our bags to their rightful places and arranging things in the apartment, making himself busy.

New Ah Ma looked very different from the old Ah Ma back at Shantou. She was a plump woman with disproportionately fat thighs. Her stomach popped out and I could spot a thick layer under her tight-fitting sleeveless *cheongsam* top. Her hair was black and her skin was tight and youthful. She had a high forehead and a broad flat nose that looked like a pig's snout. *How old is she? Is she younger than Ah Mm? Or just a little older?* She did not look like a kind woman. Keeping a distance from us, Ah Ma crossed her arms over her chest as she spoke quickly in her low and hardened voice, sometimes eyeing us from the corner of her eyes.

My lips pressed tight into a grimace and my hands hung loose and lifeless. The big reunion tied a big knot in my stomach and set me off in trepidation.

Even though I was relieved by Ah Beh's decision to bring us over, I had doubts about it the very moment I met Ah Gong. The mere presence of him had terrorized me right from the beginning.

* * *

For the first three months after arriving in Singapore, Ah Mm kept me at home. It was not fun at all. Ah Mm said that outside was dangerous. She did not want me to risk my life in a foreign place.

The only thing that was fun was a brown box with a loudspeaker hidden behind a weaved screen and a black knob at the side, placed on a base that was mounted onto the wall. It had long thick lines connected to it. I was curious about it when I first came. Ah Beh told me it was a 丽的呼声, re-diffusion radio set. And Rediffusion was the only cable-transmitted radio station in Singapore. With just five dollars a month, we could get a box, install it into our home, and listen to dramas anytime we wanted. With Ah Ma's little income from selling grass jelly drink and Ah Beh's income from being a kuli, we could still afford it.

I admired it for a long time. Early in the morning when Ah Beh turned it on before he went out to work, Teochew stories would be read out. Operas, news, entertainment-based programmes, and sometimes even Ang Moh rock 'n' roll music. It kept Ah Mm and me very entertained. In fact, it helped us to assimilate into Singapore's way of life. Everywhere we went, we could see this brown box. Kopitiams and neighbours' apartments all had it. People gathered to listen to stories and we could join in if we were outside. Sometimes, Ah Mm even used those stories to strike up conversations with one or two neighbours. That brown box connected us to more people, and live the stories it read out.

Sometimes on Ah Beh's rest days, he brought me to Ah Ma's grass jelly drink stall a few miles away. Ah Ma gradually accepted me, probably because, as I had heard her and Ah Mm discuss before, she had no children of her own even though she yearned to have one.

Her stall consisted only of a large tank filled with black-coloured water, strips of black jelly, and ice cubes. Scooping black mixture into cups for customers was her way of selling it. Occasionally, she would pass a cup or two to an Indian hawker next to her. In return, that Indian hawker would invite me over to his stall and make a big hair puff on my head with his comb using the coconut oil he was selling. When he passed a yellowed mirror to me, I was shocked to see a big puff firmly anchored to my scalp. The Indian hawker said it was *stylo!* Really stylo!

That was how I got introduced to people of different skin colours. Soon, I became brave enough to approach them on my own, those street hawkers I saw along the streets where I lived. Eventually, I also managed to pick up a few phrases in other languages.

After Ah Mm grew more assured of our district, I could go out to play. I often had elastic wars with the boys living along the same street. Armed with rubber bands and paper missiles, we took joy in running along streets, aiming at one another. Other times, our victims were wary cats or birds, or poor old unsuspected hawkers peddling feather dusters and brooms in the neighbourhood. Occasionally, we played catch and challenged one another's balance while standing on empty tin cans. We also ventured into the bushes and woods to catch spiders and watched them fight in bowls or matchboxes.

To be honest, aside from facing Ah Gong, Singapore was heaven on earth. During my first year here, I had a great deal of fun. However, eventually, my happy memories of Singapore were replaced by more complicated negative emotions when Ah Mm had more babies. About a year after we came to Singapore, my second brother, Dak, was born. His arrival marked the end of my free days.

* * *

'Kuang, feed Dak! Kuang, carry Dak! Kuang, bring Dak with you!' My ears were ringing with those orders all the time.

My other siblings arrived one after another in a short span of the next few years. My world collapsed. From Kuang, I became just a big brother. Ah Hia, they called.

We also stopped subscribing to Rediffusion stories because of the lack of money. I was very sad.

Ah Gong doted on my younger brothers, Dak and Siu especially, and always compared me with them. In his eyes, Dak was always clever. I was always stupid. I only knew how to act clever. *Geh Kiang*, Ah Gong always used these words. Dak's limbs could move so fast though he was still a young child. But my hands still worked like a pair of useless legs though I was already a big boy.

Many times, when Ah Beh was away at work, Ah Gong would flare over the tiniest issue such as me spilling a little water on the table during lunch. Sometimes he would even cane me with his old, tattered belt while yelling, 'Jinxed son. Your Ah Beh must be so ashamed to have you as his son. You're nothing but trouble.' Staring at the red marks all over my body, I wondered what was missing in me that made Ah Gong hate me so much. Was I not his grandson too?

I dared not tell Ah Beh about all these. I did not want to bring troubles to Ah Beh. Furthermore, I did not know how to share.

Every time when Ah Gong barked at me, I would exchange fearful glances with Ah Mm. But she never uttered a word.

She would frown and look down at her hands. Then she would look up again to check on me but remained silent. The edges of her lips trembled while she shrugged weakly. I could see red veins occupying Ah Mm's reddened eyes.

Not only did Ah Gong make my life bitter, but his existence also took away Ah Mm's right to speak freely. Ah Mm's voice had never been so faint. Her suppressed desire to protect me was evident on her face, but she was powerless to change anything.

I wondered if Ah Mm ever told Ah Beh about all that were happening at home. Every night when Ah Beh returned home, with his skin all tanned and burnt, he would go straight to bed after washing up and having dinner. He looked really tired. And I did not see them talking to each other at all.

It got harder at night when I was alone with my thoughts. Listening to the occasional barking of faraway dogs, I longed for those carefree days at Feng Mei village. The rows of courtyard houses and the sound of the ever-flowing river, with just my parents, Ah Ma, two Ah Gou, and me. I was certain about their love for me even though they lectured me at times.

But now, in my new home, I started to question my own worth.

* * *

Over time, I began to notice some changes among the friends whom I played with. As the younger children got older, they would disappear in the morning, then appear again in the late afternoon. This happened every day, except on weekends. If I spotted them on the streets in the afternoon, they would be dressed in some uniforms, carrying bags on their backs, going home.

They told me they went to school. *Why don't I go to school like they do?*

Education became secondary when the family was fighting to survive.

Perhaps, my parents had no clue how to enroll me in school. They must have forgotten all about it amid their busy schedules. When I asked Ah Mm about it, she replied, 'I'll ask Ah Beh.' But she never did.

As the sole breadwinner of the family, I knew Ah Beh had enough to worry. In addition to feeding so many mouths, he had to send money back to Shantou. That was a lot on his plate. Therefore, I believed he cared more about money than anything else.

If not for Uncle Tham's kind reminder, my education would be far from Ah Beh's thoughts.

Ah Beh finally decided to enroll me in a school after rounds of persuasion by Uncle Tham. I had been in Singapore for four years before I started attending school. However, it was difficult to get into a *cheng hu* English school as I was considered too old to enter primary one. Ah Beh enrolled me in a Chinese private school instead.

It was my first time feeling privileged as not many children could go to school at that time. My school fee were relatively higher than those charged by public schools. It was five dollars per month!

I was over the moon. It gave me a valid reason to stay away from home every day.

As I had never been to school, I was nervous at the same time. It was uncomfortable for me to be the tallest boy in my class because I was two years older than the rest. In addition, my Mandarin Chinese was not so good even after settling in Singapore for a few years. We still spoke Teochew the most at home, after all. I could not catch up on my studies and I appeared really stupid, not knowing so many words despite being two years older. But soon, I managed to adjust my frame of mind to fit in. All because I became good close friends with one of my classmates, Geong. He was a nice fellow to hang out with.

Geong was a Teochew too. He was born in Singapore. His parents came to Singapore much earlier than mine did. It was my good fortune to have known him in school. He sat diagonally in front of me in class. When I first entered school, I knew no one. Geong was the only person who initiated a dialogue with me. He even helped me with my schoolwork. His sincerity touched me and we became best of friends. Besides being of the same age, we also shared many similar interests. One of them was watching *Teochew-hee*.

Gradually, school was where I felt that I could accomplish something. I promised myself to devote much attention to learning in school. It was at least something I could do for myself.

Five

I returned to reality when Uncle Tham called out to me, bringing my thoughts about the past crashing to a halt.

'Take these to your parents, Kuang!' Uncle Tham tossed another three galy poks to me. 'I haven't seen them since I stopped peddling along Singapore River a year ago.'

'Thank you, Uncle Tham,' I answered warmly with my high-pitched voice betraying my emotions.

Uncle Tham's gesture reminded me of all the wonderful things he had done for my family. As I thanked him for the galy poks, my heart was swelling with eternal gratitude for his generosity.

Food tasted best when it was gobbled quickly. I devoured the whole pocket of goodness in just a few minutes.

The roads shimmered in the heat of the midday sun. Shadows of the stretch of shophouses in front of me were cast on the ground.

'I'd better go home now. Ah Mm will be looking for me.' Sweeping crumbs away from my shirt, I stood up, patting my burning hot bottom and then waving goodbye to Uncle Tham.

He looked at me, his lips quirked upwards in a joyous smile. 'See you, Kuang!'

I turned my head around. But before I even took a step forward, a booming voice exploded out of nowhere.

'*DI GU* IS HERE! *ZAO*! RUN!' For a long time, the same booming voice echoed in the background. A crazy scene soon followed. My skin tingled with discomfort as I watched on.

Hastily, the street hawkers started packing up, shoving their cutlery and utensils into big carts or large rattan baskets.

'ZAO, KUANG! RUN! That way!' Uncle Tham gave me a hard push on my shoulder. 'GO HIDE!' He urged before disappearing from my sight.

I could also hear ceramic bowls and plates smashing onto the ground. Some hawkers rode off, lifting their mobile kitchen on their shoulders using a bamboo pole, while others scampered away after abandoning everything. Exactly like rats escaping cats. The inspectors immediately gave chase to the roving hawkers as they fled the scene.

I dashed towards the shophouses and hid behind a pillar. My nostrils were flaring like those of a piglet. I was also panting and gulping for air while I watched absorbedly at what was happening.

The street filled of peddling hawkers was cleared in the blink of an eye. This changing of scene felt rehearsed, and I could not help but wonder how many times Uncle Tham had to run away from these aggressive inspectors every day.

I also had another question in my mind. Despite this constant cat-and-mouse game, how did Uncle Tham manage to help so many others?

* * *

Before anyone could catch me, I ran for my life. Insanely. Faster than my legs could take me. They felt numb and out of my control, almost giving way. I wondered if Uncle Tham had escaped those murderous inspectors.

The run-down shophouse where I lived gradually came into view as I dashed back home. It was a simple three-storey structure with minimal ornamentation.

My family lived in the apartments on the second floor. The ground level was an old-fashioned eatery. The shophouse also had a five-foot way that was sheltered by the second storeys.

The five-foot way was always filled with activities. Locksmiths, barbers, clog makers, newspaper sellers, and fortune tellers occupied the verandahs, providing service for the residents who stayed nearby. Every day, the five-foot way of our shophouse was cramped up with an endless stream of people. It allowed people to window-shop, look for refreshments, and gather for chit chats.

Arriving at the shophouse, and walking past the food and drinks stalls, one would see a long timbre staircase that led to a long corridor on the second level.

The corridor was so narrow that when I walked along it, it was nearly impossible to spread out my arms. A small common kitchen branched out from the corridor. It contained four stoves, one for each of the residential households staying at the second level.

Away from the kitchen, there were four units located side by side. My apartment was the second one from the left. I lived in it with Ah Beh, Ah Mm, and my five siblings while Ah Gong, Ah Ma, and two of their beloved grandchildren lived in the apartment next to ours.

A single living space with no bedrooms was all that we had in our apartment.

In this space, there were wooden drawers in a corner. Ah Beh and Ah Mm seemed to have placed many important things in those drawers, constantly locked. No one could open them, except Ah Beh and Ah Mm. I always wondered what was in there.

Next to the drawers, there were a foldable table and a few wooden chairs. The table had a few cracks on its plastic green-marbled surface and one of its legs was loosely secured using some brown tape that Ah Beh bought from the nearby market. All the chairs could not stand stably. They were either made imperfect, or deformed due to my brothers' bad habit of sitting at the edge of the chair and rocking it continuously.

At the other corner of this space, there was a small altar that housed a deity that looked stern and proud. He looked scary to me, but I knew he was Ah Mm's most cherished object of devotion.

Mattresses piled up next to the altar. Rats and cockroaches occasionally roamed around. The badly parquetted floor was torn and could scratch. Once in a while, we were badly cut by it.

This space was sufficient. At least, we did not have to stack on top of one another like those huge sacks of rice piled up at a warehouse. Ah Mm taught me to be contented with what I had. Whatever we had was good enough.

But, to be honest, this space was significantly smaller as compared to my house back in Feng Mei village. My heart desired for something better all the time. I did not tell Ah Mm about it.

* * *

I stood at the entrance of my apartment, panting like a dog that had wandered for long and finally returned home.

The evening sunrays travelled into the apartment through the little windows, painting all four boring walls orange. Ah Mm sat silhouetted in the auburn space, her hands patting my baby sister, Ing, to sleep. Her long-braided hair looked like a big weight placed on her depressed shoulder. She turned and looked at me. Her sunken face was an old, bruised plum, dark and creased.

'Where have you been?' Ah Mm pursued with a voice that had turned hoarse due to her persistent coughing.

'Uncle Tham's stall. He has got some galy poks for you and Ah Beh,' I replied, gently placing those savory puffs on our chipped wobbly table.

'Kuang, Ah Beh . . . will be gone from tomorrow onwards and he won't be returning home so soon,' Ah Mm spoke with a monotonous voice.

'Why? Where's Ah Beh going?' I asked, blinking rapidly as I tried to process what I had just heard.

'He's taken up a job as a ship deck worker with an Indonesian fishing company. He'll be gone for a week at least.' Ah Mm tried to explain. 'I . . . I'm still waiting for him to pass me some monthly allowance. Moreover, Ah Ma had stopped working at the grass jelly stall too. Her aching back cannot take it anymore. We have no money now . . . so could you . . .' Ah Mm did not finish her sentence. Or could she not? She seemed to lapse into a silent refuge, lowering her head.

What? My heart sank to my feet.

No, Ah Mm, I don't want to hear this. I dreaded such moment. *Please, Ah Mm, please don't ask me to do this again.* I screamed in my head. *NOT AGAIN.*

Trying hard not to reveal my reluctance to my sick mother, I asked before Ah Mm could finish her sentence, 'Ah Mm, do you need to borrow some money from Auntie Lim?' At the same time, I also hoped that my guess was wrong.

' . . . Yes, Kuang. Get a few dollars to last us through the week. Your Ah Beh will return the money to her when his pay is here,' Ah Mm looked up to answer me. After a while, she turned away from me again, lowering her head to respond to my little sister's soft cooing.

I kept still, almost rooted to the ground, trying to seek excuses within to avoid what was to come.

* * *

Why was I always the one to do this? Not Dak. Not Siu. Not Ang. Not Gia. Not Teng. Not Leng. But ME!

I gulped my reluctance.

Was it my bad luck to be the first-born? Jin suay.

I trudged along the corridor and arrived at the long flight of stairs. I sauntered around the staircase for a good half an hour before I finally looked up. The long flight of stairs appeared longer than usual. It was trying to even lift my foot and place it on the stairs. My heavy steps pulled my whole body towards gravity, making me slouch terribly, almost crawling.

Sometimes the hardest thing to do in life was to convince myself to do the easiest thing.

Kuang, just open your mouth and ask for those few dollars. Not that hard. Not that hard. I chanted in my heart as I pleaded the air to make time pass faster.

I stopped in front of Auntie Lim's apartment. Her door looked like ours. The only difference was a piece of half-hanging and beautiful yellow, lacy, linen in front of her door.

If I walked closer, I could smell the fragrance of freshly-bloomed jasmine. That wonderful scent could send people to paradise, even if paradise only existed in the mind. And that made a world of difference between staying in apartments with an adorned door and a plain one with cracks at the edges all over.

Humbly and carefully, I knocked on the door, as though my request could be conveyed with the gentlest knock. A few seconds later, it creaked open. A lady with messy curly hair, dressed in a floral cheongsam with a line of Chinese frog buttons embroidered on it stood in front of me, yawning away.

'You again, Kuang! How may I help you this time?' Auntie Lim asked in her penetrating voice. My guess was she would roll her eyes dramatically, like when I asked her for the same favor before.

But today, she restrained herself. Auntie Lim stared at me blankly, her body leaning listlessly against the door frame.

'Hello Auntie Lim. Sorry, but . . . but . . . could I borrow five dollars from you? Just five dollars this time. My Ah Beh . . . he will return you when he gets his pay next week . . . we promise, we promise!' I replied quickly with some trepidation, staring at her with my eyes wide open, trying to move her with my sincerity.

Auntie Lim was the wife of Ah Beh's Shantou friend. Having sharp features, Auntie Lim looked like a shrewd person without opening her mouth to speak or smile. She had a big mole on her chin. Some people said it was a beauty mark. Some said it meant stubbornness. Some also said she had luck with men.

Auntie Lim was a Singaporean and unlike most married women in Singapore who spent a big part of their lives managing domestic chores and taking care of children, Auntie Lim worked in a factory to earn a living for the family. She had raised three children of her own with the help of her parents.

Girls and women in Singapore in the 1960s were encouraged by their parents and husbands to focus on bringing up children and managing the household. Education for women was seen as pointless and prospects for women were limited. Therefore, Auntie Lim's career-seeking mindset was always frowned upon. But she did not seem to care how others viewed her.

'Here! Take it, Kuang!' Auntie Lim called out to me as she pulled out a few notes unenthusiastically from her perfumed lacy purse.

Auntie Lim had never looked down on us. Even though she loved to make fun of my bowl-cut oily hair and pull my ears, she had never criticized or spoken badly about my family, behind our back or in front of us. She was a soft-hearted person with a razor-blade mouth who used sarcasm with appropriate humour that was not offending at all.

Perhaps that was the reason why Ah Mm always asked me to borrow money from her.

'*Gam xia*, Auntie Lim!' I cried out in gratitude. 'See you around!'

'You're welcome, Kuang. *Mai keh ki*. But can I not see you again, standing outside my door at this time and waking me from my beauty sleep?' Auntie Lim sneered cheekily, waving to me. 'See you, Kuang!'

Exactly five one-dollar notes. Gripping them tightly in my hand, I dashed home.

The most unpleasant moment was over in split second. I closed my eyes and sniffed kindness in the air.

Auntie Lim's chirpy personality cheered me up. But at the same time, for some reason, there was a sour taste in my mouth. Deep within me, my integrity was somehow thrashed. I felt strangely defeated even though I was not involved in any game.

I made a promise to myself never to knock on Auntie Lim's door for the same purpose again.

* * *

I handed those notes to Ah Mm.

She took a quick glance at them and stuffed them into a biscuit tin. Tensely, she placed the container back into the drawer and locked it up again. She then quickly proceeded to the common kitchen to continue frying vegetables.

I was puzzled. Why was Ah Mm behaving like a thief in our own house?

'Time for dinner, Kuang,' Ah Mm prompted me as she walked back from the common kitchen and placed the same old dishes on our table.

I stood up from the floor and dragged my feet out of the house again. My body was slapping on the walls as I swayed left and right, moving clumsily and stiffly towards my grandparents' apartment. I felt a heaviness in my stomach whenever I had to go near Ah Gong.

'Time for dinner, Ah Gonggg . . . Ah Maaa . . . Daaaak! Siu!' I dragged my words and howled impatiently.

After a while, Dak opened the door, trying to shoot rubber bands at me. His cheeky face occupied by upward-slanting brows and narrow eyes popped out and was annoying the hell out of me.

'Your Ah Gong is not around. Let's go, kids,' Ah Ma answered, getting up from her old rattan egg chair and hurrying my younger brothers over to my place.

'Where's Ah Gong?' I could not tame my curiosity and asked at the dining table while waiting for my turn to have access to the dishes.

Stabbing hard into the cai pou neng with her wooden chopstick, Ah Ma shot back a reply filled with disdain, 'What else? Enjoying himself with his new hobby!'

There was a moment of silence amongst those who could sense Ah Ma's annoyance, while the younger children fought over a piece of vegetable leaf, making a lot of noise in the background.

Ah Mm looked into my eyes and shook her head slightly. *I know. I should stop asking anymore questions.* We continued to eat our dinner in silence.

Six

My hand trembled as I poured a few drops of condensed milk from a Milkmaid tin into a small, yellowed container at our common kitchen.

Ten drops of milk, a little bit of hot water, and nearly half that container of lukewarm water. Not more than ten drops of milk. Recalling Ah Mm's instructions, I measured the required amount carefully before shaking and mixing everything together. I then stretched a rubber teat to wrap the top of the container.

Every night, Ah Mm went for her quick bath at the shared bathroom straight after dinner and I had to prepare milk for Ing.

It had become one of the most important chores I did at home. Ah Hia's job. However, tonight was different. I made her milk with exhilaration, bouncing from foot to foot in the kitchen.

My favourite Teochew-hee was here to celebrate the 'Month of Hungry Ghosts'. Ever since I was a child, I was taught that, in this special month, it was believed that departed souls needed to be pacified. The Chinese people also worshipped gods using offerings and entertainment. It was common to see wooden makeshift stages for performances along the streets. Chinese operas were mostly free-of-charge and available to those who turned up early, so this was my rare chance to watch Teochew-hee.

After many days of persuasion, Ah Mm finally agreed to let me watch it with Geong today! I was over the moon. Just thinking about it made mundane chores like making milk for Ing enjoyable.

I returned to my apartment and saw Ing wailing hungrily on the mattress. Seeing no one around, I took the initiative to feed her. I tilted the container, and gently poked the rubber teat into her mouth. She began sucking the milk with all her might.

After a while, Ah Mm strode in with her long hair wrapped up like a big bun on her head. 'Kuang, bring Ing with you tonight. Ah Mm has an urgent matter to attend to,' she instructed with a soft but firm voice.

My head pulled back as my shoulders pushed forward. *Not again!* I took a steeling breath and caved my chest in. My brain seemed to have broken down and packed away.

Closing my eyes, I inhaled loudly.

What fun could I have, bringing her along, Ah Mm? I questioned loudly in my heart. *It was not like she could understand Teochew-hee and I did not wish to bring a crying baby to the show. She's definitely a fun-spoiler!*

Left without a choice, I murmured assent while turning away from Ah Mm. I glided my feet into my torn slippers, lifted Ing with one hand and let her sit securely onto my right waist.

With resentment boiling in my heart, I stomped out of my apartment reluctantly, expecting to return home soon.

I surely looked like a picture of misery.

* * *

'Geong!' I cried out excitedly, running towards him. Sitting on my waist, Ing was jerked to the front and back as I ran.

'Kuang!' Geong waved his hand back at me. I could see his bunny teeth sticking out from afar.

'Oh! You're bringing your baby sister along?' Geong asked curiously.

'Well, there's nothing I can do, Geong. My Ah Mm had to be away so, sadly, this little fellow had to come with me.' I replied, lowering my head, sighing.

'Never mind, Kuang! I'm sure she'll be a very good girl tonight!' Geong patted my shoulder and grinned widely. 'You'd better be a good girl. Let your brother finish the show, please! *Mai kao ah.*' Geong attempted to coax Ing, who was making sounds very similar to pigeons cooing.

People affect one another, sometimes in great ways that are very subtle. That night, without Geong's graciousness, I would have blamed Ah Mm for making me carry Ing around. Geong's words made my heart expand a little, stamping out traces of resentment I held towards Ah Mm.

'Let's enjoy the show tonight!' I cheered, staring at Geong's lit-up face as he smiled sweetly at my sister. '*Meh*, meh! Hurry! Let's go!'

The three of us quickly advanced along Singapore River and arrived at the makeshift opera stage.

* * *

There was a crowd standing in front of the stage, admiring the performance.

As we approached the stage, I could see fighting scenes going on. Actors were like acrobats, lavishly dressed in elaborately embroidered costumes and headdresses, running and even jumping on the stage.

Their faces were curiously covered in thick symbolic makeup and their features stood out from a distance. There was nothing more captivating to me than hearing drums and cymbals clash and bang. Whenever a man was struck in a fighting scene, the drum would be hit, and another crash of music would follow as the victim fell onto the ground.

The music played by the orchestra at the back scene was simply fantastic. It never failed to lift my spirits. This whole theatre experience indeed made a great sensation, waking me up from the slumber of my mundane life.

The most exciting part about watching Teochew-hee was buying snacks to go with it. There were street vendors pedaling and selling all kinds of tidbits near the outdoor theatre.

I was rejoicing when Ah Mm gave me ten cents as my next day's allowance before I left home for the show earlier. I decided to use those coins to buy snacks to go with the show, instead of bringing them to school the next day.

I loved *kachang puteh* the most!

Far from the stage, an Indian man stood beside a metallic cart. Among the items on his cart were sugared and steamed peanuts, cashews, chickpeas, green peas, and even *murukku*, one of the staple Indian snacks.

'Cashew nuts and sugar-coated peanuts please!' I exclaimed in delight as we approached the Indian vendor. He then scooped the nuts from the containers and poured them into a paper cone, wrapping the nuts up like a precious gift. Each small cone cost exactly ten cents.

Geong and I managed to find a space in the crowd to accommodate our two lean bodies.

Ing was surprisingly calm. She clung onto me like a baby monkey. Her small hands were trying very hard to grab my right shoulder tightly and refusing to let go.

As we watched the performance, our hands diligently picked nuts from the paper cones and popped them into our mouths, nibbling like two starved rats. Occasionally, I chewed on a nut, and spit out tiny pieces for Ing to try. She loved it and kept asking for more.

A deafening crash of music was suddenly sent to our ears. The climax of the show was especially riveting. As I looked at Geong, he also turned to me, laughing excitedly with two neat rows of teeth all exposed. His curly eyelashes stood out to me. Under his brows, they looked like toothpicks lined up in a fence.

Surprisingly, Ing did not throw any tantrums that night. She even slept through the last twenty minutes of the performance.

That night with Geong and Ing, I watched Teochew-hee with more peace and joy than I ever had imagined.

Seven

My stomach rumbled all day the next day. Having no money in my pocket, I could only swallow my drool when others had lunch at school.

Recently, the girls in my class fell in love with making animals using brown fallen leaves. During recess, they would gather and share the brown leaves they had each collected, handweaving all sorts of creatures together.

Boys did not like such stuff. However, Geong did.

Today, along with a few other boys in class, Geong joined in the girls' fun. I tried to persuade him to practise calligraphy together, but he rejected me, for the very first time.

I was stunned. *Why are you abandoning me for the girls?*

'Kuang! Quick! Come join us!' Geong randomly called out to me.

Sometimes, Geong disappointed me.

I raised my head. Geong did not even make any effort to look at me. As I watched his eyes, I was not quite sure where they were looking. The leaf grasshopper in the girl's hand or her soft rosy cheeks?

No, I am not going over. I sat at my desk, pouting. I held my calligraphy brush and wrote atrocious Chinese characters that failed to impress even myself.

I could hear Geong chuckling away, trying to crack some jokes to impress the apple of his eye. I rolled my eyes at him. As young as eleven years old, I was unbelievably overcome by jealousy.

I could not take it lying down. I stood up and marched towards them, all prepared to win my friend back.

'Kuang, fold one for Geong!' Ngia, our class monitress, casually suggested, not knowing that friendship had just torn my heart.

I stood next to Ngia and she demonstrated how to weave a butterfly. It did not seem like an impossible craft to make.

Alright, I will do it.

I was finally convinced, not by Ngia's words but my desire to share a little something with someone on this gloomy day. *But I'm not folding one for you, Geong. You don't deserve it. I shall fold one butterfly for Ah Mm. That's her favourite.*

Ah Mm had always loved butterflies.

Back in China, Ah Mm would always sit on the sill of our courtyard house door, admiring the fast fluttering of butterflies. When her chores were done in the late afternoon, she would wait for me to return home to tell me interesting tales.

Ah Mm had always been a great storyteller. Those stories about my family that she told me in secret left a deep impression on me. To me, she was even more skillful than those I had heard at *puay ko* near my home in Singapore.

Street storytellers here often embellished their tales with tonal flourishes, dramatic facial expressions, and theatrical gestures. Ah Mm did not have to do that to tell amazing stories. Her tales were filled with so much emotional turmoil and sincerity that merely listening to her voice already captivated me.

I loved listening to stories very much.

In Singapore, street storytellers set up a burning incense stick at the start of the session. When the incense stick burnt out, it signified the end of the session and everyone would leave.

I did not like this idea at all.

The entire storytelling session was rather short, and I could not bear to leave every time. Ah Mm's storytelling was better. There was no time limit to it. I could spend the entire evening just listening to her repeat stories. How I missed those days!

Ah Mm's most told tale was *The Butterfly Lovers*. It is a Chinese legend of a tragic love folktale of a pair of lovers.

Once upon a time in China, there lived a young girl who dreamed of learning. Unfortunately, she lived in an era when girls were expected to be obedient. They were required to stay at home, learn household work, and marry the man their father chose for them. They were born to stay quiet about their destinies. The lovers in the story were eventually transformed into white butterflies, fluttering their wings, as they finally got together after a grueling struggle for real love.

Whenever Ah Mm recited this tale to me, her eyes would drift and stare off into the air, studying the surrounding for butterflies. If one or two appeared, she would raise her index finger, as if suggesting to the butterflies they could lean on her should they turn weary.

I was not sure what exactly Ah Mm had on her mind. Especially on days when Ah Beh had just left for Singapore, Ah Mm was often in a daze, sitting alone at the entrance of our courtyard house.

Nevertheless, butterflies would always, at least arouse her interest, making her stay connected with the present by fluttering around her.

With the help of Ngia and a few other girls, I clumsily weaved the ugliest butterfly one could ever find. I brushed the sand off my first handmade creation, admiring its imperfection with pride. I then laid it carefully between the pages of my Chinese textbook. *May this little creature bring Ah Mm solace for all her troubles.*

The loud bell rang. My most dreaded English class had just begun. And I continued to bear with my rumbling stomach.

* * *

School ended on time. The minute I got out of school, I rushed back to our shophouse, hoping to get some plain buns or biscuits from home to ease my hunger.

As usual, Ah Mm was sitting on the mattress, playing with Ing. But these few days, Ah Mm was not herself.

Her cough was getting much worse. Her fever came fast two days ago, robbing her of her strength.

Childbirth without proper rest led to a cruel transformation of her body. Her health had been greatly sacrificed after giving birth to so many of us. Her immunity was reduced and could not withstand the impact of even a minor viral flu. From having a curvy fleshy body, she was reduced to almost a pack of bones, always shaking and pale.

Now, this sickness showed no sign of shifting, no hint of changing to a milder form. Her throat kept clenching as she coughed her lungs out. To make it worse, her occasional asthmatic attacks made it hard for her to breathe properly.

Ah Mm looked up and saw me standing at the door. She stood up and stumbled towards me. With each step, her stomach tightened as she coughed, making her slouch terribly. 'Kuang, you're back. Ah Mm made some kueh today. Let me warm them up in the kitchen now,' Ah Mm said, wetting her quivering lips as she limped to the door.

Hastily, I tried to take the leaf butterfly out from my deep pocket but it was stuck. It was enmeshed in those terribly done stitches in my pocket. When trying to pull the butterfly from the tangles of the stiches, the leaf cracked into pieces.

'Mui ah, give some money NOW. I need to buy it again!' a voice, so familiar yet detestable, bawled from behind me.

I turned my body around and gulped in fear upon seeing Ah Gong struggling to keep his balance at our doorstep.

I could smell a combined harsh scent of coffee beans, vanilla, and white flowers from him. He lurched into our apartment, paralytic, as if the ground was the deck of a storm-tossed boat.

'Give meee money! I want it NOWWW!' A string of words slurred loudly from his odour-filled mouth.

Ah Mm jostled me next to her, attempting to hide me away from this violent old man. She shook her head feebly, looking at Ah Gong with stern eyes. 'I don't have any money. *Bo lui. Wa* bo lui.'

I looked up and gazed at Ah Mm. Her pale face was whiter than before. Her lips were purplish. But her voice was different. I had not heard such a low-pitched powerful voice from Ah Mm for the longest time.

It reminded me of the days in China, when she spoke of warriors in Chinese legends, describing how they fought the toughest battles. At that instant, Ah Mm's weak front was totally concealed by her inner determination to protect our money and me.

She had become the heroine arisen from the tales she once shared. Her muscles toughened into jade.

'*Si zha bo*! Wretched woman! GET LOST!' Ah Gong roared, shivering in cold sweat. He looked like an insane man, lashing out in uncontrollable anger.

Ah Gong then took a quick scan around the apartment with his half-closed bulging eyes. He picked up a rusty pan from the table. It was stained with bits of sticky dough left from the kueh Ah Mm had made earlier. With his fingers curled tightly around the black handle of the pan, he raised the pan and heaved it towards Ah Mm's head.

The pan fell clanging onto the ground.

Ing was lying on the ground, shrieking from the corner of the apartment.

I screamed with my whole body, my eyes wide with fear, my mouth open and rigid. Adrenaline surged through my veins.

I did not know what to do. I felt like a man bursting with anger trapped in a child's helpless little body. I let out a louder piercing scream of wild panic. Tears burst out from my eyes as I squeezed them shut. 'AH MM!' I screamed again.

Ah Mm's body jerked as she fell. She collapsed onto the floor with the loudest thud. Her head was struck badly. Conscious yet giddy, she remained sprawled on the floor. I was afraid a single inch of movement could cause her to lose consciousness.

My legs bent and I knelt beside her, trying to grab her arms.

Ah Gong continued to lash his tongue loudly. He kicked the pan to the corner and started flipping our thin and flimsy mattresses crazily. I turned and stared hard at him. Though shivering, my heart palpitated so quickly that it might explode.

'WHAT ARE YOU DOING?!' Ah Ma yelled at our door, trying to figure out what exactly happened while she was away. She returned from the market just in time.

'Ahhh you cursed woman! You finally came! GIVE ME MONEY NOOOOW!' Ah Gong thundered, his body swaying to the door, and his palm striking Ah Ma on her face.

Ah Ma fell and nearly hit the sidewall. She stretched out her arms wide just in time to prevent herself from crumpling against the walls. Fortunately, she managed to recover her balance.

She limped in quickly. Her uneven hips were rocking front and back like a boat floating on high tides, her corpulent apple-shaped bottom wiggling along with it.

With all her strength, she attempted to pull Ah Gong out of our door. 'Money, money, money! Where to get so much money for you to spend on this worthless addiction?'

Never had I heard Ah Ma talk to Ah Gong in such a straightforward manner. She was usually quiet like Ah Mm. But today, she exposed her thoughts on the verge of anger.

Only heavens knew how she might be dealt with after they had returned to their apartment.

Ah Mm and I sat on the floor, silent. The room was occupied with only Ing's wailing and the smell of fried potatoes drifting in from the common kitchen.

'Ah Mm . . .' I knelt up and faced her, touching her head with my trembling hand.

Ah Mm's eyes shifted towards mine. She blinked doubly hard, trying to force a smile while her frowns gave her fear away. '*Bo si la*. Ah Mm is alright. Just a little giddy now,' she assured me, coughing away.

'Luckily he did not find out about the money you borrowed from Ah Lim the other day.' Ah Mm smiled, her pale lips stretched and trembled, looking at the set of locked drawers at the side and then back to me.

My hand reached into my pocket and pulled out the distorted leaf butterfly. 'Ah Mm, I made this in school today. It's for you.' I lowered my head and spoke with my littlest voice.

Ah Mm's trembling smile softened into a comforting beam. As she touched the cracked leaf butterfly, a spark returned to her eyes. It was that same old spark I saw when she was looking for butterflies at Feng Mei village.

A tear trickled down my face. I smiled, embracing Ah Mm for the very first time.

I want to keep Ah Mm safe in my arms for as long as time permits.

Thinking back, I loathed myself for not being able to stand up and protect Ah Mm in time. I was crushed by an overwhelming sense of defeat. I gritted my teeth as I recalled how Ah Gong shoved Ah Mm to the ground. My heart ached so much when I caught a glimpse of Ah Mm's pained look. That sharp ache in my heart grew into an adamant pulsing from within my chest. It seemed to will me to want to push through and protect Ah Mm. Even though I did not do so eventually, at that instant, I realized I had a ball of vigour burning on the inside of me. It felt very powerful.

Eight

'欢迎！欢迎！'
'欢迎! 欢迎!'

I vigorously shook a flag in my hand as I cheered with my classmates on the field near my school.

The day had dawned crisp and clear. We were standing under the blue sky dotted with fluffy white clouds, all ready to greet and welcome a leader, most loved and feared.

It was the year 1965. A very crucial year for this small piece of land I was living in.

It seemed like the day I came here with my parents in 1957 was just yesterday. I did not know what to expect. We packed a bag of our best clothes and little money and moved to Singapore. I did not even know what Singapore was. Or was it a part of China? Was it another piece of land?

Years were short. In a blink of an eye, my fleeting childhood was almost over. Yet, days were long, facing the harsh treatment from Ah Gong, coping with bad living conditions, and doing my best to help to take care of my family. Although so much had happened, little seemed to have changed. I still felt like that little rascal from Feng Mei village. How had I grown without knowing it? It was a strange and confusing feeling.

Whenever I spoke about myself to others, I mentioned my past and my story as an immigrant's child. Seldom, I spoke about my future.

What do I want to do? What do I have now and what else do I seek?

Meanwhile, new thoughts had also begun to sprout within me. A part of me had gradually grown out of playing kites and catching fish. Sporadically, I wondered what this country held for me. *Why am I here and where do I go?*

Is this part of growing up?

I did not know.

Perhaps, only adults would have a good answer.

* * *

For the past few years, Singapore had been fighting for a merger with Malaysia.

Merger was a very complicated thing. During this period, I saw people running around with thick piles of leaflets in their hands. The voice coming out from those brown boxes at kopitiams sounded urgent and firm. People on the streets talked less. There were also hushed whispers going around. But some people talked more. Even louder than before. They went around to share their thoughts about those in authority, as well as different races. Our neighbours sometimes could not communicate with one another peacefully. They got into heated arguments because they stood for different plans for this country. Bursting with self-importance, they tried to outstare each other, to see which one would be the first to lose his nerve and admit his mistakes. There was even pushing between them, each insisting they were right.

As we looked down from our shophouse apartment, sometimes, we saw people of different races fighting. Different shades of skin colours brutally clashed and gashed against one another, betraying the same red beneath.

Trust among people was broken. Our society became deeply divided.

Brows were easily raised at any racist words spoken by anyone in the public. Ah Mm told us to shut our mouths in order to avoid unnecessary attention.

Social unrest was truly a nightmare, not only because lives were taken and properties were lost, but also because everyone had to live with fear, be forced to have lesser than what was already lacking, and cope with a sense of endless futility every day.

I could vividly remember 21 July 1964.

It was a quiet day. An island-wide curfew was imposed in Singapore after a series of racial riots.

My siblings and I were all dying to peep through the small window in my apartment, pulling and pushing one another in order to steal a glimpse at what was happening downstairs.

The empty streets of Singapore gave me cold creeps as we looked down. It was eerily silent. We could no longer hear vehicles moving on the busy streets. Shops and stalls were mostly closed. And people were muted. A bustling city murdered by the words and actions of its own people stayed afloat in front of our eyes.

We could see Malaysian soldiers standing stiffly in their starched and pressed uniforms, guarding the bridges that spanned the Singapore River. They looked intensely fierce. No one dared to approach an inch closer. Barbed wires formed in large coils also fenced up the bridges, acting as barriers to deter people from crossing them.

A curfew felt like lifelong imprisonment. I felt chained up at home. We were not allowed to leave our homes the whole day, except during an allocated period when Ah Mm went down to the market to grab some groceries like eggs, rice, and vegetables.

Cramming into a small apartment with many siblings was a disaster. I literally became a horse for all of them to ride on. My hair was pulled out like weeds from the land.

While trying to be accustomed to the dead silence outside my home, I also kept my ears closed from the crazy clattering inside it.

I did not fancy this new norm.

Never did we expect the curfew to persist for another two weeks, adding a few more rounds in the later months.

Rioting did not end. There were more clashes. Life continued to be hellish as we were forced to hide in our own houses, only dependent on word of mouth to understand the outside world.

How I longed to be back in school.

These few years of strife and social unrest reminded me of the few days I spent on the boat coming to Singapore. The wait seemed long and I felt suffocated. I did not know what to do at first. Ah Mm said we got to be brave, to have quiet confidence that we would pull through all obstacles. And to remember what we set out for and have faith it would all come true.

So, during this period, I constantly reminded myself to be patient. I thought of those happy times and prayed for the very first time.

Ah Mm was right. A rainbow surely arched ahead. Difficult days were soon over. My quiet confidence won the battle.

Finally, I could go back to school.

* * *

'欢迎! 欢迎!'
'欢迎! 欢迎!'

Every student was handed a flag during assembly in school and was asked to follow our teacher to the field early that morning because we would be hearing from one specific leader that we all knew very well. After all, we had seen him many times before in our own neighbourhoods, delivering impassioned speeches about how Singapore and its people did not have to worry about the future or anything else. I was keen to meet that great leader again.

Amidst the loud cheering, I lowered my head to look at the small piece of cloth flag attached to a thin wooden stick. It was a beautiful piece of cloth divided into two colours—red and white. The red portion had a crescent and five stars arranged in a full circle.

I raised the flag up and held it against the glaring sun rays.

The beam made it slightly golden. The countless tiny holes in the fabric were glistening. The crescent and the stars looked brighter than those in the dark skies at night.

Our Singapore flag had a new meaning now. I wondered in excitement as I stared at the fresh symbol of independence.

We were finally on our own.

'欢迎! 欢迎!'

'欢迎! 欢迎!'

From afar, that great leader walked with dignity towards the people. His white shirt looked neatly pressed, just like a smart soldier's uniform. Head held high, bringing an answering smile to every face he met, he paced steadily up the stage and started his speech with composure; in the firmest tone, I had ever heard.

I held the Singapore flag close to my chest and listened to that long string of powerful words punched out from that leader's mouth. At this instant, I felt detached from my past identity. I was no longer just the little rascal from Feng Mei village.

I was a Singaporean, an immigrant turned citizen standing on my own piece of land and deciding what I could do in the future now that I was a part of this very new nation.

The crowd cheered excitedly. Thunderous claps rumbled.

Singapore was reborn. And I felt a burst of pride within me.

* * *

I lie motionless on the mattress, head touching the parquetted floor, body angled to one side and neck flexed like a fetus in a womb. Rats were nibbling the skin under the free edge of my nails.

'Kuang ah, *ki lai*! Meh! Quickly!' Ah Mm flung my uniform and it landed right on my face. I scratched my backside and drifted off to sleep again.

6.30 a.m.

Every morning, I was woken up by Ah Mm to get ready for school. It was the most challenging moment for both of us.

Ah Mm sometimes resorted to chanting Teochew rhymes over and over in my ears in order to force me out of the bed. Other times when she was more impatient, she would sprinkle water right onto my face.

At this time, the streets just got busy. The rest of my siblings who were too young for school spread-eagled on the floor around me like a swarm of zombies waiting to rise and lumber.

Today, I woke up slightly earlier.

I looked out of the window. Large heavy clouds gathered in the sky, coughing out gouts of water that pitter-pattered on my window. Puddles on the ground began plinking as the rainfall became heavier.

People on the streets were galloping like horses in a craze. Some used pieces of cardboard to cover their heads, while others quickened their pace to look for shelters.

Soon, there was so much rain falling that it blurred into one long, whooshing sound. I could no longer witness the chaotic streets through the misty curtain formed in front of me.

As I dressed for school, I rubbed my arms to tame those goosebumps. I then tiptoed towards the door, trying hard not to step on my siblings but I failed. I almost crushed my youngest brother's little toes.

That little zombie drew some rattling breaths and made low growling moans.

'Ah Hia!' Teng opened his eyes and smiled innocently at me. 'Are you going to school now?'

'Yes, I'm. Are you cold? You can take my dry towel to cover yourself,' I whispered to Teng in my softest tone, trying to divert his attention.

Teng nodded.

I sneaked back into the room and took down my hanging towel. 'Here you go, Teng. Quick, go back to sleep.'

He nodded again.

I crouched next to my little brother, watching him close his eyes and drift off to a state of unconsciousness.

His chubby face was a clean red apple. His skin was ruddy, and not as dark as mine. His bushy eyelashes curled in both directions, forming many crosses as he shut his eyes. Disproportionally, his big nostrils occupied half of his nose cone. He looked exactly like a little monkey.

I giggled, staring at Teng's face.

I rarely looked this closely at my siblings. Usually, they roamed around the neighbourhood, so we had few chances to meet one another. Sometimes I went about my days not seeing some of them at all. Today, I realized even my youngest brother had grown up.

'Have a good sleep, Teng. Ah Hia shall see you tonight,' I patted his head gently, stood up, and left home for school.

* * *

The rain had stopped. Streets were washed clean. Grasses and trees, polished with wetness.

My pocket sagged with a ten-cent coin and a five-cent coin. Ever since Ah Beh changed his job, from a kuli to a fishing vessel deck worker, Ah Mm would sometimes increase my daily allowance to fifteen cents.

It used to be only five cents and I could only buy a cup of grass jelly drink during recess.

Now, I could afford a bowl of rice topped with curry before I went to school. I stood at the side of the road, ogling at the shiny white grains painted with golden gravy.

Deep pits of water were formed on the ground in just an hour, suggesting increased risk of flooding.

November was the start of the most dreaded monsoon period. Stretching until January, storms and flash flooding were common. Exceptional heavy rains would cause poorer folks living in the *kampong* areas to become temporary refugees, losing their homes and livelihoods.

Black clouds continued to roll over the sky. Observing the frowns on people's faces, I swallowed my curry rice as fast as I could.

The holes on my torn cotton shoes allowed rainwater to seep right through, soaking my socks. They gave off a stench of a rotten egg. I could randomly smell it as I walked. The moistened surfaces of my socks and shoes were rubbing against each other. Those squelches were unbearable.

When I arrived at my classroom, I saw Geong removing his wet shoes and laying them beside his feet. I sat beside him and did the same. And the both of us laughed at each other's smelly feet. The nails on our dirtied toes looked equally black.

The bell rang. A plump figure strode into the class, demanding order even though she had not spoken a word. She had a hawkish air about her. Even her nose curved like a hawk's beak. Her beady eyes and blunt words would kill any strong-hearted individual. Dressed in a high-collared shirt and bell-bottomed black pants, her big antique glasses sat on her beaky nose. Her short hair seemed to have oiled and glued to her scalp. There was not a single strand standing out of the uniformly sculpted greasy patch. Her eyebrows were so bushy, they looked like two lines outlined with tar.

This was my calligraphy teacher. And she was our school principal. We addressed her as Madam Khoo.

Neat and alive, her effortlessly-drawn calligraphy words were near perfection. Whenever she spoke about calligraphy, we all fell silent. Some students adored her lessons and followed her instructions wholeheartedly while others pulled their hair.

Initially, I hated Madam Khoo as she loved giving us heaps of calligraphy homework every day. Most of us grew tired of it after merely a month. But, a handful of students were still passionate about it. They wrote beautifully and Madam Khoo would always praise them for their hard work. Gradually, I was motivated by these students to write neatly.

It was the end of November, less than two months before the Chinese New Year. Madam Khoo could not wait to engage us in writing spring couplets. She gripped onto her biggest brush.

Gracefully, she painted four big Chinese characters that signified the arrival of great fortune on a big piece of rice paper pasted on the board.

'Wash your brushes in warm water. Take them out when the hairs are no longer stiff. Squeeze out the excess water. Pour ink into your container and wet your brushes with ink completely. Smooth out excess ink on the edge of the container. Write your words now!'

Madam Khoo had effectively drilled us into this routine for the past year.

I tried to hold my brush like what Madam Khoo had demonstrated. However, my fingers would always move out of place uncontrollably.

My brush was kangarooing from side to side as I adjusted my grip. Ink splattered onto the rice paper, forming big dark patches all over. I was flabbergasted.

Madam Khoo slowly roved her way through the gaps between tables and arrived at mine.

I was looking down with my hands trying to cover all the black patches and praying in my heart she would walk past me without noticing anything amiss on my paper.

Warm air gusted out in two straight lines, beating against the top of my head. A huge shadow was cast on my rice paper. My heart almost stopped for a moment.

'Kuang, what are all these?' the powerful voice rang from above like a transcendental being.

Refusing to turn my head to her two small scrutinizing eyes, I apologized quickly. Silence rang in my ears as I waited for her to rebuke in irritation.

However, that did not happen.

Instead, my red rice paper was slowly drawn away from my table and a fresh new piece landed on it like a God-given gift.

'Try again, Kuang. A person who could move a mountain begins by lifting small rocks.' A hand patted gently on my shoulder. 'You can do it.'

I was immediately blushing. My cheeks became two red apples.

Madam Khoo's words instilled more than just confidence in me. I was deeply nourished by the hopes she had pinned on me in that instance.

I had always thought I was an invisible student. Never going against teachers, and never standing out either in my grades and behaviours. I was never that naughty child that made teachers angry. Neither was I the most obedient child whom teachers wanted to praise. I was a silent figure, drifting in and out of school every day, doing work accordingly so that I would not be noticed.

But today, I received a rare praise from the teacher I feared yet respected the most. It was the first time Madam Khoo noticed me.

At the end of Madam Khoo's lesson, I wiped my sweaty palms and stood up to stretch my back. Holding my spring couplet with both hands, I approached Madam Khoo at the teacher's desk.

Courage washed through my body like the downpour this morning.

'Madam Khoo, I am done with my spring couplet. Do you want to have a look at it?' I mumbled to myself.

That was the longest string of words I had ever spoken to her.

Madam Khoo looked at me and let out a genial smile. Her eyes spoke of affirmation. 'Well done, Kuang. See? You can do it.'

I was stained with pride. This moment was etched in my mind, like calligraphy words written in ink on rice paper, soaking me with happiness.

'Thank you, Madam Khoo! See you tomorrow!' I waved unreservedly at my teacher.

I had never wanted to succeed so badly before. But today, I wanted to be someone whom my teacher could be proud of. An eager desire to become a better student filled my mind.

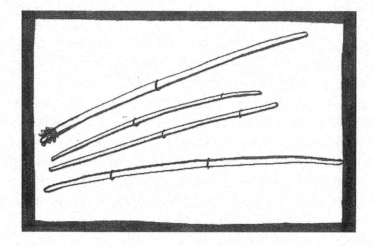

Nine

The recess bell rang. Together with Geong, I strolled to the canteen to get our drinks.

We sat on a bench, holding the diluted fruit syrup in flimsy cups tightly. A big sandy field spread in front of our eyes. Birds were dancing in the strong wind above this plot of vastness. Some leaves somersaulted to the ground.

Students arrived at the field in big groups. A trail of gunpowder seemed to have lined in their veins, waiting to be lighted. Like caged birds set free, girls and boys played to their hearts' content during this half an hour. Some were absorbed in a game of marbles, while others crossed over rubber ropes as they gradually got inched higher each round, from the ankles, to knees, then waist, shoulder, ears and over the head.

Of course, it was our long-awaited time of the day to roam freely. We became animals in the wild.

A teacher sat at the side of the sandy field, gawking at his watch, with his half-closed eyelids.

My eyelids turned heavy too, as I took sips of the diluted fruity syrup. The monsoon rain in the morning certainly did not convince the blazing sun to hide behind the clouds this afternoon.

What strange weather. I was yearning desperately to be in bed.

A group of boys from the next class gathered opposite us, hiding in the bushes. Through my sleepy eyes, I could roughly see white rods in some of their hands from a distance.

What are they doing? It doesn't look like a game.

I turned to look at Geong. He was writing Chinese idioms on the ground with a tree branch. His words spread out neatly on the sandy field.

I glanced back at the boys. I could see them distributing the white rods amongst themselves. Some of them were cracking their knuckles while others had eyes that seemed to bulge. Those eyes were scary. They were staring intently at us. Then, the boys nodded slightly to one another before slowly approaching in our direction.

I eyed those suspicious-looking fellows like a guard on duty.

Fifteen minutes into recess, an abrupt outcry shocked everyone at the field.

'CHARGE! FINISH THOSE PESKY BOYS FROM 5A!' Boys from class 5B dashed towards us, holding long light bulbs vertically up in the air.

All the other children scrambled around, looking for hiding places.

'GEONG! GEONG! RUN!' I was flustered. I pulled Geong up by his back collar while screaming my head off. Geong did not have time to even lift his head. Anxiously, he took to his heels and broke into a run in a direction different from mine.

I stretched out my hands to reach for him but he was gone in seconds. 'Geong! Geong!' I shouted. I squeezed my eyes shut as Geong dashed further and further away from me.

My flight instinct got me to race to the teacher sitting at the side of the field and begged for his help. To get more help, he continuously blew the whistle around his neck. Loudly and continuously.

Teachers could be seen running around the school to catch those dangerous bullies.

There was something familiar about this scene. It was like the communal tension that broke out last year, as described by my neighbour—rioters chasing after people and police constables chasing after rioters.

* * *

Thinking about what might happen to Geong, my knotted belly cramped, and my limbs turned weak. He was running like a frantic rat, not even turning his head to look back at me. *Why didn't he?* If he had done so, I would have gestured to him to stay. Help was just on its way.

But it was all too late. Geong was gone. There was no sign of him anywhere.

There were many rooms tucked away in those old buildings, away from the classroom blocks in the school compound. They were the dark places no one would go to. Not even sunlight could reach them.

Had Geong run to those secluded rooms?

Having reached those dark places, would he have nowhere else to run to? Could the bullies find him there and bash him up?

CAN SOMEONE TELL ME WHERE GEONG IS? I clenched and unclenched my fists. I was gasping to control my breath while trying to still my quaking.

At the same time, I struggled to understand why we had to be punished for Gee's nasty act.

* * *

Last Tuesday, Gee, our classmate, and Hock, a boy from class 5B, were suspended from lessons on the same day. Both of them were chained to tables and chairs outside the teachers' room, sitting just next to each other. Gee was assigned calligraphy practices while Hock had to complete his Chinese Language homework.

Hock had a tough time doing his homework. Out of frustration, he rubbed the pencil markings on the worksheet numerous times with his eraser. His elbow accidentally knocked onto Gee's.

Gee had just dipped his calligraphy brush in the container, ready to write but the push caused it to splatter black ink all over his rice paper instead.

'Darned you! Are you blind?' Gee roared at Hock, throwing his brush at Hock's face. Anger was boiling up in him.

Hock's forehead was slashed with Chinese ink. His sweat mingled with it, forming a long black bead. It stretched and rolled down his nose bridge. 'What's wrong with you?' Hock yelled back, crushing Gee's rice paper into a huge ball and hurling it onto the floor.

Gee was infuriated further. Out of rashness, he grabbed Hock's pencil and lounged it into Hock's lower arm. The sharp tip of the pencil lead pierced right through Hock's flesh, making him shriek in extreme pain. Blood oozed out from his wound and smeared all over the wooden tables.

Words spread in school like fire. Boys from class 5B could not take it lying down. They aimed to seek revenge on the boys in my class.

* * *

For the past few days, the boys from class 5B had been playing pranks on some of us. Splashing water at us when we were using the latrine and burning our books with matches. Their vindictive acts had caused misery to us. Today, chasing us with light bulb rods and threatening to wipe all of us out was another of their ruthless attempts.

I hoped Geong managed to escape their vengeful claws.

'Geong! Geong!' I searched the school with a heavy heart, pacing in and out of classrooms frantically, asking if anyone had spotted him.

My mind was occupied with all the worst-case scenarios. I stood in the corridors, looking out at the school compound and searching every spot I could find.

Time felt like it was slowing down. I was almost hyperventilating.

'GET OUT OF MY SIGHT. LEAVE THE SCHOOL RIGHT AWAY!' Madam Khoo's voice boomed across the entire vicinity. I could hear her voice reverberating from the old school building. Bullies from class 5B were finally caught near the storeroom. They were expelled on the spot and sent home immediately.

I dashed towards the old school buildings as fast as my legs could take me.

When I arrived, the noise around me was deafening. Girls' shrieking could be heard in the crowd. Students were pushing one another around as if starting another fight. The whole scene was like a ball of chaos. Teachers were having a hard time dismissing it.

I wanted to put my hands over my ears to shut out the pounding on my eardrums. The crowd swallowed me and I had to push my way through.

Through the gaps among the onlookers, I could see two male teachers lifting Geong up. His head was bleeding and he was using a big ball of cloth to press against his injury. I was flabbergasted. I rushed forward to have a closer look at him. 'Are you alright, Geong?' I asked several times, holding my breath.

Geong had bruises everywhere on his body. He parted his lips but did not say a word. Unblinking, his eyes moved slowly and rested the moment they met mine. His stare, however, was intentionally cold.

'Where were you, Kuang?' Geong finally spoke. 'Why didn't you help me?' Geong raised his voice a little. His lips coiled downwards into the saddest eclipse. He stared at me for a while before shifting his focus away in disappointment.

I did not know how to reply to Geong.

Indeed, I was late.

I was searching high and low for him but I was too late. The fact was, I was not there for him when he most needed help. *What kind of friend I am? Did I run to the teacher to save myself and leave my best friend in the lurch?*

I could not recall my intentions as clearly as I wanted to. It was so hard to reconcile with the past reality when my heart was aching with guilt.

'Geong, no. I didn't mean to leave you behind . . .'

I could not finish my words before the teachers rushed Geong to the hospital. The bell rang again and it was time to go back to the classroom.

'Geong, I'm sorry. I didn't mean to leave you behind,' I continued to mutter. Wasn't it just a moment ago when Geong and I were writing calligraphy together? I stood at the school gate, watching Geong as he disappeared from my sight.

Leaves continued to fall as the strong wind blew. My torn cotton shoes had dried up.

As I walked back to the classroom, sand filled my shoes through the holes. The grains of sand created unbearable pain on my soles, making each step a torture. I hobbled with an aching heart.

* * *

Three days later, Gee returned to his seat in class.

His suspension was over and it was a relief for him, but not for us. We were not looking forward to having him in class at all. Glances were darting about the moment he dragged his feet into the class. No one welcomed him back.

I missed Geong. Staring at his empty chair made me feel lonely.

Mr Wang, our Chinese Language teacher, hurried into the classroom in a fury. He did not even look at us before he started lecturing. At times, I wondered what made him so angry every day.

His lessons were the most awful.

As he chanted non-stop to himself, he wrote many unfamiliar Chinese characters on the black board. I had to stop myself from dozing off by spinning my pencil with my fingers all the time. And when I looked around, my classmates were performing all kinds of interesting acts to perk themselves up.

The classroom was almost transformed into a silent circus.

Ngia was touching her right eyelash. She pulled a strand out to compare with the one pulled out from the left. Her good friend was trimming her nails with a pair of small rusty scissors under the table.

Geong's puppy love was repeatedly tying her long glossy hair into two neat braids. Some were drawing on their tables with chalk, while others were biting their nails. Gee was pretending to shoot table legs with rubber bands, but in truth, he was aiming at some of the boys' legs. How annoying.

After writing a whole chunk of difficult words on the board, Mr Wang turned around and spoke, creasing his nose to move his fallen gold-rimmed glasses back.

'Alright, complete pages in your book, thirty to thirty-five now.' Mr Wang instructed us after chanting for almost forty minutes.

And no one did.

No one was committed to completing the work. We stared back at him blankly.

Upon seeing our reaction, Mr Wang turned mad. 'Are you all dumb? Can't even do this simple assignment? Raise your hand if you're not sure how to?' Mr Wang barked.

And everyone did. We all raised our hands. We could pretend to know but that would not do us any good because rubbish work, according to him, would land us in deeper troubles.

'LINE UP BESIDE MY TABLE NOW!' Mr Wang roared at all of us.

He then pulled out a long wooden rod from his bag and pointed it in our direction, flicking it up and down, bulging his eyes, and reprimanding us with all sorts of vulgarities.

The whole class hated Mr Wang. I always felt less than a human when he was talking with us. Sometimes, as a form of punishment, he would ask a few of us to buy groceries for him during lessons. We had to skip our lessons because of his ridiculous demands.

When our turn arrived, we had to place both of our fists on the teacher's table and remain motionless. With all his might, Mr Wang would raise the wooden rod high up into the air and lash it against our knuckles. The pain was bone-breaking. Our skin would split, and blood would tint his wooden rod. Every one of us would get ten strokes each for our ignorance.

We looked like a row of prisoners waiting to be caned at a camp. Being the last in the queue, I was able to witness the entire caning process.

None of us were spared. Girls and boys, no matter our size and stature, were hit with the same amount of force. Somehow, I felt my classmates of smaller body built had to endure more excruciating pain than those who were bigger-sized. Their knuckles were much smaller. A stroke from the wooden rod could break them easily. Ngia, the smallest girl in our class, had her knuckles all bloodied with swells.

Being punished seemed like a matter of fact. We deserved to be whacked if we did not follow instructions. Children knew nothing about the world, people said. Children lacked correct perceptions about everything. Therefore, we were told to learn from adults. If we failed to learn, we would be punished.

Gee was standing in front of me. He remained shockingly quiet as the queue shortened. He was not his usual self today and I was not used to his indifference.

Soon, it was Gee's turn to be smacked.

'Ahh! I know you! Chained outside the teacher's room for so many days and still, did not repent. Serve you right to be punished!' Mr Wang cursed as he struck Ah Ghee's knuckles like how Ah Mm chopped the chicken with a cleaver. His strength could break bones into pieces.

He struck ten blows on Gee's knuckles and was still whacking.

I was counting silently behind him. *Eleven, twelve, thirteen, fourteen...*

Worriedly, I took a quick glance at Gee. Even though he had been such a notorious bully, I felt sorry for him. He certainly did not deserve such unfair treatment on the first day he returned to class from his suspension. But Gee did not step back from the perceived threat.

Seventeen, eighteen, nineteen...

Gee's skin flushed, and veins began to surface on his protruding forehead. His breathing turned noisy. His muscles quivered. He stared at Mr Wang with cold hard eyes.

Standing behind him, I could feel hatred blistering every part of his body. Gee then lifted his left hand and grabbed Mr Wang's hand. My jaw dropped. Everyone was appalled.

Mr Wang tightened his grip on the wooden rod. He tried to shake off Gee's hand. 'HOW DARE YOU, RASCAL!'

Gee clenched his right fist and brought it forward. He walloped Mr Wang's stomach with the most forceful punch I had ever seen.

Mr Wang threw up straightaway, spitting out the water he had just drunk before the hitting session. He plummeted to the floor, shrieking in agony. Finger pointing and shaking relentlessly at Gee, he lifted his head and scowled, 'Good-for-nothing! Be prepared to die la you!'

I could foresee a forthcoming battle for Gee. He might be expelled from school again. Various public schools had chased him out before he came to ours and such a misfortunate incident had to happen.

Strangely, even though what Gee had done to Mr Wang looked terribly wrong, a corner of my heart admired him for being able to rebel against unfairness. It was something I had never had the guts to do.

I did not have the courage to stand up and push Ah Gong away when he hit Ah Mm. I wanted so much to stop him but my will to rise against him did not result in any action. If Gee were me, he would have punched Ah Gong in the face, wouldn't he?

Obedience was safe. Since young, I had been following instructions. Obey, obey, obey. Following instructions was the easiest. However, recently I started to doubt obedience. It felt like parasites feeding on my dignity. Very uncomfortable.

I shall learn to be like Gee. Let me stand up against unfairness. The next time Ah Gong yells and hits me for no good reason, I'll rise up. Watch me. I'll stop him. Ah Gong, I'll not bow my head to you anymore.

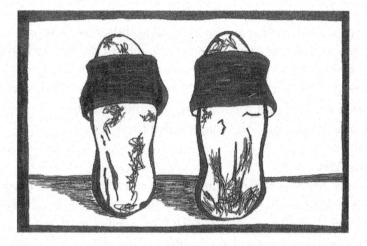

Ten

That afternoon, after having my bloodied knuckles washed and bandaged with my soiled handkerchief, I decided to go home earlier. Geong was not around, anyway. I had no one to hang out with after school.

The street market near the shophouse I lived in was a busy place, always drowning in the sea of people. Not a single empty place could be spotted between the stalls.

Walking along this avenue, I witnessed so many activities.

Children were playing cricket and catching one another. One little girl was wailing for her mother. Shopkeepers were yelling offers to attract customers. Women were picking the best vegetables from stalls to put into their baskets, and many rickshaw riders were placing paper fans above their foreheads, shielding their eyes from the Sun.

The market also had a unique scent. The air was filled with the garble of sweat and raw meats, a lingering odor of human and industrial wastes, with drain sewage mixed in.

As I approached closer to the shophouse where I lived, I saw Ah Gong and Siu pacing around a drain.

Siu was crying loudly and Ah Gong was trying to pacify him. He certainly did not wish to see his beloved grandson wallow in sorrow.

I believed something had gone wrong. But I did not wish to find out. Anyway, I had been deliberately avoiding Ah Gong. A clever thing to do now was perhaps to leave them alone and not stick my nose in. I sneaked past them, trying to avoid their sight.

'Come here, brat!' Ah Gong snarled from afar.

I froze.

'KUANG AH!'

I shut down, groaning at my failure to escape. I could have just walked on, pretending not to hear anything. But my natural reaction was to stop and cringe whenever Ah Gong yelled hard at me.

'Siu dropped his wooden toy into this drain. Get it for him!' Ah Gong boomed, holding me responsible for Siu's unhappiness as if I was the one who had dumped his toy into the filthy drain.

Why can't Siu pick his own toy? I wondered. *Why do I have to be responsible for others' carelessness?*

I lowered my head and stared at the drain. I had to stop breathing to prevent myself from becoming nauseated.

It resembled our common latrine at the shophouse—a single black oval bucket under a hole in a leveled-up squat toilet, filled with waste of different shades and emitting a putrid stench. It did not matter that the afternoon sun shone high in the sky, there was no way I would be able to find Siu's toy under all of that.

'What're you waiting for? Go on, dig it out!' Ah Gong instructed, casting a merciless glare at me.

The air around me seemed to solidify, causing my body to shrink in on itself. I squatted down, took a deep breath, and dipped my entire right arm into the filthy drain. My left hand was pinching my nose so hard that it became swollen and was triggered to sneeze many times. Tears began slipping out of the sides of my eyes.

Like finding a needle in the haystack, my hand circled in the repulsive pool, trying to feel for a wooden toy but to no avail.

Ah Gong stood beside me. His left leg was shaking ceaselessly. I was not sure if he was getting impatient, or his opium addiction was acting up.

A small gathering of people soon emerged around us. They just watched on and whispered among themselves. No one spoke a word of justice for me. No one stopped Ah Gong from torturing me.

I withdrew my right hand from the dirty drain. I could not bear the horrendous smell anymore. 'I can't find it!' I exploded, frowning and gasping for air as I released the grip on my nose.

'Did you even search for it? *Dor mia gia*! Go on! Find it! Don't you dare leave without retrieving it!' Ah Gong widened his eyes. Unsympathetically, he moved his body in front of me to stop me from leaving.

Siu had stopped crying. He lowered his head and looked at me with his big glossy eyes. Snot streamed out in a string in his nostril. *This boy, is he even aware that his carelessness has just landed me in deep shit?*

'No, I can't find it.' I insisted firmly, not giving in to this mean-spirited old man and allowing myself to be trampled by his ridiculously biased and hypercritical behaviour.

'Siu is not upset anymore. I'm going home,' I added.

When I was about to get up and take my leave, Ah Gong hurled a long list of Teochew vulgarities at me. '*PWA BEH GIA! YAU SIU GIA!*' His temper had been violently bad these few months. With his fists firmly locked by his sides, the words he used on us were threateningly blunt.

None of us in the family could go near him.

As usual, Ah Ma and Ah Mm received the most condemning treatment from him, especially when Ah Beh was away for days working in the fishing vessel. Ah Gong would push them onto the floor and throw things like spittoon and walking stick at them whenever he lacked money. He was the most detestable and disgusting person on Earth. How I wished he would just vanish one day.

I mustered my courage to persist on fleeing this suffocating situation. I ignored his words for the first time.

Ah Gong snapped.

He did not expect me to react in such a disrespectable manner. His rage came out faster than before and consumed him in seconds. He stooped lower, trying to pull his clog out from his left foot.

As he cursed behind me, Ah Gong loomed forward and swung his mud-stained clog at me forcefully. '*DUM BAI*! DUM BAI! DUM BAI!' Down flung the red clog onto the top center of my head, producing a loud thump.

My heart almost stopped beating. It was an unforgettably wounding moment. I was more shocked than scared. My hands tightening into fists, enduring the insulting blow on my head.

I lifted my head and stared at Ah Gong. My eyes welling up with angry tears. I wished him a terrible death in my heart and reincarnation as a cockroach for lifetimes ahead.

Brownish water was still dripping from my right arm. Ah Gong continued to curse like a lunatic. I diverted my attention to the small window of my apartment that could be easily seen from the busy streets. And I noticed Ah Mm standing by the window.

Ah Mm's eyes were fixed on me, and her sunken face was wet with tears. Neither did she move away nor did she lean closer to the window when my eyes met hers. She was standing in a daze, looking like a ghostly figure, white and petrified.

There was nowhere I wanted to run to but home. I needed to rid the dirty stuff off my arm, but more desperately, I was craving for safety and comfort, to be around people whom I could trust.

I wanted to be with Ah Mm so badly.

I could not help but think about the incident with Gee and Mr Wang again. Didn't I swear that I, too, would be a braver person who could stand up for myself? Why didn't I fight back? Why did I allow myself to be trampled on again?

Swallowing hard, I refused to let out a whimper. I realized to make the decision to be brave was easy. But the becoming was harder than I thought. Maybe . . . I did not have to do it overnight. I had to do it gradually. Slowly, I would be braver.

I had already done my best to fight back against Ah Gong. This was enough for now.

So, I ran, leaving a trail of brownish water on the road after splattering some on Ah Gong's shirt while squeezing my eyes shut.

Eleven

'Ah Hia, what're you doing?' asked Ang, raising his brows and staring at my homework.

Ang was my second brother after Dak. He was six years old when I was thirteen. A lovely boy with a snub nose and small eyes, Ang had a melancholic temperament, unlike the rest of my siblings.

Ang was very curious by nature. While the rest of my siblings were out playing in the evening, Ang would be at home, watching vehicles pass by and making simple woodwork using small wood pieces and shavings. Watching me do my homework was one of his favourite things to do. He urged me to teach him calligraphy but I refused. My skills were not fantastic at all.

'This is English Language, Ang. These are the names of some animals I just learned today. Cokcokdile . . . Gilaffe . . . Hippomas!' I shared with Ang, feeling embarrassed for being unsure at some of the words I read out.

'Wow, Ah Hia! This looks fun!' Ang replied with excitement, revealing his two cute bulging central incisors. He leaned nearer to the table, raised his shoulders and bent his head down to have a closer look at my homework, drumming his feet against the floor.

'Ang, you'll have your chance to go to school soon. Next year! Then you will have a mountain of homework like I do now,' I assured him, smiling.

'Ah Mm told me I may not be going to school next year.' Ang answered in a high-pitched voice, slightly perplexed at the conflicting statements he received from Ah Mm and me.

'Why not?' I questioned further, my mind racing and searching for answers. 'Did Ah Mm say more?'

'*Bo lui*. No money. Ah Mm said so.' Ang replied, scratching the base of his neck.

I could not believe this fellow, so passionate about learning, would be missing school in his tender years. *Aren't we doing pretty fine? Isn't Ah Beh doing well working in the fishing vessel?*

My stomach dipped at Ang's words. A million thoughts plagued my mind. *Why? Why did Ah Mm say that to Ang? What does she mean?* I turned away, glancing around as if looking for answers to all my questions.

Ah Beh had been working as a ship deck worker with an Indonesian fishing company for almost three years. This job secured a fair sum of money for our family's survival. Thank goodness. But Ah Beh was seldom home, each time leaving for two to three days, depending on the speed of the vessel he travelled on.

We missed him but at the same time, we felt assured with his absence.

So why can't Ang go to school? I was determined to find out more.

* * *

It was Sunday morning. I was at home, washing a pile of dirtied cloth napkins while Ah Mm sorted out her grocery.

This was certainly the most arduous chore for me.

'Ah Mm, I'm done with washing!' I went back to the apartment, heaving a sigh of relief and letting my head fall back. Ah Mm nodded. She was sitting on the shakiest chair, sewing an inner pocket in my shorts.

I approached Ah Mm and sat next to her. 'Ah Mm, I've something to ask you,' I muttered.

Ah Mm nodded again as she placed a new thread onto her tongue and wetted the end of it with her saliva.

'Mm ah, Ang . . .' I fidgeted and squirmed. 'Ang . . . told me the other day that he would not attend school next year. I mean, he told me that . . . you said, he . . . could not attend school.' I asked softly, fiddling with my sleeves.

Ah Mm remained silent for a while before turning her head to face me. Her eyes, however, were unable to meet mine. 'It depends, Kuang. Ah Beh . . . he . . . no job.'

I gulped.

'Why . . . what happened, Ah Mm?' I asked, softening my expression.

Ah Mm looked into my eyes. Her eyes resembled those of a dead fish. In a low and mournful voice, Ah Mm continued, 'Last Friday, your Ah Beh was out in the vast sea on a vessel. Halfway to Indonesia, the vessel stopped moving. Something went wrong. Your Ah Beh and a few other men were ordered to check things out.' Ah Mm paused to catch her breath. Her helpless expression told me many things in life were just not within our control.

'So, they dived deep into the waters but your Ah Beh didn't manage to solve the problem. He was gasping for air after some time. The captain commanded him to try again but your Ah Beh refused to do it. Fortunately, one of the other men managed to adjust the propellers and they could return to the shore safely.'

'And then?' I continued to ask, leaning closer to Ah Mm.

'Lost the job.'

'Just like that? Why?' I persisted in my questioning, enraged and feeling sorry for Ah Beh that he had to go through such hardship.

'His bosses had decided to fire him. They thought his refusal to dive back into the water was a form of defiance. He left the company three days later and now . . . back to be a kuli,' Ah Mm paused her sewing and looked at me. 'Ah Mm can't be sure if we'll have enough money for your siblings to go to school.'

As I listened to Ah Mm, my nose got stingy, and tears began forming in my eyes.

I had always thought that being born the eldest was my bad luck. I had to help with so many chores at home while the younger ones could play all day. Being the eldest also meant that I was the only one mature enough to borrow money for the family. I hated doing it. But at this moment, I felt privileged. I could go to school, a private school where school fees were so much higher than the ones at public schools. I should be glad, however, deep in my heart, I felt a strange sense of injustice.

Who am I to deserve such a privilege? How can I enjoy school when my younger siblings are denied the chance to even go to school? That just doesn't make sense.

No, it shouldn't be like this.

* * *

The gabble of several-hundred voices buzzed like a swarm of bees.

All students and teachers gathered at the sandy field for the morning assembly. After the flag raising ceremony, Madam Khoo paced up the podium and spoke to the school. Her tone was serious and solemn, causing all of us to be in a grave mood.

'Good morning, school. Today I've a piece of bad news to share with all of you.' Madam Khoo paused, looking hard at all of us.

She cleared her throat and coughed, before continuing her speech. Occasionally, she let out a bitter smile. 'Since Singapore gained her independence, our government has been trying to integrate the different kinds of schools in order to lay the foundation for the ideal single education system. The Chinese school committees, including ours, are asked to submit the autonomy that we used to enjoy in running the school to the government . . . '

Despite my efforts, I could not suppress my frown as I felt that familiar pit of unease in my stomach. What did she mean?

'The changing reality of declining enrollment into our school has also posed a great challenge to us financially and we can barely survive. After considering for a long period of time, our school committee has decided to close the school for good.' Madam Khoo paused and took a shaky breath. 'We would rather shut the school than to accept the government's terms for integration. Therefore, all of you would have to look for another school to enroll in. Our last day of school is . . . '

I stared at Madam Khoo in disbelief. *What? Did I hear wrongly? Did she just say our school is closing?*

Taking a quick glance around the school while standing on the sandy field, it was hard to imagine that this place would vanish soon.

I looked down at my feet. The rain had dampened the sand this morning. As I walked back to the classroom, my footprints were embedded, leaving a piece of me on the school ground. It felt like five years' worth of memories were going to be pulled down together with the buildings. I could not bear to say goodbye.

I spent the whole day in school, pondering where I should go after our school's closure in a month's time. *Will a public school want an over-aged student like me? Thirteen years old, which school would want me? Can I even cope in an English-medium school?*

It was difficult to accept the impending change.

Even though it was upsetting to leave this school, the thought of Ah Mm paying a cheaper school fee for me in the future lightened me up.

How about Geong? Will he want to move to a public school?

Geong had not been talking much with me since he returned to school. Our relationship had soured. It was hard to clear things up with him.

Every time I approached him, he would simply walk away. When he ran out of excuses to avoid me, he would answer me briefly. Recently he had been joining another group of boys for their games during recess.

It seemed like the school was closing for a good reason for me. I lost my good friend and I could not turn back time. Ah Mm was right. She said a broken relationship was equivalent to a shattered mirror. Even if the pieces were glued back together, the crack would always remain.

That was true for Geong and me. I could never have imagined a small misunderstanding could break us apart. I thought our friendship could last forever.

Perhaps, that was just my wishful thinking.

* * *

Upon hearing that my school would be closed, Ah Beh went around different public schools to ask for the enrollment requirements. Some were already full while others did not want to accept over-aged students. Two schools asked me to sit for an English Language proficiency test before enrolling me.

Why English? I had never done well for it. I always merely scraped through English exams after working very, very, very hard.

Just visualizing myself sitting for the deciding test made me shiver.

Should I give up a place in school, Ang could be enrolled in a more affordable English-medium public school? Ah Beh and Ah Mm would worry less about the family's expenses. I could then work to support my family financially. Everyone would be better off. So why not?

After giving it a second thought, I eventually gave up fighting for a place in a new school. I was not good at English anyway. There was nothing to lose.

* * *

This year's Lunar New Year's was depressing.

There was no sumptuous feast on the table and all of us were dressed in clothes sewn by Ah Mm using all sorts of reusable cloths. Nonetheless, as children, we still looked forward to it in great anticipation.

It was the only time of the year we could have soft drinks and sweets. Besides that, we would also receive *ang-pows* from the adults. We could receive up to two or three dollars.

It was also exciting to see adults and children playing with firecrackers that were used to deter evil spirits and pray for prosperity and happiness. Shops lit long trains of huge firecrackers hung from the top of the shophouses while children lighted strings of mini firecrackers in their pajamas. The deafening sound of crackers going off at the stroke of midnight to announce the arrival of a new lunar year was always music to my ears.

On the first day of the lunar new year, more firecrackers would be lit and they were usually accompanied by lion dances. I loved to observe those lion mascots. Their blinking eyes were out of the world.

New year, new beginning.

I looked forward to soaking in the entire streets filled with bits and pieces of the red wrappers of firecrackers. Such a scene always made me feel rejuvenated.

Ah Mm gave me a few dollars to buy some pork belly meat, seasonal vegetables, and fizzy drinks to cheer everyone up. Even though there was no lavish feast, Ah Mm tried to compensate by putting more red decorations at home.

She coloured a stack of rice paper with red ink and cut out big fishes and ingots from them. That was a lot of hard work apart from all the chores she had to do. Ah Mm always amazed me with her creativity, like those invigorating tales she created and shared with me at Feng Mei village.

Coincidentally, Ah Mm also found the spring couplet I wrote in school last year.

I kept it at one corner under one of our mattresses. I was not sure how she found it and how she felt when she first saw it but I definitely got a very big surprise when I saw it pasted on the inside of our main door during our reunion dinner on Lunar New Year's Eve.

As I looked at my work on the door while gobbling my dinner, I was once again filled with pride. It was the same feeling I had when Madam Khoo patted on my shoulder. Somehow, I missed that particular moment in school. The thought of not having another chance to experience it formed a lump in my throat.

I swallowed my rice quickly, hoping to push the lump away.

Why am I here and where do I go? This Chinese New Year, I could no longer chuck these questions aside.

Part Two

Growth

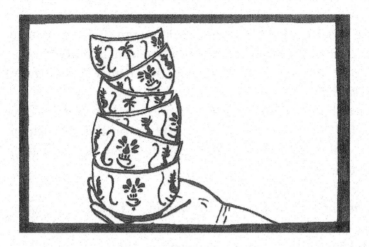

Twelve

Tok, tik, tok, tik, tok, tik, tik, tik, tok.
'Tok Tok Mee!'

The same tok-tok mee hawker and his assistant always promenaded the busy streets near my shophouse on weekdays. They continuously hit a bamboo striker against a piece of split bamboo to attract customers and their rhythmic 'tik-tok' sound had become their distinctive call.

I peered out from my window, waiting in anticipation for the tok-tok mee hawker to pass by. And he never failed me.

'Ah Chek, here!' I shouted out to the tok-tok mee hawker, gesturing for a bowl of hot noodle soup.

'Kuang! You're up so early?' a high-pitched chirpy voice sounded from diagonally above me.

'Ey, Auntie Lim! Good morning!' I turned my head and greeted the cheery lady who was smiling away, exposing her pearly whites.

Auntie Lim had just lowered her basket to get her noodle soup. She was earlier than me. I bet she needed a bowl of goodness for breakfast before heading to work.

The tok-tok mee hawker nodded at me and replied, '*Ey!* It's coming!' While he was cooking, I started lowering my basket using a long rope. This was the benefit of staying in a low-rise shophouse. I could receive my food without stepping out of my apartment.

The hawker got his assistant to place a small porcelain bowl of hot noodle soup in my basket. I would then haul it up, trying my best not to spill the contents in the bowl.

I had been waking up at 6.45 a.m. every day ever since school ended for me. I used to dread waking up on time for school but now it was hard not to wake up at this time despite having no school to go to.

Life is such an irony.

I finished my noodles in five minutes. I placed a twenty-cent coin in the bowl and lowered it down again in the same basket.

Huffing and puffing, the hawker's assistant ran towards me to collect the bowl and money. The white face towel hanging around his neck was dripping wet with perspiration. He had been running about to tend to the customers while his boss stayed put in his mobile kitchen.

We waved to each other and they soon left for another street, pushing their three-wheeled cart and creating the same 'tik-tok' rhythm as they walked.

* * *

I strolled to the kitchen to get some hot water. On the way, I met Auntie Lim at the staircase.

She was all dressed up for work. A loose collared white shirt and her usual yellow and pink flowery skirt. She even had a white scarf on her head, preventing her long fringe from falling to her face. Her face was pinkish with blush powder and her lips were glossed.

I was envious of Auntie Lim's optimism. She was always ever ready for work in the morning. Standing next to her made me stand out in contrast. Like an aimless vagrant, just trying to get by life, I was especially downcast during this period.

Other than helping to take care of Ing, sending Ang to school, and running errands for Ah Mm, I had no goal of my own. Emptiness filled my heart after I left school and I began to wonder if I had given enough thought to that decision.

'Kuang! Why are you up so early in the morning? Haven't you quit school?' Auntie Lim's words stabbed my heart once more, digging my regrets and letting them surface.

'I don't know.' I replied honestly. 'I guess this habit is going to stick with me for years to come.'

Auntie Lim stared at me from head to toe. One of her eyebrows shot up after frowning for a short while. 'Do you want to find some work to do then? Earn some money for the family.' Auntie Lim suggested, injecting a dose of her optimism into her words.

'Well, Auntie Lim, I tried but I was always rejected.' I dropped my eyes then looked up at her. 'I'm probably too young.'

'Nothing about age, Kuang. Everyone is looking for a job now, that's why it's hard to get one. Did you see that tok-tok mee hawker's assistant just now? Would you like to try out something like that? You need a lot of energy to become a hawker's assistant.'

Finally, an opportunity came knocking at my door after a month of search. My mood was immediately lifted and I felt a surge of happiness.

'*Ai Mai*? Want it or not?' Auntie Lim asked again, raising her brows and blinking rapidly.

Without hesitation, I replied in exuberance, 'YES! Of course!'

* * *

In front of Thong Chai Medical Institution at Wayang Street, rows of pushcart hawker stalls were open for business every day.

There were all kinds of food—*char kway teow,* charcoal-grilled *satay, lok mei, hokkien mee, loh kai yik, lor ark png,* chicken rice, pig innards hot soup, chili crab, *bak kut teh,* etc.

It was a bustling street filled with drool-inviting aromas.

Auntie Lim's husband had a friend who was selling Teochew fish porridge at Wayang Street. His stall stood just beside an old kopitiam.

Customers who had bought fish porridge from his stall could sit in the kopitiam to enjoy their food. As these customers would usually purchase a drink to go along with their meals, it would help to boost sales for the drinks stall located in the kopitiam.

This was how profit-seeking hawker businesses collaborated with one another. Laws were loose and there were loopholes, giving chance for street hawkers to set up stalls without proper licensing and to share space without legal permission.

Auntie Lim's friend needed a young assistant urgently. She brought me to his stall on a Monday evening with Ah Mm's approval. Even though I was skinny, I was tall and that convinced Auntie Lim's friend to think that I was strong enough to handle the job of an assistant.

'Ah Di ah, let me tell you, it's not easy to earn a living nowadays. You'll need to be prepared to work really hard,' Auntie Lim's friend reminded me in a stern voice, crossing his arms with a silent look.

'Seven days to rest in a year—Chinese New Year Eve, Lantern Festival Day, *Qing Ming* Festival, Dragon Boat Festival, Ghost Festival, Mid-Autumn Festival, and *Chongyang* Festival. Report to work at nine in the morning. You can have a short break from twelve to three in the afternoon. Then come back to work from three in the afternoon all the way to one in the morning. Fifty dollars a month. Are you good with these terms?'

I froze. My ribs tightened slightly upon hearing the employment terms. *Is it possible for me to work those long hours each day?* Worrying over what my days would be working at this porridge stall, I felt like backing off. Shoving my hands into pockets, I pursed my lips and looked away.

On the contrary, Auntie Lim's eyes gleamed with assurance as she turned to look at me. I bet she could feel my hesitation to accept these terms.

'Kuang, ai mai? He's asking you.' Auntie Lim smiled, looking at me and pointing at her friend.

I kept my hands in my pockets, lowered my head, and stared on the ground.

'Can la, can la! What a great opportunity! Kuang, work hard. You can do it. Take it!' Auntie Lim urged.

Somehow, I trusted Auntie Lim so much that my limiting self-belief was overridden by her encouraging words.

'Erm, yes, Ok, I'll . . . take it up.' I looked up and replied. A slow smile built on my face.

'Come tomorrow then! See you at nine in the morning.' The fish porridge hawker cleared his throat as he poured a large pack of fish bones into the boiling stock.

I stiffened slightly. I could not believe I was employed.

Am I becoming an adult? Does it mean I can finally earn money like Ah Beh?

I held my breath. A lighthearted feeling filled my heart as I envisioned how I would help make ends meet at home and perhaps, carve my own path in life. I clasped my hands under my chin. My heart was filled with so much gratitude and relief.

* * *

The dark morning sky seemed to be plastered on my windows. Could it be possible that the sun had forgotten to rise?

I woke up and could not get back to sleep. My mind was wild with thoughts. I was visualizing all sorts of worse-case scenarios working as a fish porridge hawker's assistant, rolling back and forth on the parquetted floor.

Time crawled like a snail.

It was my first day of work. Ah Mm did not have to pull me out of bed today. Every fiber of my being was vibrating with anticipation.

I arrived at the stall earlier than nine and Boss was slicing ginger for the fish stock. 'Good job, Ah Di! You're early. We're preparing ingredients for the fish porridge. You, wash the vegetables over there and cut them into pieces.' Boss instructed, pointing to a red pail next to the stall.

I blew out a series of short breaths, attempting to gain control of my pounding heart. *First task of the day. Alright, I'm ready.*

The other assistant, Boon, was a man in his early twenties. A compact, clearcut man with precise features, a lot of soft black hair, and thoughtful dark brown eyes. He had a look of wariness, which could change when he felt relaxed. At the same time, the caution spread across his face made him look aloof. Although it was a burning hot day, Boon was dressed in a loose dark brown tee shirt that looked rather thick.

He had been working with Boss for the last five years and was familiar with his role and Boss' expectations. Boon took to cleaning and descaling fish as a fish takes to water. His actions were swift and natural, yet error-free.

Boon was a friendly chap. He helped me several times on my first day. It seemed like nothing could go wrong as I was guided step-by-step on what I needed to do.

In fact, things seemed easier than I thought.

After washing and cutting the vegetables, I grew confident. I was keen to take on other tasks, like the one that kept Boon occupied. 'Let me wash the fish too!' I said aloud.

A doubtful look crossed Boon's face. I squatted to get closer.

'Since you want to . . . alright. Scrub the scales, cut a slit at the side like this, and pull out the internal organs gently. Remember to save these roes. These are treasures. Incredibly nutrient-dense. They add so much flavour to our porridge. Don't discard them. Place them here.' Boon advised, demonstrating the cleaning of fish in a quick manner. 'There are many fish, as you can see. Clean as many as you can,' he added.

I scratched my jaw and stared at my palms as if they held clues on how I should get started.

'Go on! Start working!' I could feel the tension in Boss' words thrown to me.

As I opened the big bag of frozen fish, it reeked of an overpowering stench, almost like the stinky smell of urine that remained stagnant for days. The fish were all stuck together, as if wrapped in one bundle with a thick layer of adhesive.

I grabbed onto the bundle of fish and tried to pull the fish apart with mere strength. It was incredibly hard. Questions began swirling in my head. But at the same time, I was worried. Would my questions invite laughter?

I decided to figure things out on my own.

Exerting my greatest strength, I used my bare hands to break the fish apart. It was freezing cold. I held onto the fish for a minute before my fingers turned painfully numb. No warm blood could flow to them. They hardened and turned white. A tinge of sharp pain penetrated my flesh at the fingertips.

I quickly put down the fish and began rubbing my hands together and using my breath to resuscitate them.

Boon noticed my odd behaviours and came over.

'What're you doing?' he asked, stunned and concerned at the same time.

'These fish can't be separated.' I tried to stop my voice from shaking. 'How . . . how do I wash them when they are all stuck together?'

'What? Just soak them in water so they will not get stuck together. For goodness' sake, let the ice first melt in the water.' Boon answered, frowning his brows and widening his eyes.

As if baffled by my ignorance, he then let out a laugh as he squatted down to demonstrate the process of cleaning a fish. 'You've never washed fish before? Ok, watch me. I'll show you again.'

'Aiyo, Di ah, you've got a long way to go. Learn on the job but don't take your own sweet time about it,' Boss turned his head and exclaimed.

Though Boss' words were far from harsh, they reminded me that there was no time to be incapable in the adult world. I had to stand on my own two feet and fend for myself.

Boon looked at me with concerned eyes while throwing a cleaned fish into a pail. 'Did you see how I did it, Kuang?'

'Yes.' I responded, concealing my anxiety with an exaggerated nod.

'Go on, try again.' Boon pursued.

Carefully, I picked up another frozen fish and began scrubbing it. Every step to completing this seemingly easy task felt like a mountain to climb. I was overwhelmed. I wanted to be like Boon, fast and skillful. But I knew it would not happen overnight.

My first morning at work went by in a blink. At the end of my morning shift, my fingers were all wrinkled after soaking them in water for a long time.

I clenched my fists and put them in my pockets, hoping to warm them up for the second round of fighting.

* * *

Around five in the afternoon, crowds began to gather.

A hot pot of aromatic porridge was made by combining the odour-filled fish with the raw ingredients I washed in the morning. Silky soft, thick, and comforting. Just staring at the porridge made me feel accomplished.

People swarmed into the kopitiam to look for seats, one group after another.

I had the busiest day of my life, far worse than rushing homework at home. In just an evening, I had to clear tables, wash dishes, serve porridge to customers, take orders, as well as to greet customers. All happening at the same time! Not to mention the most important and difficult of them all—matching customers' faces to their respective orders.

I either tagged orders to the wrong faces or took down wrong orders that invited criticism. I felt entirely thrashed in the second battle.

Trying to multitask on this job was a challenge for me and sure enough, I made a blunder this evening.

With one hand, I was cleaning a table with a rag; with the other, I was holding a stack of used bowls. My stomach was rumbling due to hunger, causing my hands to tremble. The stack of bowls collapsed against one another, producing repeated tolls of clinging and clanging, all falling onto the ground.

In a frenzy, I spilled leftover porridge onto a customer's pants. That man was maddened. Straightaway, he got up and swept the hot porridge off his pants.

'Sorry, sorry, sir!' I apologized profusely, trying to clean his pants with my dirty rag.

'What're you doing, idiot? Get lost!' The man pushed my hand away and took a step back. He almost tripped on the table's leg and fell.

All eyes around us were fixed on me. My dirty rag dangled in the air as I grabbed it tightly at one end, dripping droplets of soup onto the floor. I stood still like a scarecrow.

The man started cursing. I got scared. I could feel my skin flushing and my chin trembling.

Boon approached us upon hearing the man's loud nasty comments. He took some clean tissue papers from his pocket and dabbed them on the man's dirtied pants, trying to remove all the porridge stains. As he wiped, Boon pleaded for the man's mercy on me.

Boon arched his back very low. His loose brown tee sagged out in the front as he bent, exposing his bone-packed chest. He bowed his head continuously while he engaged that angry customer. His stiff smile was mortared onto his face. Occasionally, he shifted his eyes to look up and smiled blushingly. His right fingers repeatedly tapped on his brow, making a gestural apology as he wiped.

The angry customer pulled his chair away and sat down like an emperor settling on his throne. His lethal stares were again injecting aversion into my eyes.

I gulped.

I was sorry for my deed. If I were more careful, Boon would not have to apologize on my behalf. Yet, at the same time, I wondered why this man had to blow his top over such a small matter.

Guilty and sickened, I walked away to attend to other customers' needs.

The crowd finally dispersed by one in the morning. We packed up and were ready to leave the stall. I approached Boon at the end of the day and apologized once more.

'Enough of saying sorry, Kuang. Don't worry about it. I face this every day,' Boon answered calmly.

'Face this every day?' I winced. 'That's truly exhausting.'

'Why?' Boon countered. Curiosity filled his words.

'It's exhausting to please customers.' I explained, sighing away. 'Customers aren't always right. Sometimes we may not be in the wrong, but we've to admit that we are. And that's exhausting.'

'Well, I can admit wrong even if I don't think I am.' Boon smiled. 'That doesn't matter. What's important is getting by each day, knowing that I've given my best.'

Surprised by Boon's reply, I added, 'But . . . how do you know you've given your best?'

'Set a goal, kid. Achieve it and ignore shallow criticisms. That's what I do. Every day, I strive to help Boss sell all his porridge. Even if I make customers unhappy, I just apologize and then focus back on selling the porridge. I feel better this way. Five years in this line, *Di*!' Boon said as he clasped his arms behind his body and stretched.

Boon's words caught me by surprise. I was amazed by how Boon dealt with his everyday life and how his perspectives differed from mine. However, as much as I wanted to think like him, a part of my heart could not be convinced.

I say only what I mean, Boon. How do I lie to myself?

Boon's walking pace was still quick at this hour. I was running behind him, trying to catch up.

The morning moon was shining brightly, but not as brightly as the setting sun I used to see when I walked home from school. I shall learn to admire the soft whispering moon.

At the same time, I also needed to get used to seeing Ah Mm and my siblings less and probably, not seeing Ah Beh at all since he slept before I returned home and left home before I woke up in the morning.

Has my life changed for the better? I had asked myself this question countless times. Over the course of my first day, there were instances I berated myself over my decision to work at the fish porridge stall. There were also moments I felt thankful for this rare job opportunity.

I was not sure. I did not know where to find a good answer. I just knew I got tired of thinking about this question until I got home.

* * *

Ah Gong lay horizontally outside the common kitchen when I arrived at the shophouse. He must have fallen asleep just like that again. It was something he did more often now.

Constantly shivering in a cold sweat, recently, Ah Gong could not even stand for long. He fell easily. Sometimes he would just stay put where he had fallen and slept.

As I ran up the stairs, producing sounds of a marching troop with my old flip-flops, Ah Gong woke up. He stared at me with eyes ringed with fatigue.

'YAU SIU GIA! SEEKING DEATH?' His voice thundered like before, hurling a train of words of frustration coupled with crudities at me.

I quickened my pace to my apartment and shut the door tight. Everyone in the family was asleep. In the dark room, my body was crumpling in on itself. I could no longer tolerate another round of verbal abuse after serving tables of impatient customers today.

I needed a break. I needed to escape into a world of less blame, less guilt.

Thirteen

Five months had passed since my first day of work at Boss' fish porridge stall.

Just like Boon, I focused on selling porridge and detached myself from unforgiving customers. That surprisingly worked for me too.

Even though life went on well, I would occasionally look at the scars on my arms that were left behind by the scalding of hot porridge and sighed at the damage to my youthful skin. Calloused and hardened, it seemed to be desensitized to the harshness of work.

Becoming an adult is akin to a snake shedding its skin. When old skin cannot fit anymore, it needs to be removed. Something new has to grow. I could no longer just remain who I was. While overcoming all sorts of difficulties, my new self emerged. A more courageous me. A more forgiving me.

I rubbed my hardened skin, hoping to scrape the dead parts away.

During my break from twelve to three in the afternoon, I could go anywhere after having my lunch at the fish porridge stall. I always chose to go home for a restful nap, or stand beside some makeshift stages to watch performance rehearsals.

However, today, I felt like doing none of these.

I was thirsting for Uncle Tham's galy poks so badly that I had to pay him a visit at his stall just a mile away.

* * *

'Uncle Tham!' I called out to him from afar, hands waving as enthusiastically as before.

'Ey! Kuang! How're you? Haven't seen you for so long!' Uncle Tham smiled affably back at me. His big eyes shimmered with joy.

Uncle Tham had not changed a bit. His wide dimpled smile still warmed my heart. He became quite animated after seeing me approach in his direction. He started singing some Teochew-hee popular tunes and twirling his fingers inwards and outwards, imitating those actors on stage.

I burst out laughing while skipping my way to his stall.

'Great acting, Uncle Tham!' I reached the stall and gave Uncle Tham a thumbs-up. I could feel an overall feeling of weightlessness whenever I met him.

'Kuang! Why do you have time to look for me at this time of the day? Uncle Tham shall give four galy poks to my rare guest today! Buy two get two free. Only for privileged customers like our Kuang, okay?' Uncle Tham joked in his bubbly voice.

'Thank you! You're the best!' I replied with a satisfied smile.

'So, why're you not in school at this time?'

'Oh Uncle Tham, I haven't told you. I . . . Actually, I already quit my studies last year. Now, I'm a hawker's assistant at a Teochew fish porridge stall, just down the road over there,' I answered with a tinge of sadness, pointing my finger to the front of the road.

'Ahh, I see!' Uncle Tham stopped fiddling with this dough and looked at me with concern.

I forced a smile but on its own, my lips arched downwards.

'You don't look satisfied quitting school.' Uncle Tham saw through me.

'Ahh, no, no, I'm fine . . . I'm ok really.'

Uncle Tham continued to look at me with much attention. His concerned gaze hinted I could share my heart without concealing anything.

'Well . . . I thought there was nothing to lose. But being out of school makes my life really boring now. Every day I just clean fish and serve porridge to others. What a lousy decision I've made!' I sulked.

I could feel a thickness in my throat. It was bubbling upwards.

'Kuang, you'll be fine! Uncle Tham didn't study at all and I could live on.' Uncle Tham grasped my shoulder firmly with his white powdered palms.

'When I just came to Singapore, I had nothing. Let me be honest with you, Kuang. Nothing decent! I didn't even have a piece of decent shirt. All my clothes had holes on them! I started making puffs because I made an Indian friend and he was kind enough to share his skills with me. I needed money to bring my family over. I missed them. That was my goal then.'

Uncle Tham paused to take a sip of water from a small tin. As he drank, he maintained unwavering eye contact with me in the same steadfast gaze.

'I tell you, Kuang, I was so lousy at making puffs in the beginning. Uncle Tham is honest here. It took me all day to sell nothing. Not even a single puff! I was thinking, *jialat lah*! *Jiak cao liao lah*. I was of course very dejected. But my heart never wavered. I needed my family to be here. Making puffs was the decision I made for myself and my family. I told myself I must make sure that decision was the best decision. So, I continued making puffs and started thinking of ways to make my puffs better. So, you see, every decision made is the best if we make it to be. Kuang, you're at a place where you're most needed to be right now. You've made your decision. Make the best out of it. Don't look back, or right, or left. Just look ahead. You'll be fine, Uncle Tham assures you.'

Uncle Tham always had a way to transform me into a more confident person. Unlike many people whom I had met in my life, his words were always comforting and encouraging.

He handed four lip-smacking buttery pockets of curry to me, but was willing to collect only the money for two. I tried to slip the coins into his pouch but was discovered and rejected.

I stood by his stall and stared at him kneading dough in awe. 'Uncle Tham, what would you be if you weren't a galy pok seller?' I asked casually.

'Teochew-hee actor?'

I laughed. 'You certainly have what it takes to be one.'

'I was kidding.' Uncle Tham covered his smile with a hand. 'Hmm . . . how about a teacher, taming monkeys in school?' He laughed, clapping his hands. 'Would you like to have me as your teacher?'

'Of course!' I responded keenly, raising my right hand up.

'Silly boy!' Uncle Tham blushed lightly while shaking his head.

Curiosity filled my mind. 'Why a teacher?' I asked again.

'Well, probably because I really love children!' Uncle Tham said, giving me an easy nod. 'Kuang, you may not know, but Uncle Tham had a wonderful teacher in the past.'

'Oh! Who's that?'

'My first son. He passed on when he was three.' Uncle Tham smiled.

I widened my eyes in disbelief. Uncle Tham did not seem to be someone who had lost loved ones. My heart sank upon hearing what he had just told me. Sharing a pained glance with Uncle Tham, I asked, 'So . . . on top of the two sons you have now, there was another one?'

'Yes, I should have three.'

'What . . . happened to him?' I asked, feeling rather uncertain if I should continue to pursue.

'Jumped over the window and died.'

I looked at Uncle Tham with a focused gaze and reached out to rub his rough arm lightly.

'Sometimes, in life, we've got to face things we don't want to. It's beyond our control.' Uncle Tham looked up and bit his lower lip.

'So . . . why is he your teacher, may I know?'

'Do you know why he jumped over the windows? He thought he could fly! That silly kid. He jumped down with a broken umbrella!' Uncle Tham laughed.

Uncle Tham seemed amused, but his sad frowns and lips gave him away.

'In his first year of life, I watched him grow from a vulnerable infant to a toddler who could flip his body, crawl, sit, and even stand. That's a lot of learning. Then after he had mastered all those, he was eager to run. When he reached three, he loved jumping. He climbed onto chairs and tables and made great leaps to the ground. Everyday!'

My heart pounded faster but I was not sure why. Perhaps it was my first time listening to someone describe the growth of a child. *Was I like that too?* A child should always be obedient, that was what I was always told. Nothing of this sort.

'Children learn so much in just a short span of time. But as a child slowly morphs into an adult, somehow, he stops learning. Uncle Tham has encountered so many people in my life. Some adults are really broken. They can't learn. Their minds are so fixated.' Uncle Tham said, his face wrinkling up as he patted his own head.

'And somehow, it's a cycle. When our minds are fixed, the things we see are fixed. When our minds are growing, the things we see are growing too!' Uncle Tham continued, making big circles in the air with his finger.

My eyebrows flashed up and held. My eyes followed his finger going round and round.

'When there's growth within, we can always count on ourselves to make sense of all kinds of experiences, to see the true values of people we encounter and things that happen to us. We will always experience victories. Even in failures, there can be victories within us.'

I stared hard at Uncle Tham, my heart rate picking up slightly.

'My son taught me so much, Kuang. I would thank him if he were alive.' Uncle Tham's eyes reddened. I could see a layer of watery glaze moving gently in his eyes as he averted his gaze.

'Excitement led him to his death. That silly kid! I want to live excitedly too. That's why I want to be a teacher, to encourage people especially children to always learn. Learn to grow. Learn how to live a rich life.'

Uncle Tham smiled. His cheekbones became prominent and raised. My mood was immediately lifted too.

'Ahh! Talk to you more next time. See how I could rattle on and on. You just quit school. I shall not remind you of school again. Go, go have your galy poks and get ready for work. I suppose you need to start work soon, right?' Uncle Tham drew in a big, settling breath.

I looked up at the afternoon sky and down at the small clock on Uncle Tham's stall. 'Oh! Yes, Uncle Tham! I'd better get going! Thank you for these extra galy poks!' I waved to Uncle Tham and left his stall, turning my head to smile at him.

'See you, Kuang! YOU'LL BE FINE! TRUST THE JOURNEY.'

Memories of school were fading. Whenever I thought of school, mixed emotions swayed my heart. I was sad, regretful, yet at the same time, I could feel hope flowing in my youthful blood. Those days burning midnight oil to pass exams were especially precious. They reminded me that I could always depend on my revolutionary determination deep within. Since I had struggled with hardships like a true warrior, I could always face challenges again and again.

Like what Uncle Tham had said, victory always lands on those who continue to grow within. I kept his words in my heart and moved on, discarding my regrets. I shall not look back.

Fourteen

I left that conversation with Uncle Tham with high hopes and in high spirits, but life continued to be monotonous.

I even begun to grow sick of the same fish porridge that Boss cooked for me for supper every day.

It was generous of him to fill my constantly rumbling stomach at this puberty stage. Seldom one would meet a boss who was concerned about his employee's well-being. However, the repulsive stench of the fish stomach was too much for me to bear. I had to force it down my throat. Sometimes I sneaked away and upchucked them in the quiet alleys.

Besides that, two years of cleaning fish and smelling exactly like one made me sick of going to work eventually. I contemplated about quitting when customers started flooding into the kopitiam every single evening.

And of course, I missed my family.

My siblings had all grown up without my knowledge. Even Ing had started running and jumping. Ah Mm became sicker due to exhaustion and overworking at home. Ah Beh continued earning a meager sum to support the family and feeling bad about it.

Occasionally, despite struggling to make ends meet, Ah Beh would ask for clothes donations from our gaginang and bought thick slices of pork belly with our savings. He then packed one or two tins of pork belly buried in salt to send to my grandmother and aunties back in China.

I heard from Ah Mm that life in China was much worse as compared to what we were experiencing. They did not have enough to eat and wear, especially during the winter. Ah Beh promised himself to guard his mother's and sisters' well-being with his life.

The relationship between Ah Ma and Ah Gong had worsened. They slept at opposite corners of their apartment every night.

As usual, Ah Gong had been asking for money from Ah Ma to buy opium. When his addiction kicked in, he would shiver all over. Sometimes, Ah Ma would ignore him for days. He would be left alone in the apartment while Ah Ma stayed out the whole day deliberately.

Work was manageable. Except for some unreasonable customers, I had no complaints about the people whom I worked with. Boss was nice. He doted on me and had not reprimanded me harshly before. He even increased my monthly pay from fifty dollars to sixty upon witnessing how hard I worked.

I managed to save up a big sum to get new clothes for all my siblings during the Chinese New Year. I did not want them to bow their heads low during important festive occasions as they ran around the streets with children who were cloaked in new clothes.

As for Boon, we worked pretty well together. He always stood up for me whenever I ran into troubles with customers and I would always be around whenever he needed a hand. Of course, there were times we did not agree with each other on how things should be done. Once in a while, in order to appease customers, Boon would scatter a lot more fish roes in their bowls and say in a pleasing manner, 'Relax, relax, towkay. More good stuffs for you. Come, free one. Kuang is still new. You've the biggest heart. Forgive him. Enjoy these good stuffs.'

I sucked my cheeks in.

Boss was usually not around during the midnight shift to help us decide. So, I supposed Boon was the boss. But I would say that was a bad move.

Some other customers who noticed what Boon was doing in secret demanded more fish roes too without paying more. It was hard to reject them. We had to be fair.

Fish roe was the best ingredient for our fish porridge. A small spoonful of roes could make bland porridge flavourful. But each fish only had little roes. Some did not even have any. Instead of appeasing stupid customers, we should use them wisely to enhance the taste of our porridge.

However, I kept my opinions to myself. Boon was more experienced. He was better at dealing with customers. I listened to him. I did not tell on him. Even if I did, would Boss agree with me since I was the one who always ran into trouble with customers?

Swallowing hard, I continued working.

At the back of my head, however, I could not move on. We could have made better porridge.

* * *

Recently, I found out Boon had probably met more villains than I did in his childhood.

That afternoon, I accidentally spotted scars on Boon's back as he rolled his shirt up to wipe sweat off his face behind our kitchen. He never did that before. The skin on his back was scaly and the many lines that ate into it were all lumpy, pale, and dark red at the same time. I realized, Boon could be hiding the truth behind the similar burnt marks on his arms. He told me he was often scalded by the boiling hot pot when he first started working at this stall. I believed his words then.

However, I doubted them now. That day when I noticed those scars on his back, I did not ask him about them. Partly because I did not know how to ask about them. I was bad with words. I struggled even with expressing my thoughts, let alone asking about others.

* * *

I was caught by surprise one night when I started sharing my own family woes with Boon on our way home. I did not expect it would allow Boon to open up himself.

Boon said his mother used to be a dancing girl. An infamous one though.

Dancing girl? I could not believe my ears. I once heard a neighbour use this term before. From her words, a dancing girl did not seem like a glamorous job. *What exactly does a dancing girl do?* I seldom heard stories about them. Ah Mm did not share about them either.

Boon said his mother was not a typical dancing girl. She was not always demure, accommodating, and caring. Sometimes she offended customers, just like I did. I did it because I was careless with my actions. For his mother, it was a different story. His mother's temper was fiery. She said what came to her mind without giving much thought to her words.

Dancing girls were supposed to dance with customers. They were sometimes hired to sit at tables and drink with customers. As a dancing girl, it was important to be sensitive to the needs of those men who craved and paid for their service. She needed to be soft, tender, and alluring, both inside and out. It was even more important to be wary of customers. Offending the wrong ones would mean trouble, especially those from secret societies.

But his mother was careless with her words. She offended quite a few nasty and dangerous men. She was careless with her actions too. She got pregnant with one of them. That was one of the worst things that could happen to a dancing girl. Abortion was risky. If she wished to keep the baby, she had to stop work. Her future became uncertain. She thought she would settle down with that man who fathered the new life in her body, but that man left, leaving her with the baby. And that baby was Boon.

Boon's current father was not his biological father. His mother got married to a man who claimed to love her and Boon. But he turned violent after marriage. And young Boon became the victim of his father's abuses. Not only that, but those nasty men also whom his mother had offended earlier knew their whereabouts. Many times, they created troubles for his family.

Perhaps that was the reason why Boon seldom allowed anyone to see his true self. His family history was complicated, far beyond what I had imagined it to be. So much violence went on in his life when he was a child. As I related his story to my own, I could imagine how hard it was for Boon to talk to anyone about his sorrows. He could not even reveal his pain to his own mother. That could result in her self-blaming amidst her difficulties.

Worse, recently, Boon told me he dreaded going home. His half-blind mother began developing cataract symptoms in another eye. She experienced double vision and halos could be seen around the lights. She had been struggling with her half-blindness due to cataract, and now she had to face the music of a double whammy. In the middle of the night, anxiety would strike her and she would weep over the approaching calamity.

Boon was her sole spiritual support.

Every morning after work, Boon had to return home to lend a listening ear to his panicky mother. As much as he wanted to stay by her side to console her, Boon found himself burdened and exhausted.

He had been trying to save up for his mother's cataract surgery. Every penny was more than precious. Yet, his father's irresponsibility towards the family would smash his plans. He was one who refused to engage in any honest work. He would gamble away the money and keep asking for more.

Many times, Boon had wanted to leave home with his mother but his mother did not wish to leave her man.

Listening to Boon made me feel that family woes were like invisible worms chewing on our wholeness, making us incomplete on the inside no matter how perfect we strive to be on the outside. I thought of Ah Gong and the way he always mistreated me. I could walk away from him, but somehow, I could not stop those worms from their quiet feasting. Ah Gong's blaring voice and those penetrating

Teochew bad words haunted me every now and then. I suspected the tiniest cochlear hair cells in my ears had recorded them all.

My life was hard but Boon's was harder.

* * *

My voice had been very hoarse for the past two weeks.

At the age of sixteen, I experienced the weirdest development of my body. Puberty was an awkward stage.

Just some days ago, I sounded like I always sounded. Then one momentous day, my voice suddenly cracked and I could not even recognize it myself. It turned croaky as if I had been coughing for the longest time.

I had always wanted to be an adult when I just started work at fourteen. Now that real changes were taking place within me to become one, I just hoped to remain a kid.

It was tedious getting used to all these big changes taking place in my body. Dark, coarse, curly hairs were sprouting everywhere, transforming me into a hairy monster. My voice became difficult to handle and it took me a lot of effort to keep it under control. I also had to adapt to the strange manly sound I was making. That was supposed to be Ah Beh's kind of voice.

Hormones must have been wrecking my mind. I suddenly turned rebellious. I longed to stop working, to stop going to bed at three in the morning and to stop missing out on all the fun my siblings shared. I also hoped to stop digging bloody fish intestines and collecting their eggs and scalding my hands with hot soup.

But I did not know when and how to stop working.

Where can I get sixty dollars every month? What would happen to the family if I quit my job?

My reality and my will seemed to be running away from each other. My will refused to face my reality. And my reality would not comply with my will. I was tempted to change something, but at the same time, paralyzed by my doubtful heart.

* * *

Across the street where our stall stood was an eating-house that attracted a large crowd every evening.

The eating-house specialized in Teochew lor ark png. I could smell the fragrance of lor ark from afar. As it dissipated into the air, it mixed with the fishy stench drifting out of our stall.

Ah Beh used to share with Ah Mm that migration had transformed him into another person. He used to be able to speak freely with any gaginang from Feng Mei village. But when he came to Singapore, he became reserved and kept his thoughts to himself.

It never occurred to me that food would also undergo transformation after arriving at a foreign land. The braised duck rice in Singapore was incredibly like the common dish of braised goose rice in Shantou.

Ah Mm once bought a pack of braised goose rice for the family back at Feng Mei village. The goose meat and head were braised with dark soy sauce, sugar, five spice, ginger and garlic, and were cooked with shrimps and yam.

Ah Mm said during the slow braising process, the goose was turned repeatedly to let the gravy soak through the meat. She also told me the Teochew people in Shantou loved to jostle for braised goose heads, especially, for their late-night second dinners.

The Teochew people were finicky about the breed of goose used in the dish. It had to be Lion's Head Goose. Such breed of goose had a majestic crown and was farmed specially for their heads and livers in the suburbs of Shantou.

It was the first time I tasted a Teochew cuisine outside of home, and I was fascinated. It was a surprising supper for the family. The oily, chewy goose meat and its salty smell were tempting. I could still remember the texture of the chewy goose meat turning and tossing in my mouth.

Totally mesmerizing and forever memorable.

Sensing this wonderful smell again made me reminisce about the heartwarming moment back in China.

Perhaps, I should pay a visit to the eating-house. Who knew what surprise another round of tasting braised meat could bring me this time? I desperately hoped I could snap out of my dull and droning life.

Fifteen

A few days later, while on my way to work after my break, I walked into the grand eating-house.

There were many spring couplets with prosperity idioms pasted on its interior walls. Black and white photographs of Singapore could be found on the walls near the counter. Bird cages hung down from its ceiling. The constant chirping of the birds filled the entire kopitiam, combining nature with its modern outlook. And round marble-topped tables and wooden chairs were arranged neatly, side by side.

I could also see a row of succulent-looking braised ducks hooked and hung behind a glass cabinet. They were dripping black gravy and oil. Inching my nose closer, I could smell delicious air wafting from them. My stomach clenched with hunger at the thought of chewing on the bouncy duck meat lined with its savoury waxy skin.

I ordered a small plate of rice topped with braised duck slices. While waiting for my food to arrive, I sat down and scanned around.

There were a few young male workers trudging about. They were all dressed in white silky tee shirts and brown three-quartered pants. They had long hair covering the ears and the base of their necks. Their fringes were falling across their forehead and touching their eyebrows.

I had been seeing young men like these more often recently. Our customers did too, and many of them would talk about how sporting such long hair was associated with these so-called 'hippies' in the West. Our older customers would often go on about how these hooligans and their laid-back culture, slovenly appearance and drug-using habits were gradually corrupting our young nation. Even our cheng hu had been encouraging young men to cut their hair short to keep them from associating with the 'hippies'.

Two ladies donned in flowery linen traditional tops were making *kopi* and *teh* at the rear of the shop. One of them was roasting coffee beans with butter and sugar in a wok while the other was straining the roasted coffee beans through a deep brown sock that acted like an infuser.

The fragrance of the roasted coffee mixed with the tempting smell of the braised duck to produce an intense bitter savoury sweet scent.

There was an old clock hanging high up on the wall, and next to it, was a staircase leading to a second floor. I could not believe there were tables and chairs upstairs. This shop was huge. It was no wonder that it could accommodate such a big crowd every evening.

Chinese folks could be seen mingling in this eating-house at a leisurely pace, speaking in all kinds of dialects. There were patrons of different races too. I could also hear English songs playing in the background. *Wow!* It was a song sung by *The Beatles*, one of the most popular Western boy bands in Singapore.

Sitting in this eating-house made me feel like a part of modern simplicity. Its embrace of cultural diversity captivated me immediately.

* * *

After some time, a plate of succulent braised duck rice was placed right in front of my eyes. I could not wait to lift the pair of chopsticks to dig in straightaway. It smelled heavenly, just like the tender goose meat I tasted back in China. I carefully placed a piece of braised meat gently on my tongue, savouring the warmth of my memories.

'Towkay, Ah Choi's finally here!' one of the young workers called out to the old man who was arranging the ducks behind the glass cabinet.

'He'd better turn up today or I shall fire him!' growled the old man, shaking his head as he lit up a cigarette with his free hand. 'Young men nowadays really don't deserve any bit of trust.'

A figure hurried past the table where I was sitting at. A gust of wind blew against my back.

I turned my head.

It was a tall young man. He had the same long hair and was wearing a similar silky tee shirt as the rest. His sloping shoulders were fleshy, and his legs were rather thin. I found his back view familiar but could not recall where I had seen this person.

Just then, he turned around, wiping sweat off his forehead. He repeatedly rubbed his forehead to spread the beads of perspiration to the side. I frowned and waited.

He then brought his hand down, revealing his whole face. Narrow forehead, thin eyebrows, almond-looking eyes, and a pimpled flat nose.

I spat out a mouthful of rice.

GEONG! My brain stuttered for a moment as my heart leapt. *IS THAT REALLY HIM?*

I quickly turned my head back to my duck rice. A sensation of being squeezed filled my entire body and my muscles were going limp.

Closing my eyes and taking a calming breath, I turned my head to steal a glimpse of Geong. He was so busy attending to customers that he did not notice me at all.

Sheepishly, I turned around. I shrank my body very, very small. My shaking hand spooned big mouthfuls of rice into my mouth, trying to clear my plate and leave the eating-house as fast as I could.

Sixteen

Occasionally when I walked past the apartment next to ours, I could smell a slight fragrance. Even though it was sweet, it made me uncomfortable. It was like an exotic blend of lush florals, rich spices, tangerine, and maybe cloves? I hated cloves. Inhaling a tinge of it made me nauseous.

That long-lasting fragrance had always been around. When I was young, I suspected it was poison. These days, it was getting stronger. My apartment too, became infused with its noxious particles. The whole stretch of the corridor was filled with this intoxicating scent, making us all secondhand smokers.

Ah Mm told me Ah Gong had been puffing on opium a lot at home. Sometimes, he would even consume opium in front of the grandchildren. I could sense the annoyance in Ah Mm's expression.

I was baffled. *Consume? How?* I asked Ah Mm how he did it, but Ah Mm only answered, '*Ah neh lor, jiak lo ke*, just swallow.' I could not picture it in my head. Didn't smokers clutch a bamboo pipe between their fingers to smoke opium? How did he do it? At the same time, I also suspected Ah Mm had seen wrongly.

I was determined to find out more, nonetheless.

* * *

One day, before I went back to the fish porridge stall for work after my restful nap, I walked several miles to the opium den Ah Gong always visited. I was surprised Ah Ma shared the location with me when I asked her about it. She must be so frustrated with Ah Gong's disappearance every now and then that she thought, probably I could help get him back.

No way. Why would I help Ah Gong?

It was a secluded two-storey brick house tucked at a corner at South Bridge Road, a place with a high concentration of Chinese trades and population. I stood near its entrance, pretending to be busy with my hands, pacing back and forth.

A trishaw rider ambled in.

Sneaking up to the windows, I touched the black cloth hanging at the side and opened it slightly.

I saw the trishaw rider walking with discomfort. His ankles were swollen, and he was inhaling shallowly yet noisily. Occasionally he rasped as he exhaled, producing a low-pitched moan.

Streams of fumes that contained a warm and spicy fragrance of coffee, white flowers, and vanilla blanketed the dark room with a layer of dreamy grey. Big wooden benches covered with thin woven straw mats were positioned against the walls, inviting those who were hooked to climb up and strip themselves off their burning yearning.

I could feel tingling in my fingers and toes as I continued to peep into the opium house. Sleazy and foggy, staring at it made my mouth dry. Even my rough skin started to itch.

There were a set of specialized bamboo pipe and antique burner lying on each side of the bench. Men of all ages, ranging from early twenties to late sixties, reclined their bodies and rested their heads on two stacked up dirty-looking pillows to cradle the long pipes over oil lamps, while half-closing their eyes as if drifting off to dreamlands. One could hear no other sound except for deep breaths of great relief and continuous wheezing.

I would say the opium house looked exactly like paradise. But those men inside, on the contrary, were eluded unto their graves.

The trishaw rider approached a narrow counter, and pulled out a few coins clanking in his pocket. His speech was slurred and his lifeless eyes darted up and down, supporting his heavy eyelids that were about to close.

A lady at the counter received his money, and handed him a small packet containing thumb-sized balls of glossy black resin.

So, those were the opium balls? So small? It was my first time seeing them. Finally, the image of Ah Gong throwing opium balls into his mouth and probably chewing them became clear. Did he chew it like how I chewed on the White Rabbit creamy milk candy? But still, I could not believe it.

The trishaw rider clumsily sat on a bench, reclining on his side. Just then, a woman dressed in a tight-fitting side slit gown slowly lounged towards him. She took the packet from him, moistened her lips with her tongue, and whispered softly into his ears. She removed a ball of resin from the packet, burnt it over the stab of a candle in the burner, and carefully poked it into the bamboo pipe. She then handed the pipe back to him.

The flame rolled over the softened mush as the trishaw rider took a few deep drags. At that instant, he looked powered up. His brows were raised, stretched far above his half-closed eyes.

Could a puff of opium solve all woes within seconds? Seeing how it worked convinced me of its effectiveness.

But opium was dangerously addictive. I bet even more so than Uncle Tham's galy poks. Ah Mm always warned me not to get close to it.

According to Ah Mm, opium smoking was common among the Chinese community in Singapore. Many labourers who were struggling with a difficult labour life were forced into sleaze to help them escape the harsh reality. The old and sickly also turned to opium smoking to relieve them from the symptoms of their illnesses. Ah Gong was one of them.

Once they were hooked on opium, they could not go without it for a day. They would experience distressing symptoms as a result of deprivation when they stop taking opium. To relieve the withdrawal symptoms, they would hunger for opium again and the cycle of opium addiction would repeat itself.

Opium smoking was not only addictive but also expensive. Many addicts could not afford to buy opium and resorted to crimes to support their habits. Countless labourers spent so much money buying opium that they could not send money back to their hometowns.

I sighed at my family's misfortune after recalling Ah Mm's words. Ah Gong's insistent and violent ways of getting money from the family, especially Ah Ma, had reduced us to mere money-churning human machines at his disposal. If we refused to hand him money, he would turn insane and start smashing things on the floor. Sometimes he would even hit us. After that, he would collapse onto the floor with a shaking body. It was truly a pathetic sight.

Looking at the position of the sun in the sky, I guessed I got to go. I released the black cloth at the window, and ran back to the fish porridge stall.

* * *

That night, business at the fish porridge stall was exceptionally good. We finished selling all the porridge by twelve midnight. We got to go home earlier and I was overjoyed.

Upon reaching the shophouse, I saw Ah Gong swaying his body uncontrollably at the staircase. He had a flushed appearance and he was laughing hysterically to himself.

I tiptoed slowly behind him, craning my neck to see what was happening to him.

Ah Gong was taking an envelope out from his pocket and opening it cautiously. He shook the envelope. Under the soft moonlight, he dabbed some black powder from the envelope with his index finger and rolled it against his thumb, forming a tiny black ball.

As quietly as I could, I leaned forward to have a closer look.

The black powder looked exactly like the leftover resin ash I saw that afternoon in the pipes sitting on the benches of the opium house. How did he manage to get those resin ash? Did he buy them at a lower price because he had not much money? Or was it given to him for free out of sympathy?

I watched on from his back, holding my breath.

Giggling to himself like a fool, Ah Gong moved the tiny ball to his mouth. He then lowered his arm, letting it hang loose at his side.

He remained silent for a while before giggling again.

WHAT? Where's that black ball?

I frowned. I was certain I did not see any ball rolling onto the ground.

At that instant, I got reminded of what Ah Mm had shared with me that morning. Ah neh lor, jiak lo ke. I blinked several times. Did Ah Gong just eat the ball? *What the hell is he doing? Siao ah!*

Ah Gong huffed deeply and shook his head.

That tiny ball of opium residue seemed to have perked Ah Gong up within a minute. His body stopped swaying.

My mind was racing to think of ways to snake past this old fellow to get to my apartment on the second floor when Ah Gong turned around and saw me. He raised his brows and narrowed his eyes.

I avoided eye contact with him straightaway. In fact, I felt hollowed out. My only desire was to flee this scene as soon as possible.

Ah Gong's head cocked to the side. His posture stiffened suddenly. With a thick and rough voice, he started swearing at me.

'AHHH!' he yelled. '*Cao liu liang gia!* Didn't you see *Dua Lao Ya* here? Where's your respect? YAU SIU GIA! See how I bash you up later!'

Respect? I blinked several times. *Did I hear wrongly?* This word made my heart burn with rage all of a sudden.

My nerves got frayed when I heard this word blasted out of his filthy mouth. *What kind of respect are you expecting from me?*

I slowly turned my head back. I could feel my forearm muscles twitch and grow taut while Ah Gong continued cursing in the background.

I was surprised by my own reaction. Somehow, that fear in my little heart in the past had transformed together with my growing body. It became hatred. I hated this person. I hated him so much that I yearned to destroy him, right at this very moment.

I thought of Ah Mm counting money day and night. Ah Beh, gone for a long while and returned only to pass his hard-earned money to this good-for-nothing. Then I remembered Boon, and how he had saved up all the money for his mother's surgery and lost it all to his gambler father.

Crooks. Bastards who did nothing worthwhile, only wasting other people's time and money on nonsensical activities. *Ah Gong, I hate you. You don't deserve to live like a human.*

While a part of my heart still cringed at Ah Gong's booming voice, at this instant, the feelings of hatred and logic dominated me. *What can this old frail man do if I just push him to the ground and punch him?*

A ball of vigour was burning within me. It was that powerful will that had always existed in my heart. I stared at him straight on. My body started growing hot. A desire for revenge engulfed me.

'DUA LAO YA IS HERE! I'M DUA LAO YA!' Ah Gong continued spouting nonsense. 'SHOW RESPECT, OK!'

Then, at a quick, erratic pace, Ah Gong knelt, with his back facing me. He began kowtowing.

I was shocked.

At this time, moonlight shone on Ah Gong's hands as he raised them up into the air and down onto the floor. His creased hands were trembling uncontrollably. His long bony fingers were pointing skywards, curling a little, as if longing to grip onto something. From his back, Ah Gong looked like he was begging for help. In time, Ah Gong's repeated movements became painful to watch. It disturbed me so much that I had to take a few steps back.

Ah Gong had become insane, spewing illogical words with his shrill Teochew.

To my surprise, the tension in my arm muscles was released. My agony had faded to a dull throb. There was no point beating up an old frail man who had been reduced to such a state. Kneeling straight was not even possible for him. Occasionally he would sway to one side.

My eyes were getting tired. I decided to snake past Ah Gong like how I always did and run up the staircase. I decided to let my revenge go.

Forget it, Kuang. Forget it.

Ah Gong's thunderous voice continued to blare into the stillness of our apartment as I opened and closed the door.

After a while, it stopped. And I fell asleep.

Seventeen

The next morning, our neighbour found Ah Gong sprawled on the floor beside the staircase. His nostrils and the floor were stained with blood. An envelope was found next to him, and opium ash was scattered on the flight of stairs.

What had happened to him?

'We need to get some help. He can't go on like that,' Ah Beh sighed, staring at Ah Mm as if she would have a solution to his worry.

'Wak. But you know your father. Asking him to go to the hospital is like getting him to put a curse on himself,' Ah Mm replied softly, helpless but rational.

The room fell silent. We could only hear the chattering of our neighbours throwing their words across their windows.

It was a rare moment when all of us were present in the house on a Saturday. Ah Beh and I were spared from work, and Ah Mm just came back from the wet market. Gia caught three special crickets which captivated all my siblings. None of them wished to venture out with the neighbouring kids.

Ah Beh and Ah Mm had been talking with each other at an abnormally soft volume since early morning. The softer they were, the more suspicious I became.

What're the folks talking about? I knew something must have gone terribly wrong. I wished I could turn invisible and creep up to them.

Out of the blue, someone came knocking hard on our door.

Ah Mm winded past Ah Beh and opened it. She was delighted to see Auntie Lim standing at our door with her body leaning against the side post of our doorway.

'Lim ah, you're fast. Have you found him?' Ah Mm asked, eager to fish a positive answer from Auntie Lim.

'Yes, yes, I did. I managed to spot him along some narrow streets at Chinatown this morning. *Heng ah*! You guys are so lucky!' Auntie Lim replied in a silvery voice. 'I asked him to come this afternoon for the treatment and he said ok. Today, 3 p.m.'

I gazed at Auntie Lim with my brows almost crossing each other. She winked back at me, pouting and waving her small palm in front of my eyes.

What treatment? Ah Gong needs treatment? Is he badly injured? Why are these adults so secretive?

'Alright. We will be waiting for him. Gam xia, Lim,' Ah Beh and Ah Mm expressed gratitude to Auntie Lim over and over again.

In return, Auntie Lim nodded her head in soundless delight.

* * *

Straight after Auntie Lim returned to her apartment, Ah Beh and Ah Mm went next door to look at Ah Gong. We could follow if we wanted to.

I went ahead as I was really keen to find out what had exactly happened but the rest of my siblings could not be bothered. They scampered to the streets to busk in the crowd of kids. Dak and Siu forgot about Ah Gong and went with them too.

Ah Gong was lying on the mattress like a dead body. He remained motionless upon seeing us. One of his legs was red and swollen and it was stiffly placed on a pillow.

Ah Gong was all framed up in wretchedness.

His entire body was slightly tilted to the side, his eyelids seemed to be weighing down, and his cheeks were deeply depressed.

Except for moments he would either moan repeatedly in dull pain or screech suddenly in a very unsettling manner, he remained quiet most of the time.

I froze upon seeing Ah Gong in this pathetic state. My thoughts went blank as if my brain had stopped working. I could not believe what I had witnessed. Wasn't Ah Gong yelling crazily at me just a few hours ago?

I walked up to him.

His opium addiction seemed to cause him to shiver under the blanket. I could see saliva flooding out from his mouth like a young child undergoing teething.

Ah Ma dipped a piece of cloth into icy water, wrung and tossed it on his forehead. Cold water streamed down to the sides of his ears. Occasionally, Ah Gong would yell and he would look at Ah Ma fixedly with his half-closed eyes. He would have walloped her if he were physically fine, like in the past. But all he could do now was to communicate his anger through his lifeless eyes.

We sat on the floor, just next to their mattress. I could not take my eyes off this old man that had left countless scars in our hearts.

I rarely came over. Painful memories of Ah Gong stopped me from entering. Every time I recalled how my heart had jarred with each verbal blow from him, how the pain had seared through my every nerve and vein and took away every feeling of safety I ever had, I had a strong urge to shed tears.

I detested and despised him for his lowly behaviour. Never would I forgive him for abusing Ah Mm and me.

But the human heart was unfathomably soft.

I thought I would applaud the calamity that fell upon Ah Gong, walk into this apartment to sneer at his retribution, and trudge off like an ultimate winner. These were the images I held on dear in my heart to keep me going when I was younger.

One day, he shall perish with cockroaches.

However, at this moment when Ah Gong was on the brink of death in front of my eyes, unexpectedly, all my previous vengeful thoughts gave up on me.

I did not know what else to do except to hope for his relief. Wounds of his abuses on me were healed at the instant when I decided to let go of all the grudges. My contempt for him melted like a green ice ball under the sun.

The wonder of forgiveness was unbelievable.

Ah Ma was a changed person.

She was usually quiet. The only sound she made in the past was a loud hissing sound whenever she tried to suck the gaps between her teeth with the tip of her tongue. But today, she behaved differently.

Ah Gong would shriek each time he tried to shift. Movements caused him to suffer a sharp pain in the hips. Instead of helping him to get into a position where he felt comfortable, I spotted Ah Ma shoving Ah Gong away! Her face was filled with disdain. Her push felt like a force that contained layers of disgust accumulated all these years. She needed not say a word to hurt Ah Gong. All she had to do was to abandon him in times of his disability and that was sufficient to kill his spirit.

'Beh, hospital, ai mai?' Ah Beh asked his bedridden father with concerned eyes.

'M-a-i,' Ah Gong struggled to mumble. His lips were like two stone slabs, rubbing against each other.

'See what opium has done to you? Still giving us so much trouble before you die!' Ah Ma glared at Ah Gong, punishing him with her judging eyes.

'Ah Yi, Lim has found a Chinese *sinseh* who can cure all sorts of fractures and sprains. He always set up his stall in Chinatown and Lim managed to find him this morning. He'll be here at three in the afternoon today.'

'An early death serves you right! *Zha si zha ho!*' Ah Ma turned her head and swore a blue streak.

Ah Gong blinked rapidly. His eyeballs moved intermittently, staring at the ceiling. His body remained stiff.

We sat with him for another half an hour before saying goodbye. Before we left, Ah Gong moved his eyes and stared at us vacantly.

I had a strange feeling about the goodbye I had just waved to Ah Gong. It was the first goodbye I had ever said to him but intuitively, I also felt it might be the last one.

Eighteen

Afternoon arrived. We were all waiting for Ah Gong's saviour to arrive.

'Coming! He's here!' Auntie Lim eagerly signaled to us from the first floor.

A man, clothed in a light brown short-sleeved shirt, walked up the staircase. His black pants hung loosely on his waist, and a big wooden case held by a rusty metal chain dangled from his right shoulder.

Ah Beh and Ah Mm politely invited the Chinese sinseh into Ah Gong's apartment. Out of curiosity, I followed them in.

The Chinese sinseh took a quick look at Ah Gong from head to toe. He then faced Ah Mm and Ah Ma, exclaiming confidently that Ah Gong's illness was nothing more than just a common elderly ailment.

'There's a lot of wind accumulated in his hips and thigh, making them swell horribly. I can get the wind out easily. Just give it another three days and he'll recover.'

Upon hearing what the sinseh had said, we lightened up, especially Ah Mm. Her fingers were gripping the bedsheets before the sinseh shared his thoughts with us. Now, her hands were on her chest, and I could hear her murmuring a prayer.

Even though Ah Gong did not respect Ah Mm at all in the past and had always accused her of being the worst woman a man could ever marry, she was the only person who took care of him unconditionally, out of her duty as a daughter-in-law.

Teochew piety flowed in her blood, nonetheless.

She went in and out of Ah Gong's apartment, checking on him almost every hour since morning.

The Chinese sinseh opened his wooden case and took out a small bottle of alcohol. He poured half a bottle on Ah Gong's swollen thigh and rubbed it. Ah Gong was in so much pain that his complexion turned ashen, whiter than before. His eyes closed and he sucked himself into a deeper place to cope.

I watched on with my mouth open. I could feel my heartbeat in my throat, as if I could feel Ah Gong's pain. *This, certainly feels like being banished to the eighteen levels of hell.*

After three rounds of rubbing, the sinseh then poured another bottle of herbal ointment on the same thigh. He used his palm to spread the brown liquid around Ah Gong's leg, making sure that every part of his leg had absorbed the herbal ingredients.

The sinseh then warned Ah Gong of the intense pain he was going to receive. 'It'll be over before you know it. Bang sim. Relax and breathe in!'

Ah Gong was scared out of his wits.

I felt my body shrinking. Hair lifted on my arms and nape of my neck as I watched on.

Ah Gong glared hard at the sinseh with extreme fear in his eyes and raised his trembling arms. His body was jolted slightly upward as he strained all his remaining usable muscles to prevent the sinseh from touching his leg.

Terror was coursing through his veins. Ah Gong was as good as dead.

The sinseh then mercilessly bent Ah Gong's thigh and straightened it out. It produced a loud cracking sound!

My shoulders raised and I covered my ears. That must have been the cruelest sight I had ever seen.

Ah Gong let out the wildest shriek that nearly deafened our ears. He then fell back on the mattress and gazed blankly with his cold eyes. His thigh turned soft and limp. Sections of his leg appeared to be disconnected from one another.

Ah Gong's throat was sealed. He did not struggle anymore. Even his widened eyes resembled those of a person who died a tragic death. They carried a mixture of shock, helplessness, and defeat.

Ah Mm and Ah Beh were traumatized by what they had seen. They asked the sinseh many questions but the sinseh did not say much. He assured them that Ah Gong's shock and pain were only temporary, and they would go away after about three days. He could then stand up to walk again.

The sinseh's voice was firm and clear. The conclusion he reached about Ah Gong made so much sense.

Ah Mm thanked the Chinese sinseh profusely and sent him to the door. 'You can look for me in Chinatown. I always hover around that area.' These were the sinseh's words before he left. And we felt so assured, assuming he would always be around when we needed him.

* * *

Three days later, something unexpected happened.

According to the Chinese sinseh, Ah Gong would feel better and could even walk again. Half of his words really came true!

I came home during my break that afternoon. Ah Beh and Ah Mm were at home too.

Ah Ma came knocking on our door hysterically after I just stepped into the house. 'Wak *ah*, Wak! Your father is conscious. Do you want to see him? Meh! Open the door!'

Both Ah Beh and Ah Mm were pleasantly surprised. They followed Ah Ma into her apartment. I gave up taking my afternoon nap after tossing and turning for a while.

Perhaps, I should visit Ah Gong again.

Ah Gong's back was leaning against the wall when I entered his apartment. His unbearably smelly hair was ruffled and greasy, exactly like a person who had just roused from a heavy slumber.

No one knew for certain how he managed to sit up on his own even though his legs were still not quite mobile. As stiff as two table legs, they appeared to be made from hard wood.

'Beh, are you feeling better today?' Ah Mm asked, leaning forward with her hands on her knees. 'You are looking much better!'

But there was no reply. Ah Gong continued to look straight.

I turned and looked at Ah Mm whereas Ah Mm turned to look at Ah Beh. I clutched my hands together, my stomach fluttering. At this instant, I could not believe I was yearning more to bear with his usual lecturing than to watch him live like a dead. When did spurting of vulgarities become such a reassuring act?

But Ah Gong was very quiet. His silence was traumatizing us.

After a minute of waiting, Ah Gong finally responded. He touched his hips and thigh in way as if they were foreign to him and it was his first time being in contact with them. He then patted mechanically on his left knee.

Following, he gawked at us and demanded some durians to eat.

'*Liu liang*! Liu liang ahhh!' Ah Gong shrieked. His breathing grew heavier.

Ah Mm was bewildered by his sudden craving but quickly gave in to his request.

'Yes, yes, Beh. I will get them for you now,' Ah Mm answered in her standard obedient tone. She took on her heels and rushed to the wet market.

I certainly did not understand why Ah Gong had to eat durians at this juncture. Did he miss it so much that he had to have a taste of it now?

I turned my head and looked at Ah Beh. His features laid still on his face. His eyes became dull.

After Ah Mm was gone, I sat down on the mattress and gazed at Ah Gong. Ah Beh too, came forward to sit beside me.

Ah Gong was a pack of bones, sickly and fragile. A push could easily be a blow to make him collapse onto the ground. I wondered how a bigheaded man could be reduced to such a pitiful state in three days' time.

Both Ah Beh and I had never sat so close to Ah Gong before. It felt awkward to even imagine us touching Ah Gong's thin and wrinkled skin on his hand. Yet, at this moment, I felt Ah Beh have something to convey to Ah Gong.

Gently, Ah Beh held on to Ah Gong's big-knuckled hand. I stared on keenly as he stroked Ah Gong's arm. Up and down, up and down.

A moment of peace enveloped us. I could only hear Ah Gong's heavy breathing and the clock ticking.

Ah Gong's aged skin appeared to be loosely attached to his flesh and bones. It moved, brushing against the bulging veins, like currents washing up rows of rocks at the shore. Brown patches of freckles and deep crinkling lines floated along with it.

Ah Beh did not say a word. He then laid another hand on top, as if trying to assure Ah Gong with both his strong arched palms.

In that moment of peace, I thought it would be best to give Ah Beh and Ah Gong some time alone. It was the least I could do. We did not know how much longer Ah Gong had, after all.

* * *

I was woken up from my nap by a familiar fragrance.

A big pack of large seeds covered by custard-like flesh was laid on the floor, against a sidewall opposite my mattress. They were fresh-looking and ready to be eaten. Someone had removed them from their spikey shells and packed them neatly.

Durians did not leave good memories even though they smelt and tasted really good.

It was my favourite fruit. I could just imagine eating it and feeling satisfied. I would say that my love for durians was on par with my love for Uncle Tham's galy poks. I simply adored heavenly-tasting food.

Ah Gong loved to eat durians too. I thought we were quite similar only for this reason. But being the only durian lover in the family was a reason too shallow to forgive him for his misdeeds.

Eight years ago, there was an evening when Ah Gong brought all his grandchildren out for durian tasting. Ang, Gia, and I were skeptical after hearing his loud assertion to bring us for a durian feast.

When did this nasty old man become so generous?

He held Dak's hand while Ah Ma carried Siu, and together, all of us walked to the nearby market. Ah Gong ordered three large spikey durians and placed them on a small wooden round table.

Everyone was seated. Ah Gong, Ah Ma, Dak, and Siu sat nearest to the edge of the round table while all the other grandchildren sat around them.

When we were about to start digging in, Ah Gong hit my hand with a flick of his fingers. I frowned resentfully in pain and looked back at him.

'Not for you, wretched kid! Durians are not for idiots!' Ah Gong thundered.

My face turned red with shame and rage in front of all my siblings. I tried my best to swallow my aroused anger.

Ah Gong then stood up to remove my chair and further commented, 'You? Don't even deserve a proper chair.'

Ang and Gia took a quick glance at me with their disturbed expressions.

I was a bundle of nerves. My eyes shifted to the sides and turned glazed with a layer of tears circling in my eye sockets. I stood very still while watching all of them savour the creamy yellow custard.

Memory of this scene was painfully etched in my heart. It made me feel I was at fault for being me and I should never have existed. Aside from that, I also realized that just words alone could further drift Ah Gong and I apart.

I stared at the pack of yellow custards in my apartment, wondering why they had been left there. Didn't Ah Gong ask for them?

* * *

A while later, Ah Mm told me the tragic news, blinking away her tears. Ah Gong had passed on just an hour ago.

In addition to a surprise bag of durians, my most hated person's life ended abruptly as well. Ah Mm's face was puffy with grief.

While Ah Beh and Ah Ma were discussing burial matters, Ah Mm told Ang and me that we could have a last glimpse at Ah Gong.

We crossed over to the apartment next door and saw Ah Gong lying horizontally straight on the same mattress that had been yellowed by a mixture of his bodily grease, sweat, saliva, urine, and herbal liniment.

No one had yet moved his body. There was a sour rotting stench radiating from him.

Ah Gong's body was covered with a long piece of pure white linen cloth. I paused for a long while before deciding to have a quick peek at his face. Ang, however, did not dare to approach Ah Gong's body. 'Ah Hia, I shall wait for you at the entrance here,' Ang whispered to me after contemplating for a short while, hunching his shoulders and backing off.

I turned and surveyed Ah Gong. An image came floating in my head, instinctively warning me of a round of harsh scolding I could get for disrupting his rest. I stopped and hesitated again. *Is he really dead? What if he suddenly opens his eyes?* But logic returned as soon as I noticed there was no elevation of his belly. There was no hint of life under the cloth.

Mustering my courage and stopping my breathing through my nose, I stepped forward.

I lifted the white linen cloth by the corner. Ah Gong's face was slowly revealed in front of my eyes.

The life that had dwelt in him was gone yet his remaining sad expression added so much gloom to his cold, gaunt face. His deathly white skin pulled tight against his bones; his eyes were closed yet bulging, exactly like the longans Teng used to hide under his blanket when he was a toddler.

Ah Gong had departed with his eyes shut forever. Never would that same pair of bloodshot eyes punish me again. I should be glad but strangely, my heart ached. I did not quite understand this grief swivelling in me.

It was grief, a kind of sharp pain that came in waves, sweeping me away. It replaced all those familiar tears I used to have and I realized that pain was also a kind of love. It was love I had yet to give but I could no longer share it. It formed a hollow part in my chest, so deep and dark that it also refused to stay to ingest itself anymore. This unspent love was begging me to let it go with Ah Gong.

Goodbye, Ah Gong. Next lifetime if we still happen to meet, if you promise to be nice to me, I'll also tell you I've long forgiven you. I don't mind being your grandson again. I let out a faint smile, consoled by my own thoughts. *But you also need to be nice to Ah Mm. Can you do it? Don't take opium again. It's the worst thing. Take good care, Ah Gong. Please leave well.*

I cupped my hands and placed them on Ah Gong's protruding closed eyes. I stayed quiet for a little while and lifted the white linen cloth to cover his face.

* * *

A small piece of cloth was given to us a few hours later. We were told to wear it on the sleeve of our white shirts. Ah Beh and Ah Mm were dressed in sackcloth while Ah Ma was in full black overall.

'Everyone, turn your body. Don't look back at us. No peeping at what we're doing.' A few strong-looking men dressed in white instructed us sternly.

Ah Gong's body was slowly raised and placed into a huge wooden coffin after being ceremonially cleansed, embalmed and dressed in his favourite shirt and pants.

No one could turn back to watch.

'Alright, now we're sealing the coffin and moving it. Don't look back!'

And the coffin was closed, almost without a sound. Quietly, Ah Gong was removed from the house.

Leave well, Ah Gong.

My family and I walked along the corridors and then down the staircase behind those men lifting Ah Gong's coffin. The image of Ah Beh holding Ah Gong's hand arose in my mind as I walked. Ah Beh did not manage to say anything to Ah Gong before his death. Was it hard for him to do so, just like how I found it hard to speak to him? Did his words get stuck in his throat?

My family had always been always shunning Ah Gong. If he had not approached us for money, we would pretend not to have seen him at all.

To be honest, his parting made me feel relieved. No one would haunt us for money anymore. But I could not find joy within. I could not stop thinking about what I might have done to help Ah Gong while he was alive instead of avoiding him at all costs.

Would Ah Gong's ending be better if we were braver and kinder to speak with him, encouraging him not to consume opium, or supporting him in doing so? Even though I knew it was much easier said than done, I had feelings of inadequacy whenever I thought of Ah Gong living a different life with our help.

I also thought about my relationship with Ah Beh. Since I was a child, I had so much to tell him, but never did. What if Ah Beh passed away one day without knowing how much I cared about him? My heart ached for him when I got to know his struggles from Ah Mm. I was happy when I knew he had been doing well at work. I felt so proud of him when he successfully sent items over to China.

How do I let Ah Beh know I love him? How do I even express how I feel to him?

Death would inevitably reach all of us. Ah Gong's sudden departure reminded me to cherish those whom I loved.

Certainly, I did not want to live with regrets over love I could not give. I also did not want to die knowing I could have done so much more to show my love to my family.

The moment of death, in fact, lives in the present. *What can I do now? How should I love and live from now onwards?*

Nineteen

Resting a fish on a small table, Boon inserted the knife tip into the fish's belly near the anal opening and moved the blade up along the belly, cutting to the head. He kept the knife blade shallow into its flesh so that he would not puncture the fish's intestines. After spreading the body open and removing all the entrails through the fish's anus in a notch shape, Boon then skillfully rinsed the cavity out with his gentle hands in a pail of water.

Boon was careful and thorough, handling dead fish as if they were alive.

For the past three years, I have watched this scene every day. Despite this, I still could not clean fish as well as Boon. Nothing had changed. I still had a strong dislike for fish, largely due to its stench. If I had to handle fish, I would always excavate the entrails like a fast-digging machine. Some of its flesh was pulled into tiny pieces, floating on the dirty water.

'Boon, will you ever change your job?' I asked, interrupting his focus.

Boon looked up from the table. 'Why not?' he replied calmly in a matter-of-fact manner.

Years later and Boon was still a reserved figure whose words always surprised me.

I sometimes wondered if I had stayed at the fish porridge stall only to hear Boon's startling words. He was one who never failed to get me thinking with his insights.

'Aren't you skilled at cleaning fish and making fish porridge? Why would you leave?' I further questioned.

Boon's eyes returned to the fish. His actions paused and I waited for his reply.

'Hmm . . . It's possible for anyone to be skilled in this or another, if he wants to, Kuang,' Boon countered and continued to descale the cleaned fish.

I was stumped. *This is hard for me. I don't even know what I want.*

'What do you mean, Boon?' I persisted in asking, 'How can a person be skilled in this and that and anything else?'

Boon paused for a little while before looking into my eyes, with a faint smile resting on his lips.

'Well, Kuang, I'm sure you know fish swim well anywhere they go.' Boon answered briefly. He then turned quiet and started placing all the cleaned fish into a big pot.

Seventeen, going eighteen. Perhaps I had a long way to go before I fully understood Boon's message.

His arrogance about life was dazzling.

* * *

I stood outside the grand eating-house, soaking myself in the savoury smell of lor ark that drifted out of the shop.

Two weeks had passed since Ah Gong's death. Sometimes, I still brooded over it. The sudden loss in our family, even if it was the man I loathed so much before, still often left me feeling lost and confused. For the past two weeks, during my work breaks,

I would wander aimlessly around the neighbourhood and occasionally find myself at this eating house. I could not exactly pin-point why I was so drawn to this place. Was it the familiar aroma of lor ark? Or . . . could it be that I wanted to reconcile with Geong? To tell him all about my life thus far? To rekindle our friendship? Logic told me it would be better not to. Anyway, we had been living our lives for the past few years without each other. The thought of landing myself in any kind of embarrassment was too much for me right now.

That was right. I came probably because I wanted to bask in the grandeur of this eating-house. I needed excitement to break up the boredom of the fish porridge stall job, to see if I could be inspired to do something new.

I did not come to seek out Geong. Neither was I interested to know what went on in his life and what he had been up to.

I'll never approach him and talk to him or whatsoever . . . I'll never . . .

And then I saw Geong.

Wearing the same silky white shirt and brown pants, he went from table to table, serving steaming hot delicious lor ark png. Geong's wide smile was obvious even from a distance. He must be having a good time working at this eating-house.

I recalled the laughs Geong and I shared together in the past. Those happy moments of friendship were unforgettable. They remained in me even after so many years.

But, at that moment, I also found my sleep-deprived thoughts spinning around with envy.

Taking a deep breath, I stroked the freshly painted exterior of the shop, feeling its fine textured gradient with my hand. I, too, dreamed of working in a luxurious eating-house someday.

Then, I had a sudden urge to approach Geong. Should I say hi to him after all? Swap stories like old times? The urge was so strong yet logic won me over. *No, Geong hates me. He might even shoo me away, look, the business is so good, who has time for me?*

I walked away, harbouring a wild intention to start my life anew and trying to convince myself to let my old friendship with Geong go.

* * *

The streets near our shophouse were as busy as before. Today, I skipped lunch at the fish porridge stall and basked in the warm perpetual chaos.

While waiting for my bowl of *kwey teow* soup to be served, I found a seat and made myself comfortable. I seldom had the time to sit down to enjoy my food nowadays.

The old woman sitting at the same table had finished her soup. She got up and went away just as I sat down. I had a strong premonition that this seat was emptied for a good reason. I eyed the seat for a while before looking up at the white clouds floating in the skies.

Soon, a bowl of kwey teow soup was brought to me. A thick layer of oil shimmered on the surface of the soup. Long white strands of kwey teow were nicely packed underneath. Two fishballs, white as flour, touched each other while sitting on the surface of the soup. I started fishing the springy kwey teow with chopsticks, eager to warm my empty stomach.

'One kwey teow soup, here!'

Halfway through eating, a voice rang next to me. I could not identify the voice, but it was familiar.

A young man came into my sight and sat opposite me. He removed his hat and placed it on the table. He looked like an adult man trying to grow out of a teenager's body—sloppy shoulders with sculpted biceps, tanned skin, and an athletic physique.

I paused for a second, feeling a mix of embarrassment and awkwardness brimming under my skin. I knew I should not have stared at him this closely for too long, but curiosity washed over me. I wanted to digest every bit I captured in my eyes and assemble them together to confirm my analysis.

Square jaw, narrow forehead, thin eyebrows, almond-looking eyes, pimpled flat nose, and a pair of thick lips.

I inhaled deeply. My insides were in chaos. Sometimes, fate did not care about my plans at all. Just when I had decided to give up this friendship for good outside the eating-house, it had to come running after me now.

I lowered my head and caught glimpses at this young man in front of me. He was flapping a torn straw fan, trying to cool himself down. Beads of perspiration were all over his face. I tried to ignore him but it was hard. Even my kwey teow soup had turned cold and soggy to make me give up on my lunch.

'Geong?' I mustered my courage and asked in my most confident voice, forced and totally unnatural.

Geong shifted his eyes and looked into my eyes for the quickest while. And his tired face lightened up in seconds.

'Kuang! Is this you?'

It was weirdly emotional. This person had not been in my life for the past five years, yet when he called my name in a manner so familiar, my heart just melted.

'Yes, Geong. Kuang, I'm Kuang.' I grinned shyly. This was not the kind of smile a teenage boy would place on his maturing face. The child in me accidentally spewed it all out.

Geong smiled widely in return.

I could not believe Geong had just acknowledged me. *Did some gods enlighten him? Or has he lost his memory?*

We talked and talked. There was so much to reminisce together. Memories indeed have great power to connect people. It felt as if we had just watched another round of Teochew-hee together and were scrambling home, chatting non-stop. I had a good time laughing. Geong was the only person who could make me burst into uncontrollable laughter like this.

I tunneled back to my childhood to bury a hatchet. A profound sense of familiarity held me to the ground as I suffused my being into this noisy yet surreal landscape, facing my favourite long-lost childhood friend.

I did not manage to finish my kwey teow soup. A few broad strands were floating in the cold oily soup, forgotten.

Twenty

A week later, something bad happened to our fish porridge business.

That morning, Boss stepped into our stall with a sullen face. His left eye was bruised and his hair was all ruffled. Whenever Boss felt anxious or angry, I noticed he would weave his hand into his hair and mess it up. He must have had a terrible moment before stepping into the stall. When he walked in, he was also erasing blood from the side of his lips with his sleeve.

It was also my ever first-time seeing Boss hurling all kinds of Teochew vulgarities. And those ugly words were directed at the man who just opened another stall of similar fish porridge down the road two weeks ago. I bet they had a fight early that morning.

We could barely earn enough these days. Our rival's porridge managed to steal our customers, giving them a fresher taste with almost the same ingredients. Boss was infuriated to know that they even offered more fish roes, more flaky strips of deep-fried egg, and more steamed little white baits to garnish their porridge. There was even a slight taste of condensed milk and nuts in their gluey white grain. That was supposed to be our secret recipe! Previously, only our fish porridge had them all in the entire street.

Boss continued swearing as he continued working.

Apart from the usual damp fish odour, there was now a sense of mistrust emanating in the air.

A month ago, the same man who opened the stall opposite us patronized ours. I remembered him, as he was a rare customer who asked about my day. I had never met a customer as concerned as he was.

He slurped our porridge loudly and praised our skills. Cleverly, he even guessed the ingredients in our porridge seemingly out of sheer curiosity. I was taken in by his deceitful friendliness, nodding and shaking my head as a form of reply to his guesses.

I did not expect he was here to sound us out on our cooking ingredients. I minced on my words when Boss interrogated Boon and me on the revealing of our recipe to outsiders.

Boon sat behind Boss, washing bowls with both of his hands clad in his torn rubber gloves. He seemed to be dipping his hands in the water for longer than he should be. A few bowls definitely did not need that long to wash. Moreover, we only had five customers in the whole afternoon that day.

I did not know where to position myself. With nothing much to do on hand and feelings of regret swiveling in my heart, I began kicking sand on the ground.

Boss stood on his listless legs beside the stall, smoking non-stop and squinting at the opposite stall through his hardened eyes. He then approached Boon and me, staring into our eyes as if searching our souls. 'If this continues, I may have to reduce manpower,' Boss' words smacked right into our faces.

I had always wanted to quit out of rashness. But at this moment, my contradicting mind did not wish to have my 'rice bowl' taken away.

* * *

The next morning, I arrived at the stall on time to start the daily routine.

I was surprised to see Boss. Usually, he would not be around in the morning on a Wednesday. He was hammering nails into the new wooden poles to support our tent. Boon was at the back of our stall, washing and slicing fish as usual. I squatted next to him and began cleaning the new batch of fish after washing my hands.

'Kuang, this isn't the way to do it. That's rough handling. Why're you grabbing all the innards out at once? It will destroy the flesh. The quality of the fish will be affected.' Boon hissed at me. 'How can you not know the basic steps of handling a fish!'

I was taken aback.

It was the first time Boon lectured me so loudly. From the corner of my eyes, I saw Boss turning his head to steal a quick glimpse at us.

'Not like this!' Boon further cried out to me, snatching the fish away from me.

I was appalled. Skipping breakfast in the morning made me feel inadequate to control my emotions. My hands were trembling at his reprimanding remarks.

I was not sure of Boon's intention. Sometimes he responded in a way that hurt me. Sometimes, he shared his woes with me. And sometimes, he encouraged me when I needed someone. But never, never had he blamed me like he just did.

Was he just as vexed as Boss?

Boss did not say a single thing.

Like the hammer banging on the nail, I felt Boss' newly formed impression of me striking on my head. Boon's questionable reaction just shattered yet another friendship I truly cherished.

Images wandered wildly in my mind. I was hurt by reality and further torn by my own thoughts.

* * *

One week later, the worst thing happened. Boss told me to leave. I could not believe my ears but at the same time, I sort of knew this was coming.

Wasn't this the ending Boon hoped of me? It was certainly a brilliant plan. His wish had come true.

On my last day of work, after the crowd had cleared, I walked to Boon. The last thing I wanted before I left for good was to reproach him.

'Today's my last day,' I glared straight into Boon's eyes and said with my lowest voice.

'I know,' he replied, glancing uncomfortably at me. ' . . . Take good care, Kuang. You'll find a new job that suits you.'

I could not sense any guilt in Boon for landing me in this state. Anger simmered beneath my controlled facade.

'Boon . . . why did you do that?'

Boon looked at me then slowly turned his head to the side.

'How could you attack me right in front of boss?' I began to unleash the hurt I had been bearing for the past few days.

'Not what you're thinking.' Boon defended.

'I know what's on your mind.' I insisted.

'No, you don't, Kuang.'

'You purposely badmouthed me in front of Boss.' I glared hard at him.

Boon sighed. ' . . . It wasn't intentional. I was having a hard time . . . '

'You even told on me!' I snapped. 'Didn't you?'

Boon raised his head a little and inhaled deeply. 'I didn't.'

'You did. It's you! You know all along I was the one who leaked out the recipe of our porridge.'

'And then? I told Boss about it?'

'Yes! Despicable.'

'I didn't, Kuang.' Boon defended again.

'I don't believe you anymore.' My voice grew rough and thick.

Keeping at a distance, Boon took another deep, pained breath and closed his eyes. 'Well, Kuang, isn't this what you've been wishing for? You'd always wanted to leave.'

'I bet it's your dream that has come true.' I retorted.

I wanted to scream, but logic warned me not to. 'See? You're always lying.' I tried my best to remain as composed as I could but my fists were clenched tight. I felt pain in my palms from fingernails digging into my skin. 'Now you're finally showing your true colours.'

'If you don't believe me, there's nothing I want to say.'

Tears started streaming out uncontrollably. I brushed them away with my hand, quickly and roughly.

'Our lives have no time for doubts.' Boon looked at me intently with tenderness in his eyes. 'Just move on, Kuang. You'll do better. You're still young.'

In the past, I was always envious of Boon's ability to appease angry customers with his invented apologetic gestures. But at this moment, I was utterly disgusted to realize I was no more than a customer in his eyes.

'You said it easy, Boon.' I took a step away from him and left without saying any more.

I ran. Faster than usual.

Random images of Boon's family stories swarmed my mind. His woes and difficulties, together with his coldness and lies all combined into a bleary heap.

Today, I did not rush back home like how I did in the past. I ran, then sauntered along the river, picking up branches and stones, and throwing them into the waters. I stood in the moonlight as I recalled something Boon once told me. *Kuang, life has no time for anything as trivial as emotions.*

I stood up, staring hard at my toes clinging onto my old and dirty slippers. Boon's face turned blurry in my mind.

No point clinging onto people who don't deserve it.

In a haste, I removed my slipper and flung it into the air. Then, under the witness of the bright moonlight, I ran home, determined to start my life anew.

Part Three

Love

Twenty-One

I broke news of my retrenchment to Ah Beh and Ah Mm. Sadly, no one asked about me.

Ah Mm frowned and stared at nothing for a very long time, tapping her fingers on her laps. I knew she was calculating expenses in her mind.

Ah Beh suggested that I work as a kuli in his company so that he could look out for me. This way, I could at least earn some money.

I pulled back slightly and rocked on my feet.

The thought of having scars on my back, just like Ah Beh's, made me uncomfortable. Nonetheless, I could not reject Ah Beh's suggestion as he was ramming it down my throat.

'Just go with me! Be a kuli while you continue to look for other jobs. I didn't give birth to you to do nothing.' Ah Beh thundered. I could see a vein becoming engorged on his forehead.

I could not go against Ah Beh so I had to agree.

I agreed so that we would have no squabbles. I agreed so that Ah Mm would not have to be sandwiched.

* * *

I reported to work with Ah Beh two days later. His towkay ordered me to carry goods that were twice my weight.

Holding up a bulky gunnysack on my shoulder and walking in the hot sun was backbreaking. Moreover, the narrow wooden planks connecting vehicles to the cargo ships were unstable. Just three kuli walking on one plank was enough to make it shake ceaselessly.

From afar, I saw Ah Beh picking up two hundred kilograms worth of goods from the cargo ship and dropping the sack on his shoulders, walking briskly towards a vehicle.

My jaw dropped.

While I was impressed with his incredulous strength, my heart was butchered.

Ah Beh had been involved in laborious work way before my birth, and was still depending on it for survival. His brawny built was not by choice. Every tough muscle of his was once a soft patch of tissue. How long had it taken to stiffen them up like this?

One week into being a kuli, I was devastated. Work was hard. Even harder than having my arms scalded by boiling hot porridge and getting scolded by customers. The pay was lower than before. Worse, I could not envision a future for myself. I had always wanted to make some kind of delicacy and use it as a way to survive. Being a kuli smashed all my dreams. I also lost track of time and began puffing on cigarettes to ease my pain. Both physical and mental. Labour work brought about a kind of chronic fatigue that did not go away after a good night's sleep.

There was nothing else I yearned for except for that meager income. I went through the days leadenly, foreseeing myself slowly getting drowned in my own pool of sweat.

No, Ah Beh, this job is not for me.

* * *

One early morning, I opened the windows wide, gazing far into the busy landscape.

Puddles of rainwater could be found everywhere. As a result of the vigorous rustling of leaves last night, many branches broke and fell. I could see reflections of shophouses and stalls vibrating in the puddles, making the whole street glisten with clarity.

I loved such a scene. It was like a refreshing shower to all my senses.

A night soil collector arrived very early for his duty. In truth, he was very late. He had to finish his night duties only in the morning due to the downpour yesterday.

He paced carefully down the spiral staircase of the shophouse opposite, balancing two giant pails of waste on his shoulders. It was difficult to walk on the curvature of the staircase. One could turn giddy easily.

The night soil collector descended the stairs with care, lowering his head and staring hard at every step he took. The puddles accumulated on the steps made his descent riskier.

Staring at him from afar, even I got worried for him.

I blinked. He moved to the next step. I blinked again. And the worst happened.

He slipped!

His body slumped onto the floor. My eyes widened and I let out a loud yell.

His pails clashed against the sidewall of the staircase as he fell. Brown liquid solid spilled out and tainted the walls like splattering fireworks. Some of the brown liquid was trickling down like yesterday's raindrops.

A middle-aged woman was washing dishes by the drain. The showering of brown waste on her head made her look like a thick biscuit stick topped with chocolate fudge.

The woman was drenched. Her face was reddened with both anger and embarrassment. She remained in a state of shock for a while before looking up and cursing at the night soil collector.

'*SI NYA PEH*! *SI NYA BU*! DEATH TO YOUR ENTIRE FAMILY!'

People around her were chuckling away. A few crossed their brows but were at a loss on how to help her.

I pressed against my stomach and tried very hard to curb my exploding laughter. I did not mean to laugh. I did feel sorry for her. I could feel her agony, I really did, but to be honest, her misfortune felt strangely satisfying for me at the same time.

My giggles came to my own ears as a tickle, landing me in hysterics. I had not laughed this hard for the longest time. My knees buckled, taking me to the floor. I turned and turned, holding the sore middle of my body.

Then, out of curiosity, I stood up to observe the angry woman.

She took a big piece of rag to wipe away the brownish liquid on her head, then disappeared into a corner. After she was gone, my eyes shifted back to the eatery, to the spot where she was drenched. And I noticed someone standing way in front of all the brown splatters on the ground, waving.

Me? Was he waving at me?

'KUANG!' Geong called out to me, standing at the spot where he used to wait for me to watch Teochew-hee.

'KUANG! Here! Here!' Geong gestured for me to go down to meet him.

I squinted my eyes. The sight of Geong lit me up. 'Wait for me!' I shouted back from my apartment.

Running down the flight of stairs to meet Geong used to be one of the most exciting moments of my childhood. It was a flash of anticipation coupled with freedom from chores at home.

If I could turn back time, and pick a moment to relive, this would be it.

I felt the same exhilaration today, like an eleven-year-old jumping with joy within the frame of a teenager. I wondered what fun thing Geong was going to share with me.

* * *

'Kuang! Want to watch a movie at the new drive-in cinema together?'
Geong asked animatedly. His brows were raised as he fished out a
ticket from his chest pocket.

I was smitten by that small piece of paper in his hands.

Recently, Singapore's only open-air drive-in cinema, the Jurong
Drive-in, was opened. I heard the cinema could accommodate nine
hundred cars and an additional three hundred people in its walk-
in gallery.

I had never watched a movie at a cinema before, let alone
watching a big screen in a drive-in cinema. It must be unimaginably
relaxing to rest in a car while fixing my eyes on a giant screen, just
like those cinemas in the Ang Moh countries.

'Wow! You mean you've got us tickets to watch a show in that
new special cinema?' I asked with my heart fluttering in feverish
anticipation. 'Let me see! When is it? Oh, and which show are we
going to watch?'

'Bruce Lee! It's an action movie, Kuang. I know you'll like it!
I still remember how much you loved those athletic Teochew-hee
actors, you know, those stiff, stern ones with long beards and painted
frowns on their faces!' Geong replied excitedly. 'It's next Tuesday,
7.30 p.m.!'

Words could move hearts as much as they could pierce. I did not
expect Geong to remember such fine details about me. Those that
even I had forgotten. Yet he remembered.

'Alright! Thank you so much, Geong!' I was jumping with
exhilaration within. 'But wait, isn't it a drive-in cinema? Which
means we need a car, don't we? Do you . . . have a car?' I asked,
staring into Geong's eyes in disbelief.

'Good question, Kuang! Don't worry about that. I have another
friend coming along with us. His name is Chun. He has a car!'
Geong answered me assuredly.

I was right.

I did not think Geong could afford a car being an assistant in
an eating-house. It was impossible for him to have one. At the same
time, I was fading away in disappointment.

So, it'll not be just the two of us? I cut myself off from a chain of senseless thoughts channeling back to schooldays.

'Oh yes, sure! See you next Tuesday, Geong.' I replied in excitement.

Geong waved goodbye to me and headed towards his workplace. I turned and walked back to my apartment, smoothing the goosebumps on my arms and trying my utmost to quell the surge of uncertainty that struck me within.

* * *

I put on my most decent-looking shirt, and a pair of neatly pressed brown pants. Ah Mm did the ironing for me, which I greatly appreciated.

I squeezed out some hair gel that I bought from the market yesterday and smeared it on my thick coarse hair, puffing it up. I looked at myself in the mirror for the last time. Satisfied, I bounced out of the bathroom.

I could hear a car honking from the second floor of our shophouse. As I slowly approached it, I could see it was built like a black tank with its doors closed like a bank vault. I paced quickly to the side of the car and waved to Geong who was already seated in it.

'Kuang! Let me introduce him to you,' Geong said in a flurry, as his eyes darted to the driver as soon as I sat down.

'This is Chun, my brother, not related by blood though,' Geong let out a smile. Though the tone of his voice was a happy one, his smile was cold, one that did not reach his blank eyes. Filled with some sort of darkness I was not sure of, Geong's smile sent a shudder down my spine.

'And Chun, this is Kuang. He's my childhood friend. I mentioned him to you last week.'

Awkwardly, I squeezed out a smile and shook hands with that Chun. I had a sudden heightened need for personal distance from this man. It did not seem like he was a simple person to me. There was something uncanny about him.

Chun had an intimidating aura that made me want to hide behind my hair. His penetrating gaze was filled with nonchalance and his smile, tight and polite but not genuine at all.

I then glanced around, admiring the interior of the posh car. My heart was fluttering. It was my first time sitting inside a private car and I was awestruck by its open-top. The starry night sky was just above me! I could admire the quilt of unmoving glitters and the bright round moon at the comfort of a soft couch as the car moved.

I kept silent and remained expressionless despite the craze within, bearing in mind not to reveal my astonishment too much that it made me look ignorant.

Also, I could not wait to watch Bruce Lee in action on the screen.

* * *

The sight of hundreds of cars parked at the drive-in cinema was breathtaking.

I had not seen such a big crowd for very long. The last time I saw a big crowd gather was during political rallies in the period when Singapore was fighting for her national independence.

Patrons were munching on snacks in their cars while waiting for the show to start. Accompanied with loud chatters and children's crying, the scene was rowdy, to a point it was getting out of hand.

There were youngsters yelling vulgarities from one end to the other and cars of people shouting unhappily in the queue at the entrance. I could also see gatecrashers sneaking into the cinema without paying for any ticket.

I was not sure how this chaos could be settled before the start of the show.

Chun heaved a loud sigh out of the blue. 'Why is this taking so long? This is absolutely wasting my time!' His frustration revealed his impatience. It was something beyond his gentlemanly exterior.

'It's coming. I'm sure it's coming. While waiting, shall we ask Kuang for his opinion?' Geong added on, trying to extinguish the flame rousing in Chun.

I stared at Geong in bewilderment, wondering what question he had for me. The feeling of being an outsider consumed my every thought.

'Well, Kuang, Chun's father recently bought over a kopitiam and was asking Chun the other day if he was interested to run a business on his own,' Geong explained, his Adam's apple bobbing nervously.

'While Chun does not wish to be at the front line of a kopitiam business, erm . . . he asked if I'm keen to make it work. After working at the previous kopitiam for quite some time, I believe it's time for me to set up my own. Braising ducks is easy!' Geong laughed, red-faced. 'I've learned the recipe of lor ark png from my current boss. I'm sure nothing will go wrong.'

I was listening intently to Geong. For one fleeting moment, I thought Geong was amazing. He was all ready to be his own boss, despite such a young age. I wondered where he got the guts from.

'Will you be keen to make it work together with me?'

I gasped, almost dropping my jaws. *What? Me?*

My reaction was immediate. 'Erm, why me, Geong? I'm not sure if I can help . . . '

I was in truth, flustered within. Heat rushed up to my face. My breathing became irregular, resulting in tightness in my chest. Even though I had patched things up with Geong, a part of my heart wished to maintain a distance. Geong just did not make me feel entirely assured. His expressions, words, and behaviours all seemed to be hiding something from me.

'Kuang, you were selling Teochew fish porridge, weren't you? You've so much experience to offer. I'll need to learn from you,' Geong tried to convince me with sweet words. 'Moreover, you're my brother. I'm sure we can work well together, just like the past.'

Deep down, I did not think I deserved such flattery just by washing fish and dishes at the stall. I did not know how to reply to Geong. I wanted to say no, an absolute no, yet, a lump formed in my throat, stopping me.

At the same time, I had to admit, Geong's offer tempted me.

It was a dream coming true. I could work in a well-furnished kopitiam, have the chance to work together with my good friend, and to experience selling a different food. The best benefit was in truth, to have a reason to stop working as a kuli.

After some hesitation, I agreed.

Did I just agree? Alright, too late to say no.

'That's wonderful, Kuang! So could you share the rent cost with me then?'

I was shocked by Geong's second request.

'Not that much. Each person merely had to fork out $100 since Chun is my brother and we've known each for long. He's giving us a discount for the starting cost. Hand me the money soon so that we could get started.'

Geong's words made me pause and reconsider my decision. Immediately, I wished to retreat. Indeed, there was no such thing as a free lunch.

'Erm, Geong, I think . . . '

And the show started. Like how he appeared on magazines and newspapers, Bruce Lee had ripped through his shirt, as always. His extremely muscular body flashed onto the screen and captured all our attention immediately. Expressions of wonder and screams filled the entire cinema.

While I stared at him in awe, wondering how he could survive his own legendary abs training routines to arrive at his extraordinary body built, at the back of my head, I was sandwiched between the choices of advancing with Geong and remaining a kuli with Ah Beh.

After a long while of pondering, I finally made my decision. I began thinking of ways to get money for our shared lor ark png business.

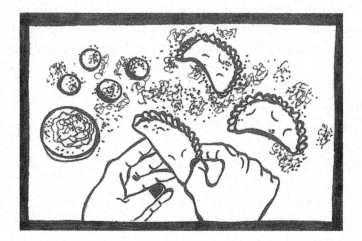

Twenty-Two

I crawled under the altar, lifted a pile of newspapers and pulled out a biscuit tin. It was where my savings sat.

With a fruit knife, I pried open the lid to reveal the notes and coins. *Ten dollars, twenty dollars, thirty dollars . . .*

I took out all my savings. The emptiness in the tin was like hollowness flowing through my veins. It was hard to accept that I was going to spend all my savings just like that. Betting my lifetime savings on a business plan that might result in a loss felt like a game of life and death.

Should I go ahead or not? This question was stuck in my head, causing my mind to be in turmoil.

Ah Mm walked into the apartment, with a pail of wet, wrung clothes, all ready to be hoisted out into the sun to dry.

'Are you in need of money, Kuang?' Ah Mm asked, looking at me with concerned eyes.

'Erm, yes, Ah Mm.' I exchanged a quick glance with Ah Mm then looked down at my meager savings. ' . . . I want to start a business with a friend.'

Ah Mm's eyes widened.

'Do you remember Geong? I hastened my pace of talking. 'My primary school friend. Remember? The one whom I always watched Teochew-hee with. He asked if we could start a business together.'

'What kind of business?'

'Lor ark png.'

Ah Mm stared at me without blinking. 'Lor ark? Are you sure, Kuang? You know nothing about making lor ark png.'

'Trust me, Ah Mm. I trust my friend. He's my good friend.'

'I know you're a grown-up now, Kuang, and I know I shouldn't interfere with your decision-making. But the outside world is complicated.'

'Aiyo, Ah Mm, don't worry. Trust me.'

Ah Mm's brows were drawing together. She then smoothed and re-smoothed her old flowery shirt.

'But Ah Mm also don't wish that you would change your mind because of me. Keep in mind, whatever happens, good or bad, come back and share it with me.'

Ah Mm's eyes were warm yet distant. Dark yet full of light.

She frowned, then smiled. The delicate skin around the eyes crinkled as her brows arched in affection.

'Just be careful. No harm trying. Men should have accomplishments.'

I knelt down, and moved closer to her. 'Ah Mm, when I have mastered the art of making lor ark png, I will make a feast for you— Teochew braised duck rice coupled with all the treasures of the ducks. Let you reminisce the goodness of Shantou braised goose.' I shared a happy glance with Ah Mm.

'You're filial, I know.' A relaxed smile crossed Ah Mm's face, her cheeks going lightly blushed.

'Ah Mm . . . but I need a favour from you.'

Worry returned to her face.

Could you let Ah Beh know? I don't want to work as a kuli anymore.' I pleaded.

'Father and son, what's there not to talk about, Kuang?'

'Help me, Mm . . . please.'

Ah Mm looked away and shook her head slightly. 'You're always like that.'

She then stood up slowly. Her thin body easily lifted up from the mattress. Limping with her slightly bent knees, Ah Mm opened the cupboard where her cherished items were kept.

She took out a bundle of notes and handed it to me.

'Ah Mm, what's this?' I asked.

'Money for condolences. This is the leftover collected from all the gaginang who came over to your Ah Gong's funeral. We've already spent a bulk of it on the bill for the funeral. This is the rest.'

'And you're giving it to me for . . . ?'

'It's not a lot of money left. Ah Mm is giving it to you to support you in your business. Take it.' Ah Mm said, shoving the bundle of notes to me.

'No, no, I shouldn't take your money.' I pushed back the notes. I would hate myself for taking money from Ah Mm. *How could I?*

'Take it, Kuang. Return Ah Mm when you earn big bucks next time. You need the money, don't you?' Ah Mm pushed the notes back to me.

I held the warm notes in my hand, looking at Ah Mm with my blinking eyes.

'Thank you . . . Ah Mm,' I said hesitatingly. At that instant, my heart was filled with endless gratitude.

Mother, who else but you, love me the most?

* * *

Geong and I stepped into Chun's kopitiam.

It was rather old and small, unlike the one Geong worked at previously.

The washes on the walls had turned yellow and there were cobwebs spun at every corner. The foul smell of a clogged up metallic sink filled the entire space. I felt nauseated upon spotting the heavy clumps of hardened dirty oil in the sink drain. They looked exactly like black soot moistened with glue.

I gagged.

And the thought of how much cleaning we had to do further prompted the expulsion of content in my stomach.

The kopitiam was incomparably small recalling the ones I saw along the streets where our fish porridge stall was located. It could merely accommodate six sets of tables and chairs. The wooden tables were slightly chipped at the corners and some of the chairs were shaky.

I was greatly disappointed. But I sucked a big mouthful of air in and forced myself to look fine. I did not want Geong to doubt my sincerity to work with him.

We sat down at one of the tables after surveying the place. Geong took out a piece of paper and started doodling and writing, trying to sketch out a rough plan with his untidy handwriting.

Both Geong and I were inexperienced at setting up a hawker business. It felt like we were stepping into the unknown together, and all we could depend on was each other.

How refreshing this new episode was. But, at the same time, it was daunting. Blind spots were everywhere in this unknown dimension. What else was needed in the shop? What did we miss out?

The fear of failure constantly kept us on our toes.

Never had I imagined myself to be able to contribute to a business plan. But Geong gave me a chance to help him and gave me a job. I felt needed and being needed made me feel good.

I came to realize little things I did at the fish porridge stall were not at all little. Without the previous experience of being a stall assistant, I might not be able to comment on even the slightest thing. I was able to connect the dots now.

For the next few days, Geong and I worked very hard to clean the kopitiam, removing all visible stains and thick layers of dirt that blanketed the entire space.

'Kuang, is this hard for you?' Geong asked me one evening, while we were scrubbing the floor together.

I shook my head hastily. 'Not at all, Geong! I'm used to cleaning and washing. I did this all the time at the fish porridge stall.'

'That's good. I knew you'll make a great partner.' Geong looked at me, letting out a tight-lipped smile.

I exchanged a smile with him.

Geong looked like he was smiling against his will and that brought up unease in me. Again, it led me to have hesitation setting up this business with him. Could it be my own anxiety striking it out on its own? It was my first time venturing out on my own, probably that was why I was jittery at times.

I pushed my doubts away and continued scrubbing the floor with all my might.

* * *

I opened my eyes wide, staring at the ceiling, and sensing fizziness in my head. Morning rays shone through the windows and landed on my cheeks.

I just had a familiar dream.

A row of braised ducks hung neatly in front of me. Some necks bent inward, revealing the duck heads, while others bent outward. A round thick wooden chopping board stood in front of me. I ran my right hand along the edge of the board to feel the rough ends and placed my left palm on the board, caressing its smoothness.

Then, I held my face upward to feel the warm light of the morning sun. The air smelt just right and I could see many birds, hopping up and down tables and chairs, waiting to pick up scraps.

It was a sweet morning. I woke up, feeling peace and contentment cruising through my veins. Yet as I slowly came to my senses, I realized my reality was different. It was shrouded with uncertainty. I longed for a conversation that could spur me on in my new business venture. Perhaps, I just needed someone to assure me that I was on the right track.

I thought of Uncle Tham.

I set off quickly, hoping to catch him before his long queue of customers formed.

* * *

In high spirits, Uncle Tham had already set up his galy poks stall by the time I arrived.

'Kuang! Didn't expect to see you today!' Uncle Tham's eyes lit up and a wide smile broke out across his face. 'Are you still selling fish porridge?'

'Not anymore. I'm on my own now.'

'Wow! That's exactly what youth is, isn't it, young man? Full of energy and changes.'

I laughed.

'I'm starting my own business.' I answered, feeling both proud and unsure at the same time. My lips quivered a little.

'Good! Good! Young people should take some risk lah. You'll make it big! I can't be wrong about you,' Uncle Tham exclaimed. His clear and powerful voice resonated and stroke my eardrum.

At Uncle Tham's mobile kitchen, a big bowl of orange mixture was waiting on the high stool. The flavourful creamy curry filled the bowl to its brim. It sparkled, releasing a mouthwatering peppery aroma. I could see hot steam rising out of the mixture as Uncle Tham stirred it with a spatula.

'Mmm, lovely!' Uncle Tham muttered to himself while bringing his face up close to the bowl.

He carefully examined the freshly rolled-out dough and ensured that every part was smoothened before spooning the cooled curry mixture onto it. His meticulousness astonished me.

'Kuang ah, so, what brings you here today? Watch this old man make galy poks?' Uncle Tham shared a playful grin.

I laughed.

'I'm here to talk with you, Uncle Tham.'

'Oh interesting! What do you want to talk with me about?'
Uncle Tham stopped fluting the edges of his pastries, looked up and
beamed at me.

Randomly, I blurted a question. ' . . . So, how do you make such
amazing galy poks?'

Uncle Tham sucked in a long breath. His eyes turned inward
and he cracked up in a quick laughter.

'So, this is it?'

I laughed again.

'Let me think.' Uncle Tham became serious. After a while, he
continued, 'When you make a dish . . . ' Uncle Tham paused and
leaned slightly towards me. 'Kuang, you need to truly love it. You've
got to love what you make as if it's your flesh and blood.' He stared
at me with unblinking eyes.

He then picked up a puff and brought it close to his nose, sniffed
it, and smiled with contentment.

'Ahh, what flesh and blood. I just realized you haven't had any
child of your own. I'm turning into a forgetful old man. Alright, let
me think . . . hmm . . . ' Uncle Tham held his head high, deep in
thoughts.

'Alright, Kuang, I got it. Here . . . Uncle Tham tell you, you
must remember, your creation creates a whole new you.' Uncle
Tham smiled, showing his whites.

'The process of bringing something into existence requires a
strong belief and a great purpose. It is always a struggle with your
own willingness to accept compromises. As you work tirelessly on
creating something unique, meeting storms and rain head-on, a
whole new you will be created.' Uncle Tham's brows raised and his
eyes sparkled.

'So, never! Never for a moment forget the effort to always create
a newer you. Go ahead and throw yourself wholeheartedly into
making your food. Carry through with that task to the very end.
You'll blossom with passion!'

I was once again awestruck by Uncle Tham's words. My eyes
glimmered along with his.

Uncle Tham put down his hand and continued twisting the edges of the soft white pastry with precision, forming a beautiful, fluted pattern while whistling a tune.

He then pulled out a bottle filled with yellow and white bits which I could not identify. He twisted the lid and sprinkled the bits onto the raw batch of pastries.

'What're you doing, Uncle Tham?' I asked, eyes darting along with the movement of the bottle, going up and down.

'This one? This is cheese! Westerners' favourite!'

'Cheese? And why are you adding them to your pastries?'

'Aiyo . . . Innovating new flavour, Kuang!'

' . . . Innovating?'

'Yes! Singapore's culture is changing, my dear young man. Can't believe I'm trendier than you are.' Uncle Tham let out a wide grin.

'Our young people are different now. They're all listening to western pop songs! Beatles! Very hot! You listen to their songs? I've got to catch up with these people's changing taste buds.' Uncle Tham said, trying to whistle a different tune.

That was an English song, mind you.

I could feel fervent enthusiasm in Uncle Tham's reply. It was something I did not sense from anyone working at the previous fish porridge stall. Geong did not give me such an impression too.

Uncle Tham's passion for galy poks coasted from every fiber of his being. Excitement about his creation wired his body like he was plugged into the mains.

It was rubbing off on me.

He continued to bounce, bending his knees up and down in a rhythmic manner in his mobile kitchen, singing and preparing the ingredients for his next batch of galy poks.

'By the way, young man, in a few months' time, you won't be able to find my stall here. I'm moving.'

'Oh! Where to?'

'Newton Circus Food Centre.'

'Oh . . . what's that?'

'It's a hawker centre, Kuang! You don't know about this?'

I shook my head in shame, knowing that I had probably missed out on important national news in the midst of setting up my own business.

'Our cheng hu has decided to bring us all indoors. No more street hawkers. *Ma da* will catch! I just got a place to sell my puffs over at Newton Circus Food Centre. Singapore is changing. Different already! I am required to get my hawker license and move. There were many other new rules too, like, what no chopping and preparing food on porous wood. Cooked and uncooked foods need to be stored separately. And all hawkers are required to wear gloves from now on too. *Lor lor sor sor . . . Jin mua huang*!

'Oh, I didn't know about this!'

'You'd better find out more. The cheng hu is going to be really strict about this. You might end up being fined if you don't adhere to the rules,' advised Uncle Tham.

'Alright, thank you so much for sharing these with me, Uncle Tham. Gam xia!'

'Don't mention about it. Here you go! Two galy poks and one extra! Run along!'

'Bye Uncle Tham! I'll see you again!'

My mind was in a whirlwind. Just two hours hanging around Uncle Tham's stall made me feel like a kid back in school again. There was so much to learn in this ever-changing society. Maneuvering in the unknown made me feel lost but yet, I felt a sense of deeper clarity from today.

Now, I confidently knew how I could improve our business. We had been fretting about the shop, the look of it especially and how customers might feel walking into it. We forgot about the main part of the lor ark png business! Lor ark! What was so special about our lor ark? What could make customers remember it and even chase after it? We got to create our own unique flavour and further innovate!

I was so glad to have talked with Uncle Tham. My heart was suffused with gratitude once again for this galy pok vendor who always shared his experiences with me. What he had learnt as a hawker, as a person too, had heightened my awareness about so many things in my own life. His wisdom had definitely turned me into a better person.

* * *

I spent the rest of my day, strolling along streets packed with Chinese restaurants. My curiosity about how businesses attracted customers grew.

There were menus placed outside restaurants. With a pencil and a small notebook in hand, I spent the evening browsing all the menus I could find, jotting down important notes for my own reference. I even attempted to peep into others' shops to see what they were selling.

What kind of soups others were making that went along with their mains? What kind of small dishes could go well with rice mains? How did restaurants sell their food? I noticed sometimes they came in sets. Could we sell our lor ark png in sets? Could it make it easier for the customers to place their orders? Were there also different kinds of chili available? How should we make our chili?

Innovation indeed required a lot of planning, thinking, and hard work.

The day after next, I met Geong at the kopitiam. He seemed to be sleep deprived. The black circles under his eyes had almost become bruises. Several times as he puffed a cigarette, I noticed him trembling.

'Geong, I'd like to share some ideas with you.'

'Yes?' Geong answered. Our eyes met and he broke it off, pretending to be busy.

'Perhaps . . . we could add more stuff into our menu, like soup-of-the-day to go with our duck rice, a few kinds of chili sauce for customers to pick from, and . . . '

Geong frowned and casted a skeptical eye on me. He interrupted, 'Kuang, can't work lah! Siao lah. You've no idea how tough it is to braise ducks. We can't add any more things into our menu. The great amount of work will drive us mad! Only three of us here.'

I was startled by Geong's strong reaction. Stress seemed to be bubbling through him. My mind was in a sudden conflict. Was I thoughtless? Or too ambitious? Or were we a mismatch? The business venture with Geong did not seem to match my vision of what a lor ark png business should be.

Unexpectedly, I felt stuck. I could not express my thoughts freely with Geong.

I longed to learn duck braising, but I had no opportunity to sneak a peek at how Geong did it. Every morning, Geong was the first person to arrive at the shop. He started preparation near seven in the morning, while I arrived one hour later to wash and cook rice, and complete other miscellaneous tasks. Our only helper was responsible for chopping and slicing duck meat.

I could sense Geong's reluctance in imparting his skills to me. I wondered the reason behind his insistent refusal. And, why was Geong suddenly acting like the boss? Didn't I chip in the same amount of money as he did for this business?

How was it a good idea for me to know nothing about braising ducks? What if one day Geong was not around? Who was going to run the stall?

I knew I needed to do something different in order to learn something new. I decided to be bold.

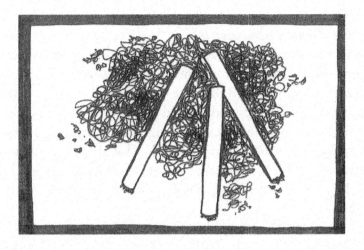

Twenty-Three

One month later, I rose early, way before the sun did.

I arrived at the kopitiam but did not enter by the front door. I tiptoed all the way to the back of the shop. Through the slightly open windows located at one corner of the kitchen, I saw Geong sitting on a stool, all flustered.

Geong lit up a cigarette and took a puff. His forehead furrowed into an agonized frown. He seemed troubled these few days. Whenever I asked about him, he would merely utter a few words.

Bowls of ingredients such as star anise, blue ginger, old garlic, and cinnamon sticks were sitting near the stove. Besides the ingredients, a big tin of dark soy sauce was almost falling off the edge of the tabletop.

Geong stood up, rolled up a white towel and placed it around his neck. He started frying the prepared ingredients in a wok. A pungent aroma drifted upwards from the wok and filled the kitchen.

It was, however, a different smell, as compared to the one I sensed outside the eating-house opposite the fish porridge stall. Something was lacking. It was pungent but not rich.

I watched in silence as Geong began pouring the sauces into the large stockpot. I could tell from his clumsy actions that he was an absolute greenhorn. In fact, he was still experimenting. *Where had all the skills he claimed he had gone to?*

I was trying to forgive Geong for hiding the truth but at the same time, I felt cheated. I watched on. In his frenzy, the bottom part of his left arm touched the edge of the wok. He yelled wildly.

A red line of flesh puffed up and caused the skin around it to swell. His hand let go of the spatula right away and it fell into the stockpot filled with boiling dark sauces. Hot steam together with huge droplets of black gravy shot up and speckled his face. Geong shielded his face with both hands, almost screaming with his whole body.

My heart was thudding like a rock in a box. I was not sure if I should approach to help him or stay put to avoid unnecessary conflict.

Geong quickly washed his face and arm under cold running water. He pulled the rolled white towel from his neck and smacked it on the table, swearing continuously at the stockpot.

Soon, the ducks arrived. They came in a huge batch with feathers already plucked off.

Geong stood up.

As if locked in chains, he dragged his feet towards the ducks. One by one, he washed them in a big pail of water, then, used a thin metal pole to poke right through their necks. With great effort, he lowered the ducks into the waiting stockpot while sighing away occasionally.

I was flabbergasted. Those ducks . . . they still had tiny bit of feathers on them! Why didn't Geong soak them in boiling water to get rid of them?

Agitatedly, I checked the time on my watch. It was soon past the time for me to arrive at the shop. Without a noise, I sneaked back to the entrance.

* * *

Business had been bad. At lunchtime, the initial crowd shrank to two or three customers. A mere six sets of tables and chairs could not be filled.

I was praying for the right time to approach Geong to share my honest opinions. I waited and waited. Finally, a moment came when he was no longer distracted by trivial tasks. I followed Geong to the kitchen and walked up to him.

'Geong . . . ' I called. His uncontrolled shivering and hand tremors caught my attention.

Geong seemed annoyed. He rubbed his temple as if to ward off a headache and turned away.

' . . . I feel something is missing in our gravy.' I shared in a low voice.

Geong turned and faced me, crossing his brows. He displayed downright unwillingness to listen. I could feel superiority slashing across his face.

'What's wrong?' he asked impatiently as if listening to suggestions given by a novice could rob his precious time away.

'It's . . . overly gooey and lacks flavour. It just doesn't taste savoury enough.'

'That's how my boss did it in the past,' Geong insisted, shutting his ears and walking away from me.

'But Geong, look at our business. Your gravy is definitely different from his.' I rebutted boldly, hoping that Geong would take my opinion into consideration. 'Would you want to work it out together? Let's come up with a recipe of our own.'

'With you? What do you know about lor ark?' Geong asked.

A moment of silence followed. Geong's hardhearted stare sealed my lips.

'You only know fish porridge, don't you? *Mai geh kiang* lah! Are you not happy working with me? *Huh?*' Geong retorted. His face reddened as his eyes narrowed.

'No, Geong. I just hope to improve our business, together with you,' I tried to explain, hoping that Geong could look at this matter with an objective lens.

'With me? You're here to help me with washing and cleaning. Listen. Those dull and mundane chores that I hated. I had enough of doing those at that darned eating-house.' Geong spoke in a penetrating voice. As dead as his eyes, his loud voice was devoid of human feeling. 'That's why I invited you to join me in this new venture. You're not here to teach me how to alter my recipe. Have I made myself clear?'

My eyes opened wide. I was appalled by Geong's selfish words.

How quickly our friendship had turned into hatred again. His hurtful words were almost unforgivable.

'How about my money?' I questioned, staring right into his eyes.

Geong grimaced. 'What? Weren't you a willing party to support me in my business, Kuang? I didn't force you to give me any money, ok?'

What? What the hell was he talking about? Heavens above knew he was the one who asked me for the money. Alright, fine, he did not exactly force me to hand over the money, but he certainly had made use of our friendship to talk me into contributing a sum for the business.

Reality had once again revealed this man's true colours.

Today, I finally saw through Geong. He was merely making use of my naivety to achieve his selfish goal. I did not know how to reply to him anymore. I felt sad, more than anything else. This blasted friendship had once again, utterly disappointed me.

Refusing to say anything, I turned around and walked out of the kitchen.

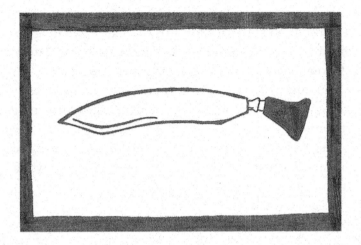

Twenty-Four

Ever since Geong and I quarreled a week ago, we had not spoken with each other. Our helper was either caught between us or had to become our messenger. It was hell, working with a self-proclaimed boss whom I could not trust at all.

Today, Chun came to our kopitiam. He was a rare guest.

Checkered suit, puffed up greasy hairdo, and a pair of shades made him look like a celebrity that had just stepped into our shop.

He sat on a chair, took off his shades to reveal his dark solemn eyes, and ordered a can of chrysanthemum tea. Noticing the empty shop, Chun called for Geong who was trying to look busy in the kitchen all the time.

'Ey! Ah Hia! Looking for me?' Geong hunched his back and scurried towards Chun like a dog cuddling up to its owner.

'Geong, how's business?' Chun asked, as if not informed by the apparent emptiness in the shop.

'*Bueh pai!* But today was exceptional, Ah Hia. Look that the dark clouds! Ha. Who would want to come here to eat duck rice?'

Geong answered, laughing awkwardly to himself. His fingers rubbing against one another.

'I see.' Chun stood up and patted Geong's shoulder.

He then continued to pace towards the stall, scratching his head umpteen times. He then stared at Geong with his predatory eyes, making Geong uncomfortable with his penetrating gaze.

'Are you sure you want to continue with this business? Why don't you consider my suggestion?' Chun asked, frowning and smiling together.

I was hiding in the kitchen, leaning my left ear against the wall, trying to listen to their conversation. Their relationship was always strange to me, but I could not pinpoint why.

Geong stayed silent.

'Geong, you know what's best for you.' Chun further added on. 'I shall not force you. You're my benefactor. I owe my life to you. But good things ought to be shared with brothers. Come and join me. Collecting money from hawkers is much easier than trying to set up your own hawker business. See? Look at all this miserable shop! I seized it at such a cheap price. From those ignorant old men who were so scared. They almost peed in their pants! I don't understand why you insisted to take over this miserable shop to try first. Try what? Try to prove that you're not so capable? I've granted your wish. And now? Look at this!'

'Let me consider, Chun. Give me two more weeks. Let me try again.' Geong requested, looking solemnly at Chun.

A wide grin spread across Chun's face.

'Of course! I'll wait for you. You'll be such a precious member of our society. I mean, potential member. But don't be too late, Geong. You know what I mean. A good life, filled with wealth and women, is hard to come by.' Chun gently patted Geong's cheek with his palm and left.

Silence hung in the air, thick and heavy.

Geong stood by a table, both of his hands were pressing against the tabletop and his head was lowered. He remained still for the longest time, muttering to himself.

I walked out of the kitchen with a pail and rag and began wiping the tables, pretending not to have heard anything. The temptation to rupture the silence was hard to resist.

My thought traced back to the moment in Chun's posh vehicle at the drive-in cinema. The way Geong talked to Chun, over-agreeable and slightly sheepish, made it difficult for me to determine what exactly their relationship was. I began to see things more clearly now. Geong must be under some kind of threat. Their association to each other was not at all simple.

Something in my gut told me Geong was in deep trouble.

* * *

Uncle Tham was right.

Singapore's landscape was changing. One by one, street hawkers were brought indoors, and squatters were reduced.

Meanwhile, our neighbours at the shophouse also started moving out of their apartments. Ah Beh said those gaginang who stayed near us had also relocated. Throughout the past decade, the Housing Development Board (HDB) had gradually built blocks of public housing flats. Tall buildings started sprouting across the island. Families were resettled from kampongs and shophouses into HDB flats. It seemed like everyone in our neighbourhood were overall pleased with the arrangement. From their chattering and jabbering on the streets, living in the HDB flats had tremendously improved their living standard. Many people rejoiced.

Ah Beh was recently convinced by the authority to move out of our old shophouse. We were relocated to a four-room flat at the east side of Singapore. My siblings and I could hardly wait to move in. We were desperate to leave this tiny apartment to start life anew. We yearned to own a proper place of our own. Best was, to have own our bathroom and toilet. No more defecating into pails. No more wriggly maggots. No more sharing.

However, moving house during this busy period was a huge challenge for me. The business with Geong was not earning enough profits to sustain my livelihood. In addition, the far travelling distance between my new home and our kopitiam made it hard for me to have enough rest. I had to wake up much earlier to arrive at the kopitiam on time. So, eventually, I made a decision to remain in the old shophouse during the weekdays.

Every family had moved out and I was alone staying in this dark and isolated apartment. Electricity and water were cut off. But I reckoned I could go without them for the time being.

The worst problem was not this but the infestation of rats, roaches, centipedes, and bedbugs. Heavenly goodness. How did they spread so quickly? These hearty creatures were raining from the ceiling every single night when I returned. The roaches were snacking on the bedbugs and the bedbugs were munching on me.

Sometimes, weird characters also sneaked into the deserted shophouse to commit crimes like glue sniffing. Occasionally, fights broke out between members of different secret societies.

Just yesterday midnight, two men were stopped by another two right next to our five-foot way. I was in our old apartment, looking out of my windows when that happened. I bent down right away so as not to be seen.

I strained my eyes and peeped through the window to find out more. The two men were challenged. 'What number do you play?' asked the other two. In a quick manner, they gestured some numbers to one another. Before I knew it, they were baring their teeth with their *parangs* and gathering their members. A staring game had escalated to a series of vengeful attacks using parangs.

Fights like this were common. Every week, bodies lay scattered. And I could smell bloodshed, metallic and salty, like many blocks of expired butter melting together.

Living alone in the old shophouse gave me goosebumps. I was fearful of those violent fights amongst members of different secret societies. Constantly worrying if I would be dragged into their affairs, the slightest sound of people talking near the five-foot ways would wake me up easily.

At the same time, I was troubled by my relationship with Geong. I needed to arrive at a decision on whether to continue working for him. So often I decided and second-guessed myself straight after.

I shut down eventually, refusing to even think about it.

* * *

Last month, Geong docked my salary. And his explanation was brief.

The cost price of ducks had gone way up and as faithful employees of this kopitiam, we had to accept low salary for the time being.

Of course, that was a lousy excuse. In truth, there was only slight price inflation in ducks. We all knew it because we had friends selling lor ark png in the neighbourhood. I was not the only one who grumbled about this unjustified treatment. Our helper made a big fuss behind Geong's back. He went down streets to badmouth Geong's actions and gave him a bad name.

I thought things would turn better this month, but I was wrong. Geong approached me yesterday and repeated what he had told me last month. The same string of words that got on my nerves. Again, my salary would be docked.

'Geong, what do you mean?' I questioned, frowning at him.

'The cost price of ducks has gone up.' Geong countered, lying without batting an eyelid. 'Told you, right?'

'Is this a reason or an excuse, Geong?'

Geong sauntered off.

'Tough times now, can't you understand? Just bear with this for a few more months!' He rattled on.

'No way, Geong. My family needs my contribution.'

'If you're not happy, then leave lah.' Geong suggested harshly.

Was he hinting to end our partnership, just like that? So much damage was done when Geong argued. Mean things just flooded out of his mouth without any control.

I shook my head repeatedly in disbelief. 'Of course, I will, Geong! I've had enough of you and the way you manage this business. I was such a fool to have followed you. I will leave OK! I will leave right now!'

'Fine. LEAVE!' Geong threw his arms angrily into the air, like a mad person unleashing his anger. 'I don't need you! GO! GO! Don't let me see your face again!'

Anger stirred within me. Flickers of irritation pricked at me, making me shake. I tried to remain stiff, refusing to let my fury take over me. My eyes glared into Geong's eyes.

'And you?' I asked, stilling my rage. 'Are you going to follow Chun?'

'What're you talking about?' Geong snapped and snarled, frowning at me. 'What do you know?'

'Of course, you don't want anyone to know. Collecting money from hawkers? What're you guys up to?' I replied with eyes widening into two glass marbles about to shoot.

'*Diam* lah! You don't know a single thing!'

I could feel my ears becoming hot.

I knew resentment was building up in Geong. He was almost choking on his rage. Another word from me could easily stir a hurricane of harsh insults from Geong. But I needed to know what could happen to him. I needed to know because . . . he was still my best friend—and *I cared*.

'Geong . . . Is Chun really a rich man's son? How did this kopitiam come about? And what is Chun involved in?' I further questioned, softening my tone. I certainly did not wish to see an old friend wander off the right path. 'Geong, you need to differentiate right from wrong.'

'I don't need your advice lah! Who're you in my life? At least Chun and his friends promise me a lifetime of brotherhood. You don't understand a slight bit about brotherhood, Kuang. You care about yourself more than anyone else!' Geong's eyes widened as he spoke. I could see both hatred and helplessness spiraling in his pupils.

'Brotherhood? What kind of brotherhood has Chun promised you? Please, Geong. Don't be taken in by his fake promises.' My voice rose above Geong's, sending each word full speed at him.

'Stop acting as if you know me best. YOU DON'T. You don't even know how I lived through these few years!'

Even though I was simmering with anger at that moment, I was also swamped with sorrow.

'Geong. Yes . . . I may not know about you but I don't want you to be in trouble.' I confessed, deepening my voice.

'Don't act as if you're concerned, Kuang. I hate that look on your face!'

I continued to stare into Geong's eyes with my furrowed brows.

'Tell me, Geong. I'm your friend. Let me help you . . . ' I softened my tone.

'FRIEND?' Geong cut me off. 'Please. Save your breath. I don't know you. And I don't wish to tell you anything! Just leave!' Veins on Geong's forehead and neck became engorged.

'Geong, don't get yourself involved in those secret societies. Don't. It'll cost you your life.'

My words were drying up. I stood with a narrow stance and hunched shoulders, completely thrashed by the feeling of inadequacy. 'Yes . . . I may not know what you've gone through for the past few years. I know you still blame me for abandoning you in school years back. I know I'm not fit to be your friend.' I choked back a watery sob, steeling myself to continue. 'But . . . at least I'm clear about my stand. Don't get yourself involved in all the illegal activities Chun has enticed you with. It's not worth it. Live with dignity, even if you have to live poorly.' I whispered resolutely.

Geong kept silent and turned his face to the rain-washed windows in the kitchen.

'Geong. No one can save you except your own decision.'

I untied my apron, pulled it away from my body, and placed it on the kitchen table. 'Keep the remaining of my salary to yourself. Use it when you need it.' I exhaled loudly and left the kitchen.

My arguments with Geong had a dull exhaustion to it, like they had been over the same bitterness too many times before.

And I wished to end it.

I was not sure if Geong's existence in my life had toughened or softened me. I could not believe I actually walked away from a friendship that I had always treasured. At the same time, I was appalled because I did not harbour a slight bit of hatred when I left.

Deep within, I still wished Geong well.

The Chinese always talked about brotherhood. Ranked above ordinary friendship, brotherhood was like a form of mock kinship that could withstand all kinds of obstacles and last long.

In ancient China, men even took an oath to become sworn brothers. As proof of their commitment, they conducted formal rituals such as toasting each other with wine into which their blood had been mixed.

In Singapore, men became sworn brothers in a different way. To think that I had almost gone to the temple with Geong the other day to pray to Guan Di Gong to make him my sworn brother. It was all inconceivable now.

So many 'brothers' have gone separate ways. So many 'brothers' had ended up in conflicts and fights.

Pursuit of wealth and fame had perhaps overshadowed people's pure intention of making friends. Nowadays, people were inclined to make friends with ulterior motives. And people became more skeptical of one another. Once motives were achieved, friendships would break up.

When I dwelled on old memories of Geong and me, there was warmth. When I thought of his eyes, it was still that pair of innocent eyes that loved and trusted me. That same pair of eyes that watched *Teochew-hee* with me.

How do I salvage a friendship that seems destined to break? Life had indeed played a prank on me, making me return to this question again.

I closed my eyes, holding on to the memories for a long while before opening my eyes to let it escape through the crack in my broken heart.

Just let him go, I said to myself.

I strolled home, dreading the images of me peering into my empty biscuit tin and Ah Beh exploding over my naivety. I was sure he would chide me for being an idiot voluntarily stepping into others' trap. And how should I explain to Ah Mm that I had lost all her money?

Strangely enough, my thoughts were still bent on helping Geong. Was this really the end of our friendship? Would I have to leave him in the lurch, yet again?

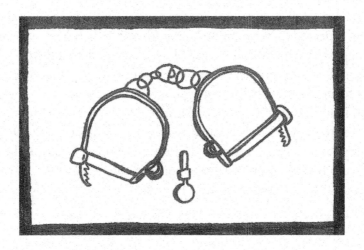

Twenty-Five

Bruce Lee says, *'Defeat is a state of mind, no one is ever defeated until defeat has been accepted as a reality.'* Yes. Bruce Lee. My new idol after catching him on the screen at the drive-in cinema. His words were stuck in my head ever since.

I repeated his words to myself umpteen times before I broke the news of my failed business to Ah Beh.

I'm not defeated. I'm not defeated.

I needed a boost of confidence before Ah Beh made me a failure with his condescending remarks. When I was mentally prepared enough to receive his insults, they would not sink in that much to gnaw at my self-esteem.

However, this time, neither did Ah Beh say a single word to me nor show me a frustrated shake of his head. He was silent. He broke eye contact with me, stood up from a chair, and walked to his bedroom. I supposed he wanted to be alone. Upon seeing Ah Beh behave this way, a feeling of dread filled my being. My heart felt like it was shrinking. I forgot to breathe. His disappointment was loudly displayed in front of my eyes through his abnormally quiet actions. His disappearing back view berated me on his behalf.

Ah Mm, on the contrary, said too much. This was abnormal too.

She repeated her comments about Geong which I already knew and suggested what I could have done instead. I swallowed hard, feeling guilty and tired, at the same time utterly disappointed at myself for making Ah Mm worry about me.

Ah Mm dragged me to her favourite deity and asked me to pray for better fortune. Hands clasped together and eyes closed. 'Do not say out your prayers,' she warned. 'Prayers said out loud would not come true. It was a secret between you and the heavens.'

I followed suit and kowtowed three times.

* * *

Previously when I was working at the fish porridge stall, occasionally I could hear young men prattling softly about the Singapore Army.

I heard them say those 'Mexican' commanders were crazy. The training they gave was crazy. Days at the camp were crazy too.

One of them said they regretted volunteering to join the army. Another one said the training was still bearable. One more joined in, commenting if the training was not hard, how could we establish a solid good army for Singapore?

Army sounded like a scary place. Fortunately, it was on a voluntary basis. I did not wish to go through such harrowing training.

But, our cheng hu resorted to compulsory conscription to expand the country's defence forces after 17 March 1967.

I was not selected for the army, thank goodness, and was called upon to join the People Defence Force as a part-timer. When we first received news from the cheng hu, Ah Mm wept.

In fact, many mothers did the same.

In our neighbourhood, we could hear mothers swearing and sharing their pain with one another.

One said, 'Dor mia cheng hu! Huh? Why? Why ask my son to join what army? I didn't give birth to my son to be a soldier.'

The other said, 'Surely very hard. A soldier's life is hard! Which soldier can have a good time at war? What would happen to my son?'

And I also heard one say, 'Those mothers whose sons are in the army say their uniform is so hard to take care of. Need to boil tapioca flour with water to make a lot of glue. Then mix the uniform with glue. Hang the whole thing to dry. So heavy how to hang? Then, iron! The whole thing needs to be stiff and hard then good. Siao lah, what's wrong with our cheng hu huh? Want to kill both sons and mothers?'

Ah Mm did not swear like how others did because she said at least I was lucky. A part-time soldier's life at the PDF should not be that hard. Only *pa niao tze* with a baton, don't need to hold guns.

I went for training during off-work hours. That was favourable for me who was trying my best to set up the lor ark png business with Geong previously.

These past few years, Singapore faced a major problem. Many youths from all races were getting hooked on hard drugs such as morphine and cannabis. Youth who longed for stability and security in life but believed they did not deserve them often became eluded. Eventually, they gave in to their cravings for easy success and pleasures, committing more crimes to buy drugs.

Maintaining addiction to drugs cost young people a lot of money. It entailed great risks and involved interactions with drug dealers who were out to squeeze people dry.

I had seen what addiction did to Ah Gong, and so I kept away from these vices. Besides going for part-time training with PDF after work, I kept myself busy with lifting weights.

I enjoyed weightlifting. It took my mind off things and it was a sport that did not need me to think too much. Just believe I could do it, and I usually did. I felt the barbells were an embodiment of my inner determination—solid, steely and simple.

My passion in weightlifting was evident on my sculpted body. I had bulky chest muscles and toned thighs after months of training. My bun-like biceps shone with a layer of gloss when I applied oil on my skin. And this was perhaps the reason why my PDF officers recommended me to work alongside the newly established Central Narcotics Bureau (CNB) to fight the rise in drug addiction among youth in Singapore.

We became additional manpower to the CNB, patrolling and supplementing the work of regular officers. We donned casual clothes and patrolled 'black spots' to catch drug addicts every week.

After everything that had gone down with Geong, assisting the CNB became my new goal in life.

* * *

Many youths succumbed to drugs because they were readily available. Pot parties were rampant. Without a care in the world, young people crazily popped pills at nightclubs and tea dances. The drugs took over their mind and drove their bodies to unconscionable acts of depravity.

Many died of overdoses and allergy. Some got into accidents while high on drugs. Every now and then, dead bodies could be found lying on the streets.

Despite the regular raids, drug activities continued.

It was hard to eradicate them altogether. Drug traffickers and abusers were undeterred by the low penalties for such offences. Many youths continued to remain shattered souls of drug abuse.

As raids became more regular, I had to spend more time on patrolling with the officers.

The end of my lor ark png business with Geong meant that I could focus on helping the CNB without worrying about other matters. Meanwhile, I continued to build a foundation of strength by adding a few pounds to lift every week. I took every chance to get in shape and get stronger so that I could be fit enough to handle those drug addicts.

* * *

That very night, the pale crescent moon shone like a silvery claw in the dark sky. We walked into Wonderland Amusement Park at Kallang late at night.

The amusement park had opened in 1969, offering many thrilling and fun rides games. The roller coaster was a big hit among young people. Nowhere else offered such a ride.

However, gradually, the amusement park became a breeding ground for drug related activities. Many youths gathered at the amusement park to exchange money for drugs. Traffickers sold drugs openly and the park offered an isolated congregation for youth to 'get high'. Some even had the guts to consume drugs secretly in the public bathrooms.

That evening, armed with an unwavering mandate, we aimed to flush out and detain drug addicts and to get drug traffickers off the park.

The significance of tonight's operation was not to punish the young people who were 'chasing the dragon', instead, the cheng hu aimed to rehabilitate them over a few months period and encourage them to turn over a new leaf.

Often, I would imagine my own brothers getting hooked on drugs and mixing with bad company. I certainly did not wish that to happen. I pledged to do my very best to save those who could not escape the claws of drugs.

We were also reminded many times to stick to collective actions. No one was supposed to chase after drug addicts alone, especially the part-timers. We did not receive adequate training. Moreover, many of the part-timers still held proper jobs in the day. The CNB did not want us to risk getting injured by crazy drug addicts when we were working. Our role was to grab hold of the addicts' shoulders and dragged them to our vehicles parked a distance away after they were handcuffed.

As we entered the park, our eyes were hooked on people's expressions. We saw people gathering en masse in some locations. They had an emaciated appearance, wasting away, and premature aging even though they were of a young age. The facial tension on their faces made my stomach feel rock hard. I gulped down breaths to stay calm.

The CNB officers, however, could not arrest people based on appearances. They needed evidence to be certain who to approach so as not to create chaos among the common innocent people.

Our strategy was to ambush a distance away from the public bathrooms and monitor the flow of people streaming in and out of the bathrooms.

Drug addicts who made use of closed cubicles to consume drugs were common. They would usually spend a long time in the bathrooms, as compared to others who went in to answer nature's call. The CNB officers would approach those addicts who had turned drowsy after drug consumption, and demanded them to open up their palms.

Somehow, the officers were able to detect traces of drugs just by looking at people's opened palms. And their judgements were always right.

Some parts of my body still trembled uncontrollably whenever I encountered these drug addicts. Their eyes were damp and dead, and had a kind of narrowed vision that were filled with hatred. They looked withdrawn and were sinking in dark thoughts. The drugs had taken them away a piece at a time.

Deliberately straightening my posture and puffing up my chest, I waited at a spot, a few metres away from the CNB officers.

* * *

A long-haired man was stopped by the officers a distance away from the bathroom.

He was not standing still, swaying a little from left to right and right to left. The CNB officer clutched his upper arm filled with dragon tattoos and demanded him to show his palm. Refusing to oblige, the man attempted to struggle off. But his dwindling strength failed him. The officers pulled him to the side and pinned him on the walls. They forced open his clenched fists. After studying it for a few seconds, they handcuffed him.

Two officers sandwiched the man and pulled him to us. As they approached us, I could smell a whiff of a mixture of herbs and wood when the wind blew. It also contained a tinge of lemon, apple, and diesel. The man's long fringe was swept to the side, revealing his face.

A square jaw, narrow forehead, thin eyebrows, almond-looking eyes, pimpled flat nose, and a pair of thick lips.

I stood still, heart thumping faster.

These familiar features wrecked my rationality. As they walked closer, my chin began to tremble.

Geong, is that you? I blinked rapidly, several times, to make sure my eyes were not lying to me. I was so scared that I felt like throwing up. Everything was crumbling around me.

Together with another counterpart from the PDF, we grabbed Geong by his shoulders and moved him to our vehicles.

Drugs had taken over his mind and body. He was skeletal, totally different from the person I had seen a few months ago. I could briefly see his collar bone and shoulder blades under his loose tee shirt. He could not even recognize me and had totally lost his sense of personal identity.

I could not acknowledge him, either. Like a stranger, I stood beside him, gripping onto his shoulder so firmly as if to assure him he would be fine. He tried to shrug off, but I pulled him back to me.

Soon, we arrived at our vehicle. I could not bear to haul my best friend into it. I hoped to call him by his name and tell him he would be fine. *It's me, Geong. Kuang here. Look at me.*

And look at you. Why? What had happened to you? But I had no choice. I had to push him in. I had to make sure he sat firmly in the car, not struggling. I held him by his shoulders, then grabbed him by his arms. And in he went, into the vehicle I used to hold in high regard, yet at this moment, a part of me wished it was not this vehicle I was shoving him into.

After Geong got in, his teeth continued to chatter. He was also laughing, on and off, revealing his yellowish teeth. The strenuous, whistling sound of him gasping for air made my heart ache. His head was lowered and his eyes were closed. His expression was a mixture of pain and relief.

As the vehicle drove away, I continued to look at Geong's back view through the rear windshield. Heavens knew what he would be going through at the rehabilitation centre. But whatever hardship Geong was going to undergo, I was sure it was for his better days ahead.

Surprisingly, the old wound of broken friendship was healed. Even though Geong knew nothing about tonight's incident, he might never know I was the one who dragged him into the CNB vehicle. I had an expanding feeling in my chest. It was an unexpected release of tension built within me over the years.

Geong was found. Finally, he was saved and that was all I needed to put everything behind me.

Twenty-Six

Ah Mm held a weaved basket in her hand and strolled towards a street vendor. I was walking beside her, chit-chatting with her, and carrying a big bag of toiletries that she had bought from the nearby grocery store—toilet papers, sanitary pads in big brown boxes, shampoo, and soap bars.

A woman with short curly hair and freckled cheeks squatted at the same spot every day. Whenever someone stopped to look at what she was selling, she displayed a grin with a few missing teeth. In front of her was an enormous pot of Teochew kueh. Pinkish peach-shaped steamed dumplings filled with the savory goodness of sticky rice filling, translucent sweet potato wrapped dumplings that contained a combination of shredded jicama, carrots, green beans, dried shrimp, and bamboo shoots, and large crystal dumplings packed with dried shrimps, minced garlic, and Chinese chives.

They were Ah Mm's newfound love after moving to the east side of Singapore.

'Ah! Mui, you're here again! And with Kuang this time,' the street vendor called out to Ah Mm, her grin stretched as she waved to us.

Ah Mm and I squatted to have a closer look at the pot of beautifully patterned rice pastries.

'I just made them this morning. There're png kueh, *soon* kueh, *ang ku* kueh, and *ku chye* kueh. Take whatever you like.'

'Juan, you're so talented. Your kueh have never failed me. I'm going to get more today.' Words of praise flowed out of Ah Mm's mouth relentlessly.

I sniffed those kueh in the pot. Indeed, they were mouth-watering.

'Alright, I want six of this, five of this, and five of that. And, erm . . . four of that.' Ah Mm said, pointing at those kueh with an unwavering look of concentration while licking her lips and smiling.

I raised my brows and ogled at Ah Mm, trying to hint to her that she might have ordered too much for the family, but her attention was too fixed on the kueh. I was afraid saliva might drip out of her lips.

'Gam xia! Thank you!' Juan nodded a few times, expressing her gratitude. ' . . . but how're you going to carry everything to your house with all those bags in your hands? Tell you what, let me send my daughter. She helps to deliver kueh to customers who stay around here.'

'That's very thoughtful of you. Gam xia ah! I'll wait for her delivery.' Ah Mm's eyes shone with appreciation.

She then passed a few notes to Auntie Juan after thanking her many times. We then left for home.

Unlike our old shophouse that stood in the middle of a few busy streets, our new HDB flat was built in a new residential town. There was perhaps only a market and a kopitiam nearby.

Auntie Juan was a rare illegal street vendor who continued to sell food on the streets despite the cheng hu's effort to bring all vendors indoors. Besides Juan, there were other vendors who pushed their food carts to the pavements to earn a living. Ah Mm was thankful to these vendors. Without them, she would have to travel a long distance to buy ready-made food. Moreover, these vendors' homemade cuisines were delicious.

* * *

For the past few years since the end of the business with Geong, I had been taking odd jobs with nothing that could lead to a good career.

Ah Beh was different.

From a lowly kuli, he worked his way to become a kuli supervisor. When the need for kulis gradually declined, Ah Beh became a supervisor for a moving company. Instead of lifting and lugging those heavy loads, he could now monitor how the younger labourers performed duties.

Twenty-six. An age that kept my parents constantly on their toes about my marriage. I had never got into a relationship with any girl and Ah Mm was terribly concerned.

How do I start dating?

I wanted a partner whom I had good chemistry with. Someone who could make my heart palpitate, just like those shown in black-and-white Hong Kong films. I could not possibly pick any girl on the street to confess my love to.

But Ah Mm thought otherwise.

'Love could be nurtured, Kuang. Who doesn't love a good girl? We don't choose the person we want to love, but we love the person that's chosen for us.'

That was certainly the trend of her times back in China. Her advice to me fell on deaf ears.

* * *

The afternoon sun-bathed the flats around us in its warm light. Huge shadows fell over the roads. Leaves rustled in the gentle breeze.

Someone came knocking at our door. Very softly. Fortunately, Ah Mm's sharp ears caught it just right. While waiting for her kueh orders to arrive, she sewed to keep herself awake.

I sat in the kitchen, trimming my nails.

'Kuang ah, *lai*, come help me receive the kueh. It's a lot.'

It turned out Ah Mm was aware that she had ordered a lot of kueh just now. Or did she realize it only after she had handed over the notes?

I jumped up and approached our door.

Ah Mm limped towards the door and opened it. She paused at the sight of two young women with neatly braided hair. I had a feeling that sight aroused a pleasant feeling in her. She was having a good posture suddenly and showing a willingness to engage the girls in a conversation. Ah Mm seldom had animated hand gestures.

The young woman standing right in front of Ah Mm had a darker skin tone. She had a much smaller built, as compared to the fair one behind. When I saw the dark-skinned girl, I just noticed how skinny she was. Small-boned and leaner than an average Singaporean young woman. Her eyes were like full moon and her lips were thin. And when she spoke, Ah Mm had to lean forward to listen.

'Hello Ah Sim, I am Huey. My mother sent us here to pass these kueh to you,' Huey uttered, looking at Ah Mm for a quick while before shifting her eyes back on her sister.

Ah Mm had been feasting her eyes on the fair lady standing at the back while listening to Huey.

'Ahh, Juan's daughters.' Ah Mm nodded, showing off some of her black teeth as she smiled. 'What fine daughters she has!'

Standing next to Ah Mm, I dragged my gaze onto her look. *Walao, Ah Mm is at it again. For sure, she would have a lot to say after this encounter with these young women.*

Eyeing the kueh presented to her on a big round red plate, Ah Mm continued, 'And such lovely kueh from your mother! Thank you so much for delivering them. Quick, Kuang, transfer them to our plates.'

'Not at all, Ah Sim. Bye bye.' The two girls waved enthusiastically, turned around, and gently strolled off.

I could hear them giggling to each other as they approached the lift while I helped Ah Mm with the kueh.

After Ah Mm shut the door, she turned her head to me, then up went her brows. 'How? Surely not married. They look very young. The one behind, *jin ngia leh. Hor?*'

Again. She's really at it again. I rolled my eyes away, while blinking rapidly.

The fragrance of the Teochew kueh lingered in the air. Ah Mm took a close glimpse at them, admiring their fine patterns. Those exquisitely homemade delicacies as well as the encounter with her possible future daughter-in-law made her so thrilled.

* * *

Ah Mm and Auntie Juan, without our consent, arranged a movie date for Huey and me.

I was, in fact, getting used to such blind dates. Ah Mm had been harassing me with a list of available girls for almost a year now.

'This girl living at the end of that stretch of road is still single. That particular vendor's daughter has reached the age to get married.' Ah Mm knew the marital status of all the girls in our town right on her fingertips.

As much as I believed in romance that occurred naturally, I did not reject any matchmaking session at all. In order to ease Ah Mm's worry, I pretended to be keen.

So, this was what happened.

Ah Mm liked that fair girl hiding behind Huey the other day. Ah Mm thought she looked like a celestial princess in those Chinese folktales she loved. She said the girl was a 仙女下凡, literally a fairy descending from the heavens.

The way she talked about that princess; it was as though Ah Mm had fallen for her. With great enthusiasm and sincerity, Ah Mm approached Auntie Juan the next day and requested for a matchmaking session. However, the response from Auntie Juan was quite unexpected for Ah Mm. When Ah Mm shared Auntie Juan's response with me, I was pretty amused by Ah Mm's expression as she narrated.

'*Bueh sai* lah.' Auntie Juan rejected the proposal straightaway.

'Why, Juan?'

'Because she's the younger sister.' That was Auntie Juan's only explanation. 'Since Huey is the older girl, she should be married off first.'

Ah Mm told me she hesitated for a while upon hearing that.

Utterly disappointed, she thought it was a great pity that that celestial princess could not be her first daughter-in-law.

I laughed.

However, she gave in to Auntie Juan's counter request after giving it a second thought. Ah Mm was the kind of person who could convince herself easily with her own logic. Getting a daughter-in-law was more important than getting a daughter-in-law that she wanted. She thought, well, at least she was respectful of elders. Ah Mm successfully sold this idea to herself.

And that was it. Just like that. A date was reserved. Tickets were bought.

'Six in the evening, Kuang. This coming Sunday ah. Dress your best. That only brown shirt you have? Wear that. Wear that.' Ah Mm reminded me, as if I were still a twelve-year-old.

I leaned back on the sofa, mouth agape.

* * *

That evening, I combed my hair into two neat puffs, curling from my center parting. I tucked my brown shirt into my most decent black pants and added a fake leather belt that I bought with my first little salary earned from the shared business with Geong. I also rubbed some cologne borrowed from Dak on the collar of my shirt.

Staring at the mirror countless times before I left my room, I was feeling much more confident and assured than any other blind dates I had gone on. *Maybe this time, things might turn out different*, I mused.

I slipped the movie tickets into my pocket and left home.

I arrived at the void deck at the other end of our elongated HDB flat. Fifteen minutes into waiting, two young ladies came out of the lift. Both of them were dressed in boldly printed long-sleeved blouses and tight bell-bottomed pants. Girls now were totally inspired by the 'a-go-go' trend. They looked pretty similar, everywhere.

'Hello, I believe you're . . . Huey?' I paced slowly towards the shorter lady and asked in a polite and curious manner.

'Yes, I am.' Huey replied in a soft tone. 'This is Hoon, my younger sister. You don't mind she comes along, right?'

'Oh, I'm fine with that. I . . . saw her before, that day?' I responded immediately. 'Oh wait! But . . . but I have only two movie tickets.' I was flustered. A drop of sweat trickled down onto my eyebrow.

'I see. I guess we can purchase another one when we reach the cinema,' Huey suggested calmly, looking at me. She then turned around and held her younger sister's hand. 'Let's go, Hoon!' And they strolled off without me.

I was not even in time to nod in agreement with her suggestion.

I followed behind them, like a watchdog keenly observing the two girls skipping their way to the nearby cinema. Their giggles and chattering were contagious. It was my first time being at ease on an arranged date. Probably because her attention was not on me.

The close bond between Huey and Hoon made me think of my younger siblings. I could relate to Huey, even though she had not spoken to me much that evening. I was eager to know more about her.

I could feel my heart thumping fast as I gazed at her from behind. *Is this palpitation? Or are they walking too fast?*

Huey was a soft-spoken girl but her guts were not average.

She took the initiative to stand in the queue with Hoon to purchase another ticket when we reached the cinema.

I noticed there were old men wandering aimlessly at the cinema, eyeing Hoon's body, from head to toe, while they were in the line. A few of those lecherous men wolf-whistled and cast lewd comments about Hoon. One of them was the worst. He was peeling a banana and offering it to Hoon from a distance. *How sickening! Lustful men who lack self-control and respect for women are outrageous.*

I stepped forward, attempting to help the girls out. Never did I expect Huey was faster in her action.

She studied the men with piercing scrutiny, not showing even a slight bit of fear in her stares back at them. She did not cower or feel uncomfortable. Attempting to shield her sister from those perverted stares, Huey stood up even straighter, displaying an upright posture that deliberately made her body curve slightly, but with great dignity.

Her small body looked superimposed onto her sister's taller built. '*De Gor Beh* . . . Ignore those dirty old men, Hoon,' Huey told Hoon, shifting her eyes to the side and back and constantly adjusting her position to guard Hoon.

I found Huey impressive in her own unique way. She was like a lotus flower that rose from mud without stains, blooming with dauntless grace and strength, rising above those plain features that Ah Mm thought were unattractive.

We finally got our ticket after a long wait and we hurried to the theatre.

Before going in, Huey turned around and looked at me. Guiltily, she muttered, 'Kuang, let's exchange tickets. Give me those two of yours. This . . . this one is for you!' Stuffing the single crumpled ticket into my hand and grabbing the two in my chest pocket, she frantically turned back and shoved Hoon to the two allocated back seats.

I was caught in a daze, staring into the air with a crumpled ticket in my hand. *What just happened?*

I dragged my feet to the first row, totally not prepared for an achy neck and dazzling spots in my vision at the end of the show.

How I wished I could tell Huey I dreaded, no, I hated sitting at the front row. The date just did not turn out the way I had planned it to be.

I sat down, closed my eyes, and decided to have a good rest while laughter filled the entire theatre as the film rolled.

* * *

Huey, to me, was a special girl. I could not erase her off my mind ever since the first day we met. I was particularly captivated by her instinct to love and protect her loved ones.

We got together after a few more movie dates. Gradually, Hoon stopped going out with us. She probably realized she had become more of a burden to Huey than a rightful companion. Thus, I finally got to sit beside Huey in the theatre.

It was my ever first romantic relationship with a girl. To be honest, I did not know where to bring her, except to watch movies and eat *ice kachang* at a stall near the cinema.

I wondered if Huey had ever felt tired of being with me. She usually nodded as I talked about the movie we watched earlier. There was once, she actually yawned so much that tears gathered in her eyes and streamed down her cheek. It was surely an embarrassing moment. I did not know how else to react but to continue with my seemingly senseless story.

Occasionally she would be amused by my words and let out a giggle. She seldom shared her thoughts with me. Once in a while, I would be surprised by her relatively short but thoughtful comments. Her ideas were always unique. Out of this world. And this made me wonder what else went on in her mind.

There was once I asked Huey out of curiosity, what image came to her when she thought of two people in love. She said a man sharing his thoughts enthusiastically with a woman, and the woman listening intently to him.

That was the sweetest image I had ever painted in my mind. I would always remember it.

I enjoyed being with Huey. Through her lens, I could always gather new perspectives. I was also convinced that I would marry none other than Huey. She was the most pure-hearted lady I had come across.

One day, after being together for about one year, I suggested a formal meeting for Huey to meet not just Ah Mm, but my entire family.

Huey did not ask me for the meaning of this formal meeting. When I proposed the meeting to her, could she have guessed I was set on marrying her? I did not know how else I could explain the reason for bringing her back to my home to meet everyone.

To my surprise, without any hesitation, Huey said yes, in a voice so certain and joyful.

'This Saturday! 7 p.m.! See you at my house!' I was immediately invigorated. With a fluttery stomach, I unglued my eyes from Huey. I did not expect Huey to agree to it so readily. My heartbeat was so fast. I was almost jumping and dancing with joy like a child. Yes! Like me, Huey was all ready to take our relationship to a more committed, long-term level. I could not wait for my whole family to meet her and know more about this special girl I had chosen for myself.

Huey inhaled loudly and continued to anchor her attention all on me. She giggled as I shook my bottom and swung my arms into the air. In her half-closed eyes, I could see a blissful gloss shining back at me.

Twenty-Seven

That much anticipated Saturday arrived after what seemed like an eternity.

My siblings were all excited to meet their future big sister-in-law. I had to remind them many times not to tease Huey or crack any jokes about us. I was very skeptical of my brothers' quick nodding. They looked like they had something up their sleeves.

Ah Beh and Ah Mm looked different that day.

Ah Beh did not go around half-naked. He put on his singlet, attempting to cover his big-breasted front and slightly protruded hairy tummy.

Ah Mm dressed up better than usual. She dolled herself up! Ah Mm's cheeks were dusted with light pink powder and her lips were glossed with a layer of olive oil. When she came out of her room in a flowery blouse trouser set, we were all enthralled.

'Ah Mm, Chinese New Year is not here yet leh!' Dak laughed. Everyone followed.

Ah Mm blushed. 'Ahh, you ah, only know how to spout nonsense!' She shook her head and pulled her blouse to straighten the creases, then walked to the kitchen.

Today, Ah Mm planned and obsessed over every detail in the kitchen. She started the preparation of dinner, hours in advance.

All of us could sense Ah Mm's eagerness to meet Huey. In her head, she must have already imagined Huey as her future daughter-in-law. Now that she was going to meet Huey more intimately, she must be over the moon.

Ah Mm had prepared a feast. All the dishes we always had for Chinese New Year. The best was a big pot of pig organ soup. An attractive bowl of light, clear broth containing liver, intestines, stomach, heart, and pig's blood. The soup is enriched with preserved vegetables, as well as fried onions for flavour. On top of that, Ah Mm's own zingy chili sauce made it perfect. It was Ah Mm's signature dish, one that no guest should miss.

Everyone was in unruly high spirits.

I looked out of the windows. The setting sun had set the sky on fire. Strips of golden orange stretched far and wide, bleeding into the clouds. As I waited for Huey's arrival, I prayed for a successful gathering where my family members and Huey could accept one another. My heart pounded fast with every breath I took, taking in as much air as my lungs could hold now in case anxiety overwhelmed me later.

Then, the doorbell rang.

'She's here!' Ing screeched as she peeped through the door hole, flapping her hand up and down, signaling for all my other siblings to get ready to welcome our long-awaited guest.

She opened the door.

Huey, dressed in a pale pinkish checkered dress with puffed up sleeves, stood very still, holding a bag of fruits in her hand.

Awkwardly, she waved gently at Ing, nodding her head politely.

'Hello! Come on in!' Ing replied in excitement.

The moment Huey stepped into the house, to my surprise, everyone turned quiet. I was expecting my siblings to chitter-chatter around us and fight their way to introduce themselves to her. But I was wrong.

What happened to everyone? Are they all tongue-tied?

Noticing no one speak, Dak exclaimed, 'Ah So is here! Welcome sister-in-law.' He then clapped, as if applauding his courage to make the first move to welcome her.

I rolled my eyes. 'Go away, Dak. Siao ah?'

A grin stretched slightly across Huey's face. I approached her, gently grasping her hand, and brought her to Ah Beh and Ah Mm who were standing at the entrance of the kitchen.

'These are my parents. This is Ah Beh and this is Ah Mm. You surely have met her before.'

'Yes. We've met last time. Hello, Ah Sim.'

Ah Mm smiled and nodded. 'Make yourself at home hor, Huey. Let's have dinner soon.'

'Ah Mm, wait. Where's Ah Ma?' I asked.

'Oh yes, resting on her bed.' Ah Mm replied, quirking an eyebrow and smiling.

I grabbed Huey by her shoulders and directed her to one of the bedrooms. When we reached, Ah Ma was seated on her bed. Her eyes were closed, and she was busy cooling herself with a straw woven fan. She opened her eyes as soon as she heard my voice, moving and fidgeting.

'*Di diang?*' Ah Ma asked, squinting her eyes as she turned towards Huey.

'Ah Ma, this is my girlfriend, Huey.'

'Ahh! *Zha bo peng you* ah?' Ah Ma blew out one long breath and smiled. She squinted her eyes again to take a close look at Huey.

'Wonderful! You've got yourself a fine woman to bear kids with. Look at her wide and fleshy bottom! She can surely bear many kids! *Ka chng dua, ho* ah!' Ah Ma exclaimed in an excitable tone, staring at Huey's hips. Her lips lifted upwards, displaying a warm glow of happiness.

I caught a glimpse of Huey's reaction to Ah Ma's words. Her dimples crinkled and the wrinkles at the edge of her eyes froze as her soft lips stretched.

I hoped Huey had taken Ah Ma's thoughtless remarks lightly. Adrenaline had certainly caused me to be hyper-alert, scrutinizing Huey's expression at every moment.

Together, we supported Ah Ma by her arms and led her out of the bedroom for dinner. We took turns to have our dinner as the dining table was too small to accommodate everyone in the family, as usual.

Huey and I had ours at the first round together with Ah Beh, Ah Mm, Ah Ma, Siu, and Ing.

Ah Beh was a quiet man. He seldom talked to his own children, let alone a stranger. His head was lowered throughout and the only sound he made was the usual loud sipping of porridge.

Ah Mm was not good with words either. But she tried to be gracious. She occasionally smiled at Huey, trying to assure her that she was welcomed into this family. She also kept picking food and putting them into Huey's bowl.

Ing and Siu gladly took the initiative to ask about Huey. Even though they might have already known the answers to those questions, they tried to strike a good conversation with her, pretending not to know. I was relieved Huey was engaged all the time.

As for Ah Ma, I secretly wished she would keep all her thoughtless comments to herself and she did.

That evening, I forgot to savour my favourite pig organ soup. I simply could not. My hands were clamped up, and I could feel muscles tightening all over. My attention was all on Huey, ensuring she was well taken care of.

What's love? I pondered. *When did everything become less important than a person in my world?*

After the dinner, it was just a typical Saturday night. My siblings were catching a show series that was coming to an end on the television. Recently they were smitten by our new colour television. Their eyes were glued onto it. Ah Beh was taking his evening nap. Ah Ma spent nearly an hour in the bathroom, scrubbing her truckload of pants. The only person who talked to Huey was Ah Mm.

In her dimly lit bedroom, Ah Mm invited Huey to sit on the straw woven mat.

'Huey, how did your mother learn to make so many kinds of kueh?'

'Oh, from our fellow kampong neighbours in the past. Almost all the Ah Sim in my kampong knew how to make kueh. They loved to gather and learn from one another.'

'How nice that was.'

'I think so too.' Huey replied with her brightly lit eyes. 'In the past, whenever Ah Mm learnt a new recipe and made new kueh, my siblings and I would be so eager to try.'

'Do you make kueh too?' Ah Mm asked curiously.

'Yes, I do. My sisters and I always help out in the kitchen. Ah Mm needs more helping hands.'

'One day, I shall consult you then. I love to make kueh too but mine aren't fantastic.'

'No, no, no, Ah Sim. I'm not good at it at all. The pastry skin I make is always ugly and thick. You'd better consult my Ah Mm instead!' Huey laughed, covering her mouth with one hand and waving the other frantically.

'I know your skills are as good as your mother's. Don't be humble.' Ah Mm responded, beaming away. Her black teeth were especially glossy under the dim orange light. 'Come to our house more often, Huey.'

I sat at the entrance of the room, gazing at them and listening to their conversation.

Ah Mm's eyes twinkled in amusement as she spoke with Huey. How wonderful it was that Ah Mm had wholeheartedly embraced her. Upon seeing them so engrossed talking about kueh-making, my heart overflowed with gratitude.

* * *

Clingy was never a word to describe Huey. She seldom phoned me. In fact, two days not talking with each other was our norm. But when she did not look me up for two weeks after the visit to my house, despite me calling and asking her out, I knew something was not right.

That Saturday when I walked her home after the formal meeting with my family, Huey did not speak a word to me. We kept to ourselves while clenching each other's hand tightly as we walked. Her hand was sweaty and she constantly shunned my eye contact.

I was confused by Huey's contrasting behaviours. She was her usual bubbly self at my home. She seemed to like everyone in my family. But when she was alone with me, both her brows and lips started to arch. It was the first time she gave me cold shoulder and that broke my heart.

For the past two weeks, I had been trying to talk with Huey on the phone. I called many times, but each time, Huey would gently decline my request to meet her.

Busy schedule. More kueh orders this week. Impossible to leave the kitchen.

Sometimes, Auntie Juan would pick up the call and ask me to dial back in a hesitant tone. Huey's sudden absence in my life tormented me, making me loathe myself.

Was I not good enough for her? I was mentally shutting down. My hopes for this relationship were slowly dashed. Not only had I lost a girlfriend, I also lost my confidante. I could only grip onto our sweet memories for comfort.

Then one day came when Huey appeared under my block in the evening. She was standing next to the lift and her eyes were staring into the distance. I walked closer to her.

Upon sensing me approaching, Huey moved away.

'Huey . . .'

Huey looked up. Through her thick short fringe, I could vaguely see sadness shrouding her face.

'Kuang.' Her voice vibrated with sadness.

' . . . how have you been?' I pursed my lips. Awkward silence filled the gap between us. 'I mean, I haven't seen you for about two weeks . . . I'm not sure . . .'

'Kuang. I've something to tell you.' Huey looked at me vacantly. I was overwhelmed by a wave of cold.

We strolled to the nearby park and sat down on a bench. Huey sat next to me. She was constantly rubbing the edge of her skirt and refused to look up. My heart was thumping uncomfortably.

'Huey?' I mumbled. 'What was it you wanted to tell me?'

Huey inhaled deeply. As she looked down at the grass she was stepping on, her eyes blinked rapidly. 'I've been thinking about our relationship, Kuang.' Huey continued softly. Her face made a strange expression as she shifted her attention back on me. It was hard to read.

'I don't think I want a relationship with you anymore.'

I stared into Huey's eyes in disbelief.

Never did I expect Huey to initiate a breakup right after a formal meeting with my family.

Tears were circling in her eyes, mimicking the whirlwind of questions winding in my heart.

My stomach hardened. I did not know what to say.

The evening sun gave way to the darkest shade of blue blanketing the night sky.

Since half an hour ago, both Huey and I had not moved an inch. I was reluctant to leave her. I was more reluctant to leave this moment for another day. I could not imagine a day without Huey.

'Huey . . . are you sure?' I asked, hoping for a different reply after a long silent wait.

Huey stood up and stepped away from me. She turned back and stared at me like a stranger.

'Yes, Kuang. I've decided. Let's not see each other anymore.'

'Why, Huey?' I swallowed hard.

'Don't ask. Let's just go on separate ways from today onwards.'

I was totally defeated by her resoluteness. I lifted my chin, forcing myself to maintain eye contact with her. Quietly, I nodded as I guzzled down a sob. 'Alright.' I mumbled. 'Let's end it.'

A thousand of thorns were pricking my heart. My heart kept ballooning, leaving me gulping for air. It was tight and painful. I was waiting for my heart to burst but it did not.

It just turned horribly sore.

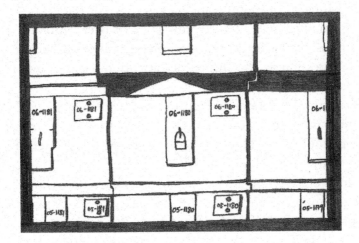

Twenty-Eight

Ah Mm sat down on the sofa, holding a plate of leftover rice from yesterday and swallowing it in big mouths as breakfast.

'Kuang ah, invite Huey home next Saturday. It's the eve of Dragon Boat Festival. I will be making some *bak zhang*. Haven't seen her for so long.'

Ah Beh was getting changed in his room. As he walked out, I held my breath while eyeing his actions. 'Ah Beh, Ah Mm,' I called out to them. 'Erm . . . Huey won't be coming anymore . . . we've broken up,' I announced with a trembling chin, creasing into myself.

Ah Mm looked at me with concerned eyes. 'I thought you were getting along well with her? What . . . what had happened?'

As shocked as I was when Huey shared her decision with me, Ah Mm had a hard time finding the right words to say. Her eyebrows squished together. I wanted to slap myself for making Ah Mm worry about me.

'I don't know . . . I didn't ask. *Aiya*, it doesn't matter.' I deliberately turned on the television and pretended to look interested in the programme while my heart wrung.

Ah Beh turned his head around. As he sat down to put on his shoes, he hurled a string of baseless conclusions about how young people dealt with relationships nowadays in the most hostile tone.

'Mui, just look at youngsters now. Breaking up this easily. Leaving each other without a good reason. And this young man here could let the matter rest, just like that. How irresponsible!'

Ah Beh's and Ah Mm's reactions made me feel worse. I had always felt like a failed son who could not provide much for the family. I could not bring in much money. And now, I could not even provide a good reason for the loss of their future daughter-in-law.

I was a failure in everything.

I could not do much for the next few days. I slumped myself in my bed, living my days wilting away, chomped on by mental lethargy.

* * *

There was no way I could have imagined Ah Beh's infuriation would last so long.

It was painful enough to lose Huey. My heart yearned for understanding and consolation. Yet, my family's expectation piled on me and made me feel worse.

Sunday arrived and without my knowledge, Ah Beh did something insane. Unpardonable. When Ah Mm told me the detailed story about what Ah Beh did, I was fuming mad within.

How could he?

Early in the morning, when everyone in the family was still asleep, Ah Beh woke up. Alone, he stepped out of the house.

He took a lift down to the sixth floor, walked past the long corridor to get to the other end of the block, and arrived at Huey's house.

He knocked on the door.

With his strength, even a slight knock could startle the family living in it. There was no answer, of course. It was 6.15 a.m. Even the sun had not risen. *What was he expecting? Why was he so inconsiderate?*

Ah Mm said Ah Beh then turned impatient and began banging on the door despite the early morning quietness.

After a few more tries, the door finally creaked open.

Auntie Juan had been the one behind the door. She was peeping through the open slit with her tired eyes. 'Di diang?' Auntie Juan had asked with what I could only imagine was bewilderment and annoyance.

Ah Beh must have stared back at her purposefully with his usual firm deep-set eyes before telling her who has was. After which, according to Ah Mm, who had heard from Ah Beh himself, this was exactly how the rest of the confrontation played out:

Auntie Juan blinked a couple of times and squinted her eyes, trying to take a good close look at Ah Beh. Her eyes carried a mixture of surprise and shock. 'Are you looking for Huey? She's sleeping. I go get her.'

Ah Beh then told her not to. He must have been speaking in his sternest voice. I was sure Auntie Juan was scared stiff.

Ah Beh then continued, 'Your daughter is a wonderful lady. Our family welcomes her. But when a lady plays hard to get and requests for a breakup without a good reason, it creates confusion for everyone, especially my son. Please tell her to be more responsible.'

Auntie Juan nodded as she listened.

Ah Beh's abrupt visit to demand for a good reason for the breakup must be beyond her anticipation. Would Auntie Juan find herself sandwiched between respecting Huey's decision and urging her to be accountable for my feelings?

Why did Ah Beh make things so difficult for everyone?

This was the first time I got so mad at Ah Beh that I wanted to leave home.

* * *

When Ah Mm informed me about Ah Beh's confrontation with Auntie Juan the next day, chaos rummaged through me, constricting my throat. Ah Mm said, she felt she needed to let me know about Ah Beh's actions, not because she did not agree with Ah Beh's behaviour, rather, her purpose was to let me know that they cared about my relationship with Huey.

How was this a way to show concern? Ah Beh's words and actions have ruined my relationship with Huey and her family even more!

I remained calm, only my eyes turned red. Anger flooded my vision.

It was unlike me to behave in this manner in front of Ah Mm. My heart was entirely crushed but I suppressed my emotions and walked away hastily.

I refused to speak a single word to Ah Mm.

Why? Why is Ah Beh such a kay-poh? I don't need help to resolve my relationship issue. Can't he understand?

I was more disappointed with Ah Beh's behaviour than Huey's decision to end our relationship.

My tightened facial muscles gave me away. Ah Mm followed me as I walked to my room. She stopped at the entrance, and spoke in her calmest tone, 'Kuang ah, your Ah Beh means well. He doesn't want to see you suffer in silence.'

My eyelids grew hot. 'Enough said, Ah Mm. Let me be alone.' I countered, urging her to leave.

I just hoped to self-medicate in private.

I sat on my bed, listening intently to the ticking of the clock. I knew Ah Beh loved me, but being loved without being respected was equivalent to keeping me safe in a house without windows.

It was mere suffocating. Familiarly suffocating.

* * *

One night, out of desperation, I wrote a letter to Huey. A blank page with only a few words

'Huey, I miss you. But please don't reply so that I may forget you.'

These few words contained so much of me. My desire, my logic, and my inability.

I placed it in Huey's letterbox the next day. I could not stop telling her about my days. Like how I always did. *Would she be listening?*

Old habits refused to change. Our love had grown rooted without me knowing. Two months were not sufficient to mend a broken heart.

A week later, Huey called. It was a surprise. As usual, we arranged to meet at the ice kachang stall next to the cinema we used to frequent. I spent the whole day preparing myself for the worst scenario.

* * *

Huey looked skinnier. Her collarbone protruded and the puffed-up sleeves of her dress hung loosely on her boney shoulders. Her face seemed to be shrouded with worries.

Her eyes, nonetheless, were different. They glittered with clarity.

That night, Huey talked more than I did in the past. I wondered what Ah Beh had told Auntie Juan and what Huey had received from her mother that made her explain so much about her previous decision.

As she spoke, tears were spilling out from her eyes.

'I'm sorry, Kuang.' Huey uttered. 'I'm sorry to have caused misery and confusion to you and your family.'

I could scarcely breathe as I listened to Huey's confession. Not knowing if Huey's apology had given me go-ahead to touch her, boldly, I gently held her hand in mine. I stared at her side view for a very long time, noticing how her fringe had grown longer and how beautiful her eyes were, even when they were soaked in remorseful tears.

'Kuang, I have thought about it once more. Our relationship. Remember that day when I went to your house? I was actually petrified and stressed. Even though I come from a big family and have the same number of siblings as you do, the thought of leaving mine and staying with yours after marriage made me want to escape. How am I able to live with so many strangers under the same roof?' Huey's eyes widened, mentally replaying how she had felt during the home visit and pouring all her fears out.

I nodded and leaned forward, stroking her back with my gentlest strength.

Huey kept silent for a while, then smiled slightly to herself as she exhaled, looking up and shaking her head at the same time. 'But I want to be brave and responsible.' She turned and gazed at me in my eyes in the same way when she asked for a break-up previously. However, this time, I could sense certainty in her overall demeanor.

'I want to be with you, Kuang. I shall not escape. Even if I may have to face my fear of living with so many strangers in the future, I am determined to overcome it for us.'

Huey's face was calm.

It was clear to me that Huey had made her own decision based upon her values and hopes for the future. I was convinced that even if Ah Beh's shocking move had caused Huey to reflect on her actions, her final decision was her own.

My face turned hot. With a quickened heartbeat, I let out a wide grin and spoke with a voice that cracked with emotions, 'Of course, Huey, let's begin again.'

Twenty-Nine

My patience was running thin.

Auntie Lim promised to come over to our house by 6.30 a.m. but here we were, sitting on our sofa, still waiting for her arrival.

Frantically.

Today was our Chinese betrothal ceremony, exactly one month before our actual wedding day. On this special day, it was my duty to show Huey's family that she would be well taken care of after our marriage. Together with a matchmaker, I would present gifts to her family.

It had never occurred to me that Auntie Lim would have such a big role to play in my wedding. Ah Mm suggested her to take on the role of our matchmaker to accompany me to Huey's house to deliver the betrothal gifts. To my surprise, she gladly agreed to it.

Ah Beh let Ah Mm be solely responsible for the betrothal. He had other things on his plate to take care of.

He spent days and nights recalling and inviting all the gaginang whom he kept in contact with to our wedding. Fifty tables of guests. That was what Ah Beh suggested to me. Out of these fifty, thirty tables were reserved for his gaginang whom Huey was not even acquainted with.

In the kitchen, I took a second look at the betrothal basket as I awaited Auntie Lim's arrival. Two pairs of dragon and phoenix candles, a red packet bearing the bride price, canned pig trotters, two bottles of wine, boxes of wedding cakes, oranges, peanut candies, four pieces of gold jewellery, raw pig's trotters, dried longan, red dates, lily bulbs, peanuts, lotus seeds, beans and grains as well as a red banner.

To be honest, without Ah Mm's help, I would never be able to gather these items for that day's ceremony. Chinese weddings were indeed rife with traditions that were passed down by word-of-mouth through generations.

I was eager to meet Auntie Lim after such a long time despite her late arrival. When I lifted the betrothal basket and bags of wedding cakes with all my strength, a familiar voice filled my house.

I stepped out of the kitchen and saw a slim figure dressed in a bright red flowery gown standing at our door. As she turned around, I could see a heavily powdered face embellished with a pair of red glossy lips.

What an exaggeratedly dressed matchmaker!

I gasped in disbelief. One could easily mistake her as my bride.

I approached Auntie Lim, trying to catch a closer glimpse at her extravagant appearance. In no way did I expect her to run to me and spin me around in circles, touching my shoulders, arms, and waist. Apparently, she had forgotten that I was a mature man. It was awkward for an elderly woman to be caressing me in such a passionate manner.

'Wow! Is this the Kuang that used to run along our old corridor, asking me for candies? Now twenty-eight and going to get a bride in a month's time, young man! How time flies!' Auntie Lim commented with her usual high-pitched voice while punching me in my chest. 'Let's do a good job later, groom-to-be!'

Ah Mm glanced up at the clock. It was 6.50 a.m.

The sun had risen and the sky had turned slightly blue. Searching for the right words to stop Auntie Lim from being engrossed in her own monologue, she also gestured for us to leave the house at once.

'Don't be late, Kuang! Meh! Meh! You can't be late for the betrothal.' Ah Mm shoved us to the doorsteps. Her reminders disoriented me despite her good intention. Now I felt more nervous than before.

* * *

Upon reaching Huey's house, we were welcomed with open arms. Everyone was excited. Auntie Juan's eyes sparkled when she saw me.

'Kuang, this day finally arrives!' She gave me a slight tap on my shoulder and ushered us into the living room. 'Have a seat,' Auntie Juan said warmly, pouring her ready-made tea into two cups and serving us.

Our betrothal was a simple affair. Huey's family did not request much.

To Auntie Juan, the promise I made to her daughter would suffice if I were serious about marrying her. The betrothal gifts were merely symbols of my sincerity. She told me not to spend too much money on them.

Auntie Lim seemed to have gathered all her energy for today's ceremony. She managed to engage Auntie Juan in a conversation and I was glad they hit it off. She talked non-stop. But thanks to her, the atmosphere was lighthearted and casual.

Firmly, I transferred the tiered betrothal basket over to Auntie Juan with both hands.

She accepted it with deep gratitude, thanking me with a bow. Her acceptance of my betrothal gifts meant that she was all ready to entrust her precious daughter to me.

'Huey! Come out now.' Auntie Juan called out. 'Please bring the gifts in return out to the living room.'

Huey, holding four big bags in her hands, waddled to the living room. She sat down and looked at me, smiling and blushing at the same time. We had not spoken for days. Days before our marriage, we were not supposed to meet.

I was yearning to see Huey, not just because I missed her terribly, but because she had told me she had started munching on raw tomatoes every evening just one week ago so as to get a good skin in preparation for our big day. I was surprised to know her plans and to be honest, I was astounded by the differences in the way we worked towards our wedding.

For the bride, nothing seemed to beat the joy of being dressed in her favourite white gown and looking the most glamorous. But for me, the wedding was about doing all that was needed to make sure all events ran well on the actual day.

Taking a second look at Huey, she was indeed glowing with bliss. Her cheeks were reddish pink and a bit fleshier than before.

Auntie Juan passed me a ton of return gifts. She also accepted a little of the bride price and returned the rest to me.

'Sharing good fortune with you, my son,' Auntie Juan said calmly with a low-pitched voice, grinning from ear to ear and exposing her uneven teeth. I smiled back warmly at her and whispered my thanks. I then clutched the ang-pow containing the remaining bride price she shoved into my hand, eyes focusing on the double 喜 inked on it, hopeful for the future.

Thirty

A month later, our wedding day arrived. It was the happiest day of my life. But it was more exhausting than a day of kuli's work.

Our wedding was held at a big ballroom at Singapore Chinese Chamber of Commerce. Ah Beh thought a proper ballroom would grant us more space to accommodate our fifty tables of guests thus, he chose this venue and managed to get it rented for a night.

I approached a friend who opened a *tze char* stall and asked if he was willing to lend a hand by preparing our banquet dishes for fifty tables of guests. He gladly took it on and congratulated me.

At the end of the wedding banquet, Huey and I were drained of energy.

Huey was squeezing her eyes shut, then opening them wide again to perk herself up as we shook our guests' hands to thank them for their presence. The only person who remained high-spirited was Ah Beh.

His smile seemed mortared onto his face as he talked with every single gaginang he met at the exit. Occasionally I heard Ah Beh use Teochew words which I seldom or never heard before when he was talking with his fellow villagers from Shantou. I could not fully understand what he was saying.

It was a chaotic scene outside the ballroom. Accompanied with loud prattling and constantly tonal changing high-pitched Teochew pronunciation, everything became a blur.

Our wedding banquet lasted for three hours. When all the guests had left, I heaved a heavy sigh of relief. Tightness in my throat was finally released.

In our haste to finish the wedding, we seemed to forget to experience it when it came. It had been a whirlwind, and I remained in a state of disbelief.

* * *

Huey moved into my house and stayed with my family straight after our wedding. The next morning, I was woken up by an emotional cry.

I opened my eyes, expecting to see Huey crying in her dreams next to me. But she was not there.

From the corner of the room came a wracking sob interrupted by a constant need to draw breath. My eyes darted from the empty space beside me to the corner filled with grief.

I saw Huey squatting next to the dressing table.

Her back was briefly touching the wall and her head was raised at an awkward angle. As if she had fallen to the ground from the bed, and was not in time to get up to a comfortable position before she had to handle her emotional outburst, her body seemed frozen and stayed very still. Lone tears traced down her cheeks continuously from her puffy eyes and her chin could not stop trembling.

Seeing Huey cry like there was so much raw pain within her frightened me.

Wasn't yesterday our happiest day?

I knelt next to her and wiped her tears. Sensing my concern, Huey attempted to stop sobbing.

'Just let me be,' she said, still gasping for air. She then slowly turned her body away from me.

I held on to her shoulder gently.

'Just let me be, Kuang,' Huey insisted, glancing down. Huey was sinking into a pit of misery, a realm I could not understand.

After a while, she mumbled, 'I . . . I just miss my family.'

I hunched my shoulders and stared at the floor for a minute before I stood up. In a quieter tone I added, 'You'll be fine soon, Huey. You can always go home to pay them a visit.'

And she nodded. A few times, as if assuring me that she would be healed for sure.

I had not thought about the real change that a marriage could bring about until the moment I witnessed Huey's free flow of tears that morning. For me, a marriage meant living with the person whom I loved. And that was probably all. But to Huey, saying 'yes' to my proposal was the beginning of a life-changing affair, altering fundamentally how she would see herself from this moment on.

She had to change her family name, move into a different house to stay, learn to love another family, and the most difficult of all, to fulfill wishes that may be against her will.

* * *

Huey, after being stuck in her unhappiness for days, was finally able to get up from bed and get ready for work without a single tear running down her cheek. However, Ah Mm, not knowing what had happened to Huey, expressed her heartfelt concerns at the most inappropriate time.

One late Friday afternoon, I came home earlier than usual as I was having a splitting headache. Ah Mm said it was because I liked to sleep with my hair wet and wind had gone into my head. It was so painful that it even made it difficult for me to move around.

I thought a warm bath would make me feel better. Just before I got into the bathroom, I saw Huey come home from work herself and Ah Mm approaching her, speaking in a quaking voice.

'I'm getting older, Huey. Going to the market to get grocery is getting harder day by day.' Ah Mm admitted frankly to Huey while they were sitting at the dining table in the kitchen. 'The family needs help.'

No one else was present. Just Ah Mm and Huey in the kitchen and me in the bathroom, eavesdropping.

After Ah Mm mentioned that, there was a pause. I was waiting for Huey to say something but it was all silent.

'Dak ah . . . Ang, and Siu have just started working, Gia and Teng are about to finish studying. Leng ah . . . seeing someone and might be getting married soon. *Zha bo gia* . . . if married, will move into her husband's family. And Ing is still in secondary school.'

At this instant, I could feel Ah Mm's words towering over Huey. Seeing Huey's tears every day, I took heart not to ask her to do anything for me. Not even waking me up in the morning for work. I was afraid requests might add on to her stress staying in my home.

There was not a single word from Huey. She remained silent still. I could almost see her weighing Ah Mm's words on her mind, her heavy breathing blending into the loud gurgling noise of my bath water flowing into the drain.

'Huey ah . . . Ah Mm has a favour to ask from you.'

My heart stopped. Taking a deep breath in, I wondered if I should dash out and stop Ah Mm from speaking altogether. But . . . Ah Mm might really need help. To be helpless required courage. Ah Mm was humble enough to ask for a favour from Huey.

Eventually after a quick moment of flustering, I decided to listen to Ah Mm first.

'The family needs help. All my children are occupied, and I need someone to help me take care of the family.' Ah Mm let out a sudden loud cough. She was coughing her lungs out. Listening to that tore my heart.

'I'm sorry to be asking this from you. To ask you to quit your job and help this old woman to take care of the family might not be something modern girls like you hope to achieve.' Ah Mm said apologetically and pleadingly. 'Maybe for just a few years before the younger brothers are married and have their own wives to take care of them?'

I wondered how Huey would reply to Ah Mm. Images of Ah Mm's hunchbacked body and frail-looking appearance as well as Huey's uplifted expression when she stepped out of the house to work at the factory every day made me very confused. Strange feelings rumbled inside me. I did not know what to do.

Huey must be having a hard time too at this moment.

Will she agree to sacrifice her work for my family?

There was again, a long silence after. I quickly scooped water from the pail to wash the foam off my body so that I could get out to dissolve this awkward situation.

But Huey spoke.

She spoke in her usual gentle tone. I was surprised as she had not been speaking like that in a long time. Her trembling voice had disappeared.

'Ah Mm . . . Bang sim lah. I will help. I will stay at home with you.'

Water stopped gurgling down the drain.

* * *

Since a few years back, I had been depositing money in a bank account instead of keeping all my money in a biscuit tin, despite the meager sum I could afford to save each time.

Looking at a figure and imagining the amount of money I had was a strange feeling. A figure merely informed a definite value, and could not allow me to indulge in a physical possession of the rewards of my labour. I preferred to hold and feel the notes in my hands.

The thicker the pile of notes I had in my biscuit tin, the more satisfied I was. This motivated me to work harder to save more.

But it was different now.

Everyone yearned to own a bank account now, especially ever since banks started to introduce interest accumulating saving accounts. Everyone said it was more worthwhile.

Catching up with the trends of times required a lot of learning, and a bulk of it came from letting go of old practices. To unlearn was harder than to learn. It took me a while to get used to looking at figures.

But the problem an absolute figure could bring about was magnifying the insecurity a shrinking amount presented on a bank statement. A constant reduction in savings may be concealed more easily if I were holding notes in my hands.

Just don't count them so often and live my life, happy-go-lucky.

Ambiguity shaped ignorance. And ignorance was bliss.

A married man just could not do that anymore. Let alone a married man with a child.

Huey and I had our first child within the same year of our marriage. We named him Hao. It meant greatness. And we hoped this boy would grow up, refined and outstanding.

Who could have known a tiny being could turn our lives upside down? Life was different after Hao was born. The hysterical cries and his constant waking in the middle of the night almost drove me nuts. Being a first-time father, I screamed inside more times than my son did out loud. There was once I threw Hao onto the bed when he was still very little, harbouring an ill intention of abandoning him.

'Cry! Cry some more! I'm going to dump you. Serve you right!' The degree of my madness was certainly beyond my own understanding.

Fortunately, Huey was a patient mother. Without her, I would have crushed my baby out of exasperation.

She often soothed him with Teochew rhythms and rhymes, just like how Ah Mm took care of me when I was a baby. Her love for Hao was immense. As promised, she gave her utmost to the family, helping Ah Mm with all the chores and taking care of little Hao. Huey was indeed a family-oriented woman who valued family commitments above all else and I knew I could always count on her in any situation.

The dwindling savings in my bank account ever since the birth of Hao was haunting me. I became bothered whenever old fears ran through my head.

What if Hao had to live a childhood just like mine? Hopping from house to house to borrow money for survival.

I could not let this go on. Holding odd jobs and earning just enough were simply not enough for me to sustain the livelihood of my family. I finally started seriously reflecting and questioning myself, *how can I give my family a better life?*

Thirty-One

At the age of two, Hao was out-and-out capable. He could wash vegetables and clothes under Huey's supervision. He was also skilled in pounding his grandmother's back and thighs, helping to allay her body aches, and rolling cigarettes for his grandfather.

Hao was also sharp. He had noticed changes in Ah Mm's movements and urged us to check on her every night. He would tug at our pants and point towards Ah Mm's bedroom.

Ah Mm, indeed, had been lying on the bed. She rarely got off her bed these days. But we were not worried. Ah Mm had always been frail and ill. Occasionally, she suffered from constant dry cough and unknown stomachache that could last for weeks. Her lips were always purplish pale and her face, as white as ghost.

We were used to her feebleness. After a while, she would return to her usual self.

Her asthmatic attacks used to make things worse for her. In the past, she breathed with a small amount of difficulty, but rarely struggled for a long time. She was cured from asthma with changes in her diet that included intake of more garlic and ginger. Natural remedies worked best for Ah Mm as she was allergic to many kinds of western medicines. We thought her life was free from asthmatic attacks until one day this old ailment slowly, and quietly crept up on her without anyone's knowledge.

'Mama, Ah Ma has a long snake on her body.' Hao pointed to a long stretch of blistered rashes hidden under Ah Mm's shirt one day excitedly.

The red and bloody-looking rashes crusted all over her body like a venomous snake wrapping its prey and had even started occupying her thin, wrinkled neck.

Huey was alarmed by such a rare condition. No one noticed it except for little Hao who crawled to Ah Mm's bed every late morning to scratch her back.

Ah Mm who had been tortured by the constant itch, sighed at her grandson's accidental disclosure of her secret. She was ashamed and disturbed at how a new health issue was going to make her whole family worry a great deal.

* * *

'It's shingles, Kuang. Ah Mm has shingles,' Huey told me about Ah Mm's unusual health condition that very night. Her voice elevated in pitch and volume.

'Our neighbour, that Ah Sim living on the eleventh floor, just died from it last month.' Huey arched her brows and took a deep breath to calm herself down. 'What shall we do?'

Recently, there seemed to be a wave of shingles spreading around the neighbourhood. Babies and elderly who were ill were especially susceptible to it. Rumours spread that shingles was incurable and anyone who had contracted it would eventually die of a weakened immune system. And by far, no elderly had survived it. We were not sure how true this rumour was.

'Ah Mm, you'll be fine. The itch may be unbearable but it's . . . part of the healing process,' we comforted her, feeling guilty at the same time as we did not believe the hopeful scenario we had just painted with our words. As much as we wanted to assure ourselves that Ah Mm would pull through this abnormal condition, we were skeptical about it too.

Ah Gong's death in the past warned us of the risk of seeking a quack doctor for help. An unlicensed medical worker was equivalent to a murderer. He could take away lives easily with false promises of recovery.

Once bitten twice shy.

Therefore, we decided to take Ah Mm to the hospital at this critical juncture while Ah Beh continued to look for licensed traditional Chinese doctors who could cure shingles.

Ah Mm was prescribed some medication to reduce the symptoms. 'At this point in time, there was no cure for shingles,' the doctor said.

Upon hearing that, we sank into misery.

The itch from her blisters had gradually transformed into excruciating pain. It was a kind of nerve pain that got worse at night or in reaction to heat and cold. For many nights, Ah Mm could not fall into deep sleep. She was either woken up by the severe pain or became overly worried in the middle of the night.

Besides eating painkillers, it seemed like nothing could relieve her pain that had been dragging on for months, killing her will to live on. Those prescribed medication did not help either.

* * *

Neighbours swarmed to us, suggesting different ways of healing Ah Mm. We became hesitant to accept kind-intended advice when they flooded our ears. We even became sick of Auntie Lim who called us multiple times to offer her help of grounding ginger and making it into paste to apply on Ah Mm's skin. We had learnt to decline methods that did not sound feasible.

One evening, Ah Beh came home with a telephone number written on a piece of torn brown paper. 'Call this number, quick! This sinseh has a clinic and claims to be able to cure shingles.' Huey and I were convinced by Ah Beh's certainty in his voice. We dialed it and fixed an appointment. And on the following day, we brought Ah Mm for a consultation.

* * *

'Poke the blisters and let the pus flow out,' the sinseh suggested. 'Continue to bring her to my clinic for the next two weeks. I want to 'catch the snake' and destroy it by nabbing its head.'

As ridiculous as it might sound to be, we followed suit. We were not aware what the sinseh was going do to Ah Mm but we were certain that this doctor would be able to cure her.

There were other patients with shingles waiting at his clinic and through their conversation with one another, we knew Ah Mm could hope for recovery.

The sinseh burnt a stick made of ground mug wort leaves and placed it on Ah Mm's blistered skin, particularly aiming the beginning of the long stretch of rashes. It was a fast procedure and Ah Mm could return home after it. At the end of the treatment, the sinseh proudly proclaimed, 'Now that the snake had been captured, with its head chopped and body cut through, your mother will recover very soon.'

Several days after the full treatment and constant releasing of the pus and water from her blisters, Ah Mm miraculously recovered. She was finally relieved of the pain and itch caused by the stretch of red blisters. She could now sit up and even tell stories to Hao.

No tale could give Ah Mm enough motivation to spend the entire evening entertaining her grandson besides The Butterfly Lovers. Every evening, Hao treaded backward towards Ah Mm, making her laugh with his funny antics. Then he would climb onto her bed and sit on her laps, urging for a session of storytelling.

'Once upon a time in China, long ago, there lived a young girl who dreamed of learning. Unfortunately, she lived in an era when girls were expected to be obedient . . . '

Hao's bright deep-set eyes stared wide open at Ah Mm.

I observed Ah Mm's eyes were watery whenever she told this tale to Hao. Those special tears circling in her eyes. They made Hao very curious.

Hao would stand, approach Ah Mm, and touch her eyes with his small fingers. Perhaps, little Hao was not fond of Ah Mm's favourite tale. He might not be able to understand it. It was the sheer emotional change of his grandmother that had captured his attention.

Huey and I would usually leave Hao alone if he cried too much. Especially for me, I could not stand it when Hao wailed. I had to leave him for a while before I turned mad.

Hao had not seen any adult cry in this house. He was the only one who was always screaming with tears. At the instant when tears started circling in Ah Mm's eyes, he must be thinking Ah Mm and him were the same. The same kind of human who could feel sad and turn teary.

I guessed Ah Mm made Hao feel better with her own tears.

From then on, Hao constantly looked into her eyes and followed her wherever she went.

Thirty-Two

Ah Mm was soon fully healed from shingles. And I got retrenched by the company that was providing me with those odd jobs. It was the worst thing that could happen at this juncture for a man with family.

Recently, Ah Mm had been telling us how afraid she was to think that she would die from shingles. That kind of bone-breaking pain was ten times worse than giving birth. Whenever she thought about the experience, she would pat her chest a few times and inhale deeply. Just thinking about leaving us made her so scared.

'Wak ah,' Ah Mm said as she limped to the living room from her bedroom. 'Wak, I need some spring onions, garlic, and honey. You go get them from the market for me, ok?' Ah Mm requested for Ah Beh's help early one morning.

Ever since Ah Mm contracted shingles, Ah Beh had been helping with household chores. Upon seeing Huey chase Hao around the house for an hour and having difficulty preparing even a pot of hot tea, Ah Beh knew he had to take leave from work and lend a helping hand to Huey that day.

It started pouring heavily last night when everyone was asleep. The wind was howling and windows were shaking. It was a horrifying sight. A strong gust of wind suddenly blew into the house, shutting the windows with a loud slam that almost woke all of us up. It had been a long time since we experienced such a torrential downpour.

When morning arrived, the day seemed much brighter and refreshed. The cool moisture remained in the washed air. Dak, Ang, and Siu left home early in the morning. Ah Beh had gone to the market. The rest except for me, Huey, and little Hao, were all still asleep.

The quiet morning amplified the sweet songs of birds that sailed in the breeze. Ah Mm sat on the sofa, closing her eyes to enjoy the rare peaceful moment while Huey sat on the floor, feeding Hao cereal that had gradually turned cold.

I was walking around, busy with those mundane household chores. Occasionally, I stopped what I was doing and approached Ah Mm to check on her.

I realized something was amiss as I listened hard.

Slight squeaky sound was coming from Ah Mm's lungs as she inhaled. If anyone else were to produce this sound when he or she fell asleep, it would not be as alarming. Usual as it might seem, this soft wheezing sound, however, preyed on my mind. After going through a struggling episode with shingles with Ah Mm, a slight change in her behaviour sought my attention easily.

Huey too, turned and looked at Ah Mm who had dozed off. She then looked at me with eyes, unable to close. The spoonful of cereal, which was approaching Hao's mouth, stopped moving too.

Ah Mm's chest was moving up and down gently, and her eyes remained calmly shut. Nothing seemed to be bothering Ah Mm. Huey and I looked at each other again and confirmed that we were both overreacting. I was relieved to know that my worry was uncalled for.

Huey turned her head and continued to pour another spoonful of cereal into Hao's mouth. I went back to the kitchen to finish up what I was doing.

But the squeaky sound grew louder.

So loud that it travelled to the kitchen. So loud that it could not be ignored anymore. I jumped up immediately and rushed to the living room.

Ah Mm stretched her eyes wide as soon as she heard air moving through her bronchioles like a musical instrument that had gone out of tune. The weird sound that came from her lungs suggested an asthma attack was on the way.

I could feel a familiar yet strange sense of anxiety filling Ah Mm's heart as she tried to inhale more air. Unable to draw in her usual lung-full, Ah Mm stopped trying and stood up. Her face slowly turned purplish, and she began patting her chest. The lack of air drove Ah Mm to start gasping.

Within seconds, she was jumping in panic.

I felt my muscles straining all over my body as Ah Mm breathed harder. Thoughts in my head turned from confusion to fear. Huey dropped the bowl of cereal on the floor and carried Hao away as Ah Mm stomped and jumped non-stop.

'AH MM AH, ARE YOU OK?' I screamed as I witnessed my elderly mother fighting to breathe. I was at a loss what to do.

Carrying Hao in her hands, Huey dashed to the kitchen, frantically searching every drawer she saw in the kitchen for an inhaler.

I followed Huey to the kitchen. We zoomed into every small corner of the cabinets, hoping to find a breathing aid. I would not mind even an old, expired inhaler. Just something to give me some hopes to save Ah Mm. We searched high and low, pulling things out from cupboards and drawers and thrashing them onto the floor.

Hao began wailing loudly at the kitchen entrance.

After a while, strange silence crept onto us despite Hao's incessant crying.

There was no more thumping sound coming from the living room. We rushed out. There was no one in sight. Terribly worried,

I went to the Ah Mm's bedroom. Huey lugged Hao and paced quickly after me.

* * *

Ah Mm was jumping on her bed, gasping even harder.

She grasped onto her own neck with both of her hands, almost digging into her own skin with her stiff bent fingers. Her face gradually turned blue-black and lips were reduced to pale nude.

I shouted at Ah Mm, repeatedly calling her. Seeing how much Ah Mm was struggling, I yelled out to Huey to quickly wake my other siblings up. Huey placed the crying toddler on the floor and darted out of the room. Afraid that Ah Mm might fall from the bed and hurt herself, I climbed up to the bed and held onto Ah Mm's legs tightly, refusing to let go.

A moment later, Ah Mm let out a sudden loud shriek, *'WAA!'* Her face turned bluish and she collapsed onto me. Her hands let loose of her neck and she fell into a deep coma.

The rest of my brothers and sisters were finally stirred from their sleep. They all raced to Ah Mm's room together with Huey.

Without saying a word, I picked Ah Mm up and piggybacked her out of the house in my tattered singlet and shorts, barefooted.

'Lao gung! Doctor!' I bawled out loud as I hurried down the flight of stairs. Huey then urged the rest of the siblings to get Ah Beh, Dak, Ang, and Siu back. Ing immediately rushed to the market.

Ah Mm's body weighed on my back like a heavy slab of lifeless flesh. With all my might, I grabbed onto Ah Mm's legs and secured them firmly to my waist. Her head rested on my right shoulder, with her nose and mouth positioned close to my ear. One more flight of stairs before reaching the corridor that led to the lift, I adjusted Ah Mm's position on my back, inhaled deeply and pushed on.

'Ah Mm, I bring you to see lao gung. You'll be ok. You wait. You wait ah,' I chanted as I ran on.

Halfway through walking with caution on the flight of wet stairs, I could suddenly feel stillness lingering around my right ear.

There was not a slightest movement of air circling between Ah Mm's nose and my ear.

Ah Mm was very quiet.

Her whole body had become numb. Her widely open legs dangled next to the sides of my waist, while her arms swayed left and right just below my eyes.

'Mm ah! Ah Mm!' I shouted.

My legs stopped at the stairs.

I found myself in a state of fear, trembling at the thought of Ah Mm's departure.

'Ah Mm.' I whispered. The bridge of my nose hurt and those steps before me blurred.

There was no movement from Ah Mm.

No reply.

No breathing.

At that moment, I pleaded insanely in my heart for Ah Mm to wake and nag at me for making a mountain out of a molehill, just like how she always did. But, deep within, I could sense that Ah Mm had left, silently, leaving a warm lifeless body on my back.

I blinked and blinked. Then, turned around and wobbled back to the house.

* * *

I walked straight into the house in a daze, dragging my feet on the floor. Silence hung in the air as the rest of my siblings crowded around me.

Huey stepped forward to take a closer look at Ah Mm.

Sniffing and wiping her tears away, she then patted on my upper arm and said in a low voice, 'Kuang, Ah Mm has passed on.'

Ah Mm's passive frozen expression told Huey she had not escaped the claws of the merciless asthma attack. The pain that burned like fire in Ah Mm's body just minutes ago had faded into icy numbness.

No one could believe it.

Leng let out a sharp cry and sank down to the floor. Gia and Teng turned away, sobbing uncontrollably and wiping tears off their faces with their sleeves.

It was a moment of indescribable pain.

Everyone broke down and wept hard like children, like how we used to do when we were young after getting scolded by Ah Mm. Little Hao too, continued to wail upon seeing everyone's tearful expressions.

Rain began to fall from the skies once more, weeping for our loss.

* * *

'Kuang . . . place Ah Mm on a mattress. Lay her down and straighten her limbs,' Huey suggested softly as she placed her hand on my arm.

Too sorrowful to speak, I followed Huey's instructions without thinking much about what she had just said. As soon as I laid Ah Mm's body down on the mattress, her body began to stiffen slowly, making her frozen expression look colder.

Ah Mm looked like she was asleep. Peacefulness spread across her face, making it hard for me to believe that she had already passed on.

'Ah Mm . . . ,' I muttered as I squatted down next to her body.

'Ah Mm . . . wake up.' I pushed her shoulder lightly.

'Ah Mm, *mai sng*. Ki lai . . . ki lai!' I sobbed piteously over Ah Mm's body, trying to convince myself that her death was not true.

A huge gap formed in my being, making me numb and confused. Heavily soaked in tears, my eyes could not even blink. I began touching and rubbing Ah Mm's hands and arms, hoping to feel more of her being before she was gone. Her cold wrinkled skin became stretched.

Ah Beh and Ing were standing behind us, entirely dumbfounded by what they had witnessed in the house.

Shaking his head slowly in disbelief, Ah Beh tumbled onto the sofa. He looked hard at Ah Mm's body. His whole back arched like a deformed rod and his head was bent very low. Lethargy must have stroked him. I believed he was too drained to cope with the present moment.

I guessed Ah Beh's heart had been resilient for too long to be soft. He did not drop any tear. Could he not? Was he torn deep within? Like me, could he not believe the drastic change a single morning could bring about? Having just gone to the market for groceries, he walked back into the house only to find Ah Mm already passed. Forever, she was gone. There was nothing we could do to bring her back. Didn't our family just rejoice at Ah Mm's recovery from shingles a few days ago? And now she had to be laid straight and flat on the floor, waiting for all her blood to be drawn and body to be placed into a wooden case.

My heavy heart was racked by sobs as I imagined how Ah Mm would be buried underground. She would be so lonely. Would the dampness of the soil reach her in the wooden case, making her body colder? Or would the bugs and lice take over her body and chomp on her skin and flesh in just a few days' time?

Ah Mm had always worshipped the gods. *But now, tell me, where're all those damned gods taking her? Return her to me!*

I beg you, return her to me.

Ah Beh closed his eyes for a long time. Was he sandwiched between trying to accept what fate had arranged for him and pleading fate to return his wife to him? He lifted his arm and touched Ah Mm gently on her white face.

'Mui . . . ' Ah Beh whimpered. It was the first time Ah Mm's name became so sad on his lips. He then remained silent in a daze.

Departure was a strange thing. It urged people to relive memories at the present.

Today, the house was very quiet. No one uttered a single word. But at the same time, it was noisy. Filled with chatters, jokes, gossips, and stories. Especially Ah Mm's contagious laughter. A mixture of present pain and past sweetness minced my heart.

The smell of Ah Mm's clothes, her favourite traditional medicated oil, and her shampoo continued to linger at every corner. For a long time, we could not bear to remove any of these.

Once in a while when a wheeze of her smell drifted past, we could lie to ourselves and enjoy a moment of her brief presence in the air.

* * *

Ah Mm's departure dawned on me a realization of some sort.

The more I wanted to shun death, the more I could not accept the pain death brought. But the moment I acknowledged Ah Mm had to leave, the pain of losing her began to heal.

When we first arrived in Singapore, Uncle Tham took a family portrait of Ah Beh, Ah Mm, and me with his new roll-film camera.

In this old photo, Ah Beh was smiling widely. How rare it was to see his smile. He was very happy to be reunited with Ah Mm and me after so long. I was standing in front of Ah Beh, frowning at the camera. It was my first time seeing such a unique device. I remember I was anxious to see how it was going to work.

Ah Mm was standing beside Ah Beh, expressionless. I guess she was still in a state of shock and confusion upon arriving at such a different world. But from her eyes, I could sense hope.

Ah Mm had by no means been entirely happy. In fact, Ah Mm had led a life filled with anxiety, fear, and worries, especially in her younger days. But Ah Mm's eyes always overflowed with immense hopes whenever she looked at me, despite the tough circumstances.

Her faith and the boundless tenderness of her love protected me from the harshness of my own childhood. She was the only person who genuinely loved and cared for me.

As I began to embrace days without Ah Mm, I found her more alive in my heart. Her departure was no longer associated with absence. Rather, the presence of her hopeful eyes dwelled in my being whenever I thought of her.

Goodbye Ah Mm.
You loved me in a way
I never imagined
was possible.

You lived hard, fought hard,
and loved hard.
And you made me laugh
harder than I could,
always.
You walked with me
through the darkest of trials,
and trusted me
with your entire heart.
I knew
I had never told you this before, but
being your son
was my greatest blessing.
I will miss your smile, your scent,
and your soup.
Your stories, your voice,
and your being.
Every part of you will be with me,
in my heart, my soul,
and my dream.
I will miss you forever,
Ah Mm.
I will miss you for
the rest of my life.

Part Four

Hope

Thirty-Three

'Ah Mm! Come, try.' I cried out to Ah Mm, holding a plate of lor ark png in one hand, and a plate of Ah Mm's favourite treasures of a braised duck in another.

Ah Mm sat at the sill of our door. The hazy brightness outside shone in and blurred my vision.

She got up and sauntered towards me. Her pace was faster than usual. I had not seen her walk like this for a long time.

Ah Mm looked at me with her brows lifted against her much youthful skin. Her curiosity was awakened upon seeing the two plates of delicacies laid in front of her.

'Wa, Kuang . . . did you make this?' Her neck tipped back as she bent to have a closer look. Her familiar scent of medicated oil made me caress gently on her back.

I puffed up my chest and gripped on Ah Mm's hands, trying to contain a jittery feeling of excitement.

'I made this just for you, Ah Mm.' I nodded, maintaining the smirk on my face.

Ah Mm's cheeks grew red.

'*Jin kiang*, Kuang. I can't be wrong about my son.'

She stretched out her hand and picked a piece of juicy duck liver. After admiring it for a minute, she placed it on her tongue. She then settled back in a chair, twitched her lips and hid a smile behind her hand.

'Ah Mm, *ho ziah bo?*' I asked.

'Jin ho ziah. My son is so capable.' Ah Mm bragged, taking deep breaths to savour both the liver and the present moment.

The dark savoury gravy on her lips gathered into a drop. It flowed downward to her chin.

I laughed.

Ah Mm used to wipe gravy off my chin when we ate braised goose at Shantou. While reminiscing, I wiped her chin with a wet cloth.

Ah Mm smiled and gave me the thumbs-up. Her boney finger seemed to be fleshier. She then held the plate of duck treasures and stood up.

'Ah Mm, where you going?' I asked.

Ah Mm did not reply. She turned around and limped forward, stopping at the sill of our door. I could not figure out where she was heading.

'Ah Mm, come back.' I called out to her.

A colourful butterfly came fluttering around her. The outside of our house became piercingly bright.

'Ah Mm ah!' I shouted.

She half turned around and looked at me. Then turned back, squatted down and faded away.

'Ah Mm!' I shouted again.

But Ah Mm did not return.

* * *

Today marked the 101st day of Ah Mm's departure.

For the Chinese, mourning usually lasted a hundred days for the family. Family members wore a small piece of colored cloth on their sleeve, signifying their continued mourning.

Huey was trying to remove the small piece of black cloth from my sleeve when I opened my eyes.

'Still don't want to take this out?' Huey asked. Her voice softened. 'Ah Mm had passed on for a hundred days already. Time to move on.'

I stared hard at the ceiling. Huey's worried look entered my vision occasionally.

'Are you alright?' Huey asked. Her eyes stopped blinking.

'Yes, I am. Ahh ya, I forgot to take it out yesterday.'

'Are you sure you're alright?' Huey popped her head into my vision again, straining her neck to get close to me. Her features stiffened.

'Erm . . . again, a weird dream.'

Huey looked at me with eyebrows drawn together. 'Was it about Ah Mm feasting on braised goose meat back in China again? My mother used to tell me that if one dreams of a family member who has passed on, the deceased may have a message to convey.'

'Ah Mm was eating my duck rice in my dream earlier.'

Huey stared hard at me. 'Hmm, maybe it's just a dream.'

'I know a little.' I bit at my lips. 'I mean I know a little about making lor ark png.'

Huey was surprised. She touched her neck, her lips parting slightly.

'You've never told me about this before.'

'I learnt it from a friend in the past. Just . . . some simple steps of making lor ark.'

'Who did you learn it from?' Huey continued to observe me. Her eyes became more widened.

'A childhood friend . . . You don't know him. Never mind about him.' I replied, pinching my lips, reluctant to bring up the past.

Huey nodded. I smiled.

I looked at Huey's expression, one that revealed understanding. Breath bottled up in my chest. I had always wanted to tell Huey about my past with Geong, about our failed business, and all that I had learnt from the experience. But every time when I wanted to share, there was something tugging in my heart, asking me to suppress my intention.

I did not feel it was worthwhile to share my previous experience with her. Would she think I was too naïve back then? In any case, it was a short-lived project that did not matter much to me, Geong, or my family.

Did it not?

Then why was I mulling over it for such a long time, keeping the experience quiet within me, yet unable to stop myself from reflecting upon it and even coming up with ways to want to relive it?

I did not know.

Huey seemed to be holding still in expectation. Perhaps I should discuss my plan with her. A plan that even I was not very sure of.

'Huey ah . . . hmm . . . what do you think about me setting up a lor ark png stall? Be my own boss.' I casually suggested.

Huey continued to look at me but doubts circled in her eyes.

'Not a good idea?' I asked.

'I don't know. But who's going to help you with that?'

'You . . . ?'

'Me?' Huey yelped. She looked away, behaving like she had not heard what I said.

I noticed her eyes move randomly, as if searching for words to reply to me. After some time, she said in a distressed voice, 'Kuang . . . I've stopped working for so long. You know me, I can't.'

'Why do you say so?' I asked, concerned.

'I can't imagine myself stepping out of the house and . . . working again, really,' Huey confessed. 'Moreover, facing so many customers and remembering orders aren't easy. My mum used to do that when she was a peddling hawker. Kuang, I've a poor memory. I can't do it.'

Huey was trying to justify her choice. At the same time, she seemed guilty for being perturbed by her own timidity.

I nodded vaguely as I listened to Huey. Her reluctance evoked some strange emotions in me. It was a mixture of guilt and disappointment.

Would Huey have become a different person had she not been married into my family?

As much I wished to persuade her to keep an open mind to this business idea, I did not wish to change her mind at the instant. Insisting what I wanted might make her retreat into herself.

'I know it's hard, Huey. I was joking.'

I stayed quiet. Even though the dream was bizarre, I felt a deep sense of wholeness waking from it. I could not quite identify with it. Goosebumps rose on my skin, and I enjoyed a brief moment of happiness.

Perhaps, dreams could prophesize. Or probably, they served to drop some hints to awaken.

I could feel a ball of vigour remained in me to unearth the dream that had been chunked away for years. Every fibre of my being was telling me that my affinity with braised ducks had not ended.

I had not made my special braised duck rice for Ah Mm yet.

* * *

Little Hao spotted a stall at a corner of the hawker centre selling golden-crusted dough of all shapes and refused to leave. I was walking way ahead of them, searching for Uncle Tham's stall.

Stepping into the hawker centre, I was deafened by the noise of people chattering, dishes clanging, and the intermittent blast of a fiery wok furnace.

A familiar scene was unfolding in a different setting.

At a hawker centre, stalls were built in and evenly distributed. An array of local dishes was neatly spread out in front of my eyes.

Some dishes had been existing for a long time ago.

Some were different from where they had originated.

And some were no longer around, anymore.

It was almost as if Singapore's own past and present cultures all converged in the walls of any and every hawker center.

'Hao, you just had them in the morning.' Huey stretched her arms and wrapped them around his chest, trying to discourage him from making a scene.

'We'll get you another one later. Papa is looking for his friend. He sells fantastic curry puffs. You'll love it. Call Ah Chek when you see him later.' Huey tried hard to pacify Hao who was hitting himself out of frustration.

Provoked, I turned my head around upon hearing Hao's endless cries from a distance. Mounting exasperation tightened my throat. I crossed my brows and glared hard at him.

Countless pairs of eyes were looking at him sprawling to the floor. Some were laughing at his uncontrollable behaviors while a few old women expressed their concern about him hurting himself.

Towards Hao, my patience ran thin easily.

Maneuvering my way through the rows of tables and chairs, I quickened my pace towards Huey and that little rascal.

I squatted next to Hao and spoke in the sternest tone, 'You'd better stop it!' I pulled him by his collar and glared hard at him.

Hao screwed his eyes shut, avoiding my piercing stares. 'Mama, mama, I want mama. Not you! I want *youtiao!*' Big beads of tears rolled down as he shrieked louder, bending his body backward.

My heartbeat got faster and I could feel my face burning with anger. I was all prepared to yell.

I stretched to pick a thick branch that lay under a table right in front of us. Grabbing Hao's shoulder with one hand, I bellowed, 'You'd better stop what you're doing and get up to walk. Don't make me hit you in public!' I warned Hao, pointing the branch at him.

Countless pairs of eyes were fixed upon us. I could feel soft exchanges of comments everywhere at the hawker centre.

'Kuang!' A hunchbacked figure strolled towards us in small steps. 'Is this your son?'

I gazed up.

A wrinkled baby face edged with a sparse fringe of white was smiling at us, revealing his almost toothless gums. That familiar pair of attractive dimples had turned into two long creases that stretched to the jawline, sinking into the loosened skin that had grown much thinner. His eyes were heavily lidded and weighed down with wrinkled folds.

'Uncle Tham!' I gasped in great surprise.

I was expecting the croak of old age but Uncle Tham's voice was more like a youthful man—distinct and powerful. His brows seemed stitched in an upward manner, moving up and down every time he talked. His curiosity remained even though he had aged.

'My stall is just right behind this youtiao stall. Over there. Heard a child crying so badly, so here I am, finding out if I can help in any way.'

'Thank you, Uncle Tham. *Paiseh,* this brat . . . is my son.' I turned back at Hao, softening my gaze and shook my head.

'Haven't met you for so long. Dropping by to pay you a visit today. So glad to see you! Hao, call Ah Chek.' I turned my head again to reply to Uncle Tham.

My mood was instantly lifted the moment I met the eyes of this high-spirited old friend. 'And this is my wife, Huey.'

Hao stopped crying. Bewildered, he quietly observed the conversation between Uncle Tham and me.

'Kids, being kids, have interesting way of expressing their wants. They're still young. Be patient, Kuang.' Uncle Tham patted my shoulder gently.

'You know, making food is the same as raising kids. Got to be really patient and flexible. Come, boy. Ah Chek has very nice galy poks for you.' Uncle Tham stretched out his hand to help Hao up slowly.

We walked to the back of the hawker centre and found Uncle Tham's stall. It was crowded with people.

Little buttery pockets of curry with the same luring smell, once again, engulfed my entirety. The familiar golden-brown pastries piled up neatly in the glass cabinet. Every single one of them was a piece of delicate art.

We noticed there was not just one kind of galy pok. Uncle Tham had invented new flavours such as black pepper chicken, yam paste with pumpkin, sardine with tomato, as well as chili crab.

Huey and I were deeply astonished.

Besides galy poks, there were other common deep-fried pastries such as butterfly fritters, sesame balls, and spring rolls. I could see other interesting pastries like deep fried durian rolls, lobster glutinous puffs, and cheese mochi in the glass cabinet.

Two young men stood in the stall. One was kneading dough for the next batch of puffs, the other was frying some in a heated wok.

'They're . . . ?' I asked curiously.

'That brat is my son!' Uncle Tham laughed. 'The other one who is frying puffs is my worker.'

'Oh, your son is helping you with your business!'

'Yes, my second son. He loves what I make.' Uncle Tham replied, caressing his own head.

'He's taking over your stall?'

'Yes, for now. He's still learning. His aim is to open a shop to continue the family business. Time flies, Kuang. I'm old. I can't do this anymore soon,' Uncle Tham confessed, giving the tiniest of smile.

'I told my son, 工字不出头. I'm sure you know that 'gong', 工, suggests labour for others will never earn you a breakthrough in life. Only setting up your own business and becoming your own boss will make you somebody. But of course, it's all up to him.'

The map of wrinkles on Uncle Tham's face told of his incredible journey of selling curry puffs. From a peddling street hawker who had to constantly avoid inspectors to a boss who could guide the next generation in setting up businesses with his experience.

It seemed like age had brought more wisdom to this man of the purest heart.

'Oh, let me pack some puffs for your parents. How're your parents?' Uncle Tham asked, turning his concerned gaze at me.

'Ah Beh is doing fine. Doing some odd jobs now. But Ah Mm . . . unfortunately, she passed on months ago. Asthma attack.'

Uncle Tham's concerned gaze remained still. But his warm brown eyes turned cold. He shut them firmly and nodded silently to himself.

'She's in a better place.' He smiled. 'Life comes and goes. Her mission is complete. She has raised so many of you up. Not an easy task.' Uncle Tham nodded again and expelled a shallow breath. He pressed his palm against my shoulder and stood up, cracking a bone, and walked towards his stall.

'Here you go, Kuang, eight galy poks for you!' Uncle Tham swung a big bag of curry puffs to my face.

Before I could fish out notes from my wallet to pay him, he was already talking to another customer, taking orders and packing more puffs.

As we were about to leave, Uncle Tham's voice rang behind us. 'Bye bye! Come again, Kuang! Bring a few more children next time! See you, Huey!' Uncle Tham grinned widely, holding his hand straight up and waving enthusiastically at us.

Hao waved vigorously back at Uncle Tham, then turned back to look at Huey. 'Mama, I want galy pok. I don't want youtiao anymore,' Hao urged, eyeing the bag of scrumptious pastries and controlling his drool.

I cracked a smile. Even a young child could not resist Uncle Tham's galy poks. Or was Hao not able to resist Uncle Tham's gentleness in his words, thus, still thinking about him after we had left his stall? I certainly needed to learn from this wise man once again. This time, it was about winning the affection of a young child.

Thirty-Four

Since the day I met Uncle Tham, I had often recalled his warm eyes and words to his son, as if they were meant for me.

On one hand, I was tempted to set up a business. On the other hand, I was stricken with fear every time I thought of losing money to a failed business.

Sometimes, I loathed a human brain.

Humans learn so well from experiences, that sometimes the past may trap us from advancing.

The failed business with Geong had landed me in bitter misery. I lost my money and my good old friend, and most painful of all, I lost faith in myself.

Unable to decide on the future course of action, I found a new place to work at as an odd job worker once again, going through the motions of life and earning barely enough to feed my family of three. However, anxiety laid in the pit of my stomach and rose when I envisioned my future, every once in a while.

What if we have another baby?

Ah Mm used to say, if I wanted something bad enough, opportunities would fall in my hands. The gods would not forsake those who were sincere and earnest.

Sandwiched between the desire to venture into a business and the fear of venturing into one, I waited sincerely for an answer to be bestowed upon me.

I prayed hard day after day.

And indeed, it did.

* * *

I chanced upon a kopitiam at Circular Road when I was out delivering goods one day.

A board with the words 'For Rent' lightly inked was hanging loosely at the entrance of a uniquely shaped kopitiam. Following my curiosity, I stepped into have a look.

A big middle-aged man slumped down into a chair at the counter. His big belly was exposed, revealing a line of thick hairs that grew sparsely from his chest to the top of his belly button. Holding up a set of newspapers right in front of his face and casting his focus on it, he had not realized I had stepped into his shop.

'Hello, are you the owner of this kopitiam?' I asked, trying to raise my voice to catch his attention.

The big man lowered the newspapers and leaned forward, looking shrewdly at me with his narrowed eyes. 'Yes?'

Captivated by the raw finishes on the walls and floors and the lush foliage surrounding the space, coupled with random rows of slender wooden chairs and tables outfitted with pristine white marble tops, I asked, 'Are you . . . are you renting out this kopitiam?'

The big man coughed a few times and frowned, making his narrowed eyes appear to be more scrutinizing. 'Yes. It's written on the board, isn't it?'

'May I know much is the rent?'

'$380 a month, lad. Why're you asking? Are you keen?' The man asked, scanning me.

'Yes, I'm. But I'd like to find out more.'

'Alright. Go on. What else is on your mind?'

'How's . . . the business here?'

'It's pretty good. Many people stream in and out for lunch.'

Surveying the empty kopitiam, I was bewildered upon hearing his answer to my question. 'Are you sure, Ah Hia?'

The big man clicked his tongue in irritation and rose from his chair. 'Today is a Sunday lah, lad! Who works in the office on a Sunday?'

'So, do you mean business is usually good on weekdays?'

'Of course! Look around you. There're offices everywhere.' The big man clicked his tongue again. 'So, are you keen or not? Don't waste my time if you're not.'

'Yes, yes, I am! But could you let me think about it? I'll come back to you tomorrow.'

Glaring hard at me, the big man warned, 'You'd better be fast . . . '

'I've one more question, Ah Hia.' I interrupted.

'What?' the man gaped. His eyeballs were about to fall out.

'If business is so good, then . . . why are you renting it out?'

The big man frowned and stared at me in silence for a while. He then turned and revealed his rotting back thigh covered with flaking skin and fungal infections. 'How to work like that, you say?'

I gulped. I could feel his pain just by looking at the inflamed wound corroding his skin. ' . . . Diabetes?'

'Yes.' The man replied, softening his tone. 'My greatest life misfortune. Soon, I can only sit down and collect money. Work for it? I doubt so. The big man bent his body to take a closer look at his own rotting skin. 'It's good to work, lad. Work frees our minds of worries. Work hard if you can.'

'Well . . . when one door is closed, another will definitely open for you. With the money collected, you may end up in a better place.' I tried to encourage him, sounding optimistic.

'Better place? Do you mean heaven?' The big man laughed. His deep voice resonated the entire space.

Limping slowly towards me, he suddenly quietened down and looked me in my eyes. 'Lad, just take it. You want this place badly, *tio bo?* I can see it in your eyes. Why're you hesitating? To tell you honestly, a few people came earlier and asked about it. I'll save it for you but just for one more day.'

I felt myself arriving at a turning point in my life and I had to make a decision. A quick one. Though I was not exactly sure what lay ahead of me, I wanted to believe the best did.

'Thank you, Ah Hia. I'll come back tomorrow if I want to rent it.'

Somehow, the big man's words urged me to live a life rid of fear. Perhaps, Ah Mm was right. The gods would not forsake those who were sincere and earnest. And opportunities would definitely come knocking at my doorstep to give me the answer I was seeking.

* * *

Over the night, the image of the kopitiam could not leave me.

It was God-sent.

Spacious and well-lit. Clean and welcoming. Exactly what I had in mind whenever I thought of myself running my own hawker business.

That big man had set my dream on fire. That stranger. That person who knew so little about me, yet he seemed to know me more than I did.

The little voice in my head grew louder. *Kuang, it's time to have a breakthrough. Kuang, just go for it.*

The more the little voice talked to me, the more I yearned to retrieve the dream buried at the back of my head. The little voice became so loud that it could spur actions. I could hear it echoing countless times into the night.

JUST GO FOR IT, KUANG. BELIEVE IN YOURSELF.

So powerful yet gentle.

It surfaced to my mind yet, it anchored so deeply in me.

I could hardly fall asleep. My whole mind was occupied with all the nods I was going to present to the big man the next day. At that very instant, I also had an urge to let Huey know about my grand plan. I turned and faced her, whispering my encounter with the big man and the good opportunity that had befallen upon me into her ears.

'Huey ah . . . I've something to tell you.' I murmured in a hushed tone.

Scratching her face, Huey opened her eyes. 'Yes, Kuang? So late already . . .'

'Today, I chanced upon a very spacious kopitiam at Circular Road. Its location is very ideal and the whole atmosphere in there gave me a good feeling. I want to rent it. And . . . start my own lor ark png business.' I shared honestly, not even blinking my eyes once.

'What?' Huey rubbed her eyes and sat up abruptly. 'Did I hear you wrongly?'

'No, you didn't. I really want to have it, to set up my own business. Actually . . . it's always on my mind. Just that, I prefer to share it with you when I feel surer about it.'

Huey tried to pry open her eyes to look at me. She looked exhausted, her eye bags were all puffy, but at the same time, I could tell she was very concerned.

'Hmm . . . Kuang, I don't know what to say. Though I am a bit worried, I believe you know yourself best. If this is really what your heart wants and you have a good plan to build this business, just do it lor.' Huey smiled with her heavy eyelids flapped back. 'Don't worry about the family. I still have a little savings left if anything happens. Just go for it. Just try lor.'

Huey's confidence in my plan surprised me.

Her assuring words were where the warmth was, the future I wanted to move into. I felt Huey's hands resting upon my shoulders, warm and soft, giving me the greatest push that I ever needed to pursue my long-lost dream.

* * *

The very next day, I arrived at the kopitiam again.

The big man was standing at the entrance of the kopitiam, as if waiting for my likely arrival. He raised his brows upon seeing me.

'I know you'd come.'

I wondered what made him so sure of his assumption of me. I was not used to people guessing my heart right.

'Ah Hia, I've thought about it and . . . decided to give it a try,' I replied in an awkward manner, admitting that he had guessed my intention right.

'That's the way, lad. That's the way to live. Don't worry too much about problems that don't exist.' The big man frowned and smiled. 'Worry only when they come. Pang sim lah.'

Holding a thin pile of documents, he invited me to sit at the counter with him. After spending a long time explaining the rental terms and conditions, I was invited to sign the contract.

I carefully sketched my name out in the most cursive manner on the piece of paper. For the first time, I felt my signature was important.

At the same time, as I left my mark on the paper, I was not sure if I was being rash or brave.

Without anyone's consent, I decided and signed, allowing myself to be legally tied to a list of terms.

And without anyone's consent, I made a decision and created an opportunity for me to live like how I had always imagined my life to be but did not have the courage to pursue it.

I was bound, but at the same time, I was freed.

Thirty-Five

The day I told Ah Beh about my decision to set up a business, I was dumbfounded by his willingness to listen to me.

Ever since Ah Mm passed on, Ah Beh had become a changed man.

He spent hours standing by the windows, gazing out, as if searching for something. Once in a while, he would call out in exhilaration, *'Toih!* Isn't that Mui? *Jin ziang!'* Then with keenness, he continued to stare at some old woman walking across the streets.

But no one replied to him.

We did not want reality to make him look crazy. We let him say whatever he wished to. Sometimes he even mumbled to himself at the windows, as if talking to Ah Mm. If he was not standing by the windows, he would be rolling his cigarettes in his bedroom and taking puffs to soothe his tired body.

Ah Mm was no longer around to help me convey messages to Ah Beh. When it became habitual not to communicate to someone, it was hard to kick the habit to start anew. Communication needed effort. And most importantly, communication needed courage.

This time, I had to do it myself.

I spent a few days mustering my courage to approach Ah Beh to share my plans with him.

Ah Beh had always been a hard nut to crack. He seldom shared his thoughts and had never been supportive in any decision I made. He usually remained quiet or questioned my actions as if he knew it best. It was hard to talk with him.

My fear of him had always been lingering at my chest. Now, I could feel it wrapping my shrinking heart.

I went into his room on the day I felt I was ready to face him. He was looking out of the window like how he always did, puffing on a hand-rolled cigarette.

I handed him some notes as my monthly contribution to his allowance. As usual, he nodded slightly without even looking at me and continued with his own activity.

'Ah Beh,' I called softly.

He exhaled some smoke out of his mouth, half-turned his head, and waited for me to continue with what I wanted to share.

'Ah Beh . . . I . . . ' Words got stuck at my lips.

Surprisingly, Ah Beh did not lose his patience. *'Zhor ni . . . ?'* He lifted his chin a little and looked at me with concern.

'Ah Beh, recently, I . . . rented a kopitiam at Circular Road.'

Ah Beh's forehead creased. 'For what?'

I took a deep breath and explained, 'I want to run a lor ark png business, Ah Beh. To continue with what I had left behind in the past. It's time for me to earn more for the family.'

Ah Beh lifted his eyebrow and nodded slightly. He turned his head away and continued puffing on his cigarette.

'What do you think?' I asked.

'So, you do know you've got to earn more.' Ah Beh said in his deep voice, looking back at me.

I raised my brows and offered a curious gaze. 'Things are getting more costly now. And Huey and I may have more children in the future. If I don't make any progress, my current earnings won't be able to sustain us.'

Ah Beh remained quiet for a while then blinked hard and nodded again, 'Good to think for the family. Be really serious about it.' He then twisted the remaining of the cigarette and squashed it into the ashtray.

'Definitely, I will.' I replied, giving a curt nod.

Ah Beh looked at me with unwavering eye contact. His squarish stiff shoulders loosened slightly; his dull expression softened into a lidded look of satisfaction. He then took out another piece of white paper and some loose-leaf tobacco, all ready to make another cigarette.

I waited for a moment for Ah Beh to say more but he did not. Ah Beh always gave me the impression that he needed to have his time for himself, instead of using it to talk to anyone.

I paused for a while before I excused myself. 'Have some rest, Ah Beh. Will let you know when dinner's ready.'

I often wondered, would there ever be a time when Ah Beh and I could truly understand each other? When words were few but hearts could be connected.

Today, I felt we could. When both of us were talking to each other not just as who we were, but as fathers who cared for our families. We could feel the anxiety that came with the responsibility of being a father. On top of that, I was willing and probably brave enough to know my father's opinion and to be known by him for the very first time, and that was sufficient for a calm exchange.

I was glad I initiated a dialogue with him. That was the first step to probably allow me a little more freedom to express my love to him. I did it. I finally did it.

Fatherhood had changed my relationship with Ah Beh, starting from now on.

In missing Ah Mm, I found myself grow more determined to mend my relationship with Ah Beh. I remembered how much Ah Mm fretted over my inability to convey my words to Ah Beh when she was still with us. I closed my eyes, letting my mind fill with Ah Mm's voice. I could hear Ah Mm being happy for me. As I thought of her, my heart filled with gratitude she would never be able to hear and praises she could not say of me when she lived.

I imagined Ah Mm's scent and breathed it all in.

* * *

After two months of planning and preparation, my kopitiam was open for business.

I employed two of Ah Beh's gaginang from Shantou as my assistants.

Ing asked if she could help at my stall to earn some pocket money. She graduated into the bad job market two years ago and had remained unemployed for a long time.

Being the oldest brother who had always been taking care of her, ever since she was a baby, I felt I was accountable for her well-being. It was a kind of responsibility that Ah Mm had left on my shoulders and I could not fail her, even though she had passed on. Taking care of Ing had sort of become my lifelong duty.

Since the opening of my kopitiam, only a trickle of customers walked into my kopitiam each day. However, I was simply grateful people came at all.

I counted customers every day when Geong and I had our business. It was a terrible feeling. Any day with fewer customers would turn me into a nervous wreck. When my happiness was heavily dependent on the number of customers whom I served each day, I became downtrodden easily.

This time around, I reminded myself never to regard customers as a figure. A successful business was not merely about the quantity of customers that it had served. In fact, every satisfied customer was a success.

I recalled Uncle Tham's words every now and then.

Kuang, you need to love it. You've got to love what you make as if it comes from your flesh and blood. Be proud of what you've created.

Warmed with Uncle Tham's unwavering belief in me, I became determined to create the most succulent Teochew braised ducks.

* * *

I got up early at five in the morning every day and arrived at the kopitiam before six.

Braising ducks was tough; however, it was not the toughest. From my experience working with Geong, I realized having control was the crucial factor in determining the taste of the ducks.

Grasping the right duration of braising, maintaining a certain temperature with the stove, and exhibiting control of ingredient input were the means to produce savory duck meat.

Sweat poured from my forehead and my entire neck every single morning as I stood in front of the braising pot.

A large amount of hot air was spread from the stove. Without sufficient ventilation fans in the kopitiam, it was hot and stuffy. My armpits were soaked in perspiration and my chest was swarmed with heat rash at the end of each day.

The need for constant standing also added pressure to my ankles, making them numb, and eventually leading to inflammation of the veins.

That was not all.

As a lor ark png hawker, working with knives was the most challenging aspect of the job. Everything seemed deceptively simple when I looked at how seasoned hawkers broke down a duck in the past. Using a cleaver, they effortlessly chopped the duck meat into pieces and placed it neatly on a bed of rice. How fascinating!

My first time working with a cleaver, I realized how hard it was to break down a whole duck with it. Among all types of knives, the cleaver had the broadest blade, making it easy to cut through tough bones. I was afraid to even hold it in the beginning. Like a bladed hatchet, it was large and heavy. I was nervous just imagining the blade of the cleaver cutting into my layers of flesh.

Sometimes, being extra careful made me careless instead. There were times I slit my own skin with the cleaver, and I was petrified. I spent weeks just holding and moving it around in the stall, hoping to understand and eventually 'tame' it.

Right now, I had discovered there were two ways to using a cleaver. For the first grip, I could choose an area closer to the blade, then curl my four fingers on one side and the thumb on other side. This grip was the easier one.

As for the second grip, I needed to hold the cleaver handle with three of my fingers, place my index finger on one side on the blade and thumb on the other side. By holding the cleaver this way, I was able to use the force of the blade to get maximum chop on the duck.

To chop stubborn meat off the bones, sometimes I had to use another hand to exert force on the blade. Constantly exerting force on the cleaver gradually transformed my palms into two hardened lumps, swollen with calluses and wounds.

On top of that, I needed to recognize the difference in the bodily structure between a drake and a duck. A duck has a thicker and fleshier bottom than a drake. Therefore, I could get more meat from a duck than from a drake. By knowing the ducks before I chopped and placed them on plates, I could plan how they would be distributed onto plates.

It was physically strenuous manipulating the cleaver every day. Whenever I felt like giving up, the image of Geong puffing cigarettes and hurling vulgarities at the braised ducks in our previous stall would come back to me.

I could wallow in sorrow and pity myself for choosing this difficult path, like Geong, or brace myself up and continue to focus on mastering the most succulent braised ducks.

I chose the latter. I reminded myself every day.

If I failed, I would strive to win again. Even if I were defeated today, I would aim to win tomorrow.

As time passed, a trickle of customers during lunch time gradually became a horde of hungry office workers tramping into the kopitiam in search of food to fill their empty stomachs. Shops in the vicinity had been closing due to renovations and cleaning so more people started to take notice of ours.

Lunchtime queue could stretch all the way to the end of the kopitiam. I found myself running from customer to customer, taking their orders, mentally calculating how much they needed to pay while struggling to remember their orders.

Ah Beh's gaginang were occupied with tasks in the kitchen and Ing was inexperienced. There was no way I could hurry them to tend to the customers. I could only trust and depend on myself.

In the mad scramble every day, I also learned many other things.

A task as simple as scooping soup into a bowl, or laying out the chopsticks and spoons in such a way there was sufficient space on the tray to accommodate the plates of lor ark png, or even packing rice using the brown piece of paper quickly and efficiently, was not at all a child's play.

I needed more help, but as a beginner hawker, I could not hire any more employees due to insufficient funds. Sometimes, the urge to get everything done well and fast made me impatient and anxious. I quarrelled with Ing, vented my anger on my employees, and turned guilty after that.

Satisfying customers' tastes was another challenge. It was common for customers to provide feedback to me and expect immediate changes.

'Too salty.'

'Too bland.'

'Meat not enough.'

Comments flooded my ears every single day. I became confused. Was I doing everything wrong? As days passed, my confusion transformed into arrogance. It was a familiar sense of dislike for customers who had so many comments about me, that feeling that I used to have when I was working at the fish porridge stall. *Who are they to criticize? Do they even know how to braise ducks? Well, if they don't like what I make, they can go elsewhere for lunch.*

There were times when I even ignored my customers. *Don't look at me like that. Get lost if that doesn't suit your taste buds.* My arrogance was definitely making me lose customers, day by day.

My confidence in myself slowly crumbled, and I was lost. Worse still, I even harboured intention to wind down the business.

It was unclear to me whether pressing on would be helpful. But the voice at the back of my head told me not to give up. And I often recalled Boon's words. *Focus on a goal. Do my best to fulfil that goal.* I had always thought I could never forgive Boon for all the lies he said. But unknowingly, his insights remained in me. Or was it the first lesson I learnt being a hawker?

I did it. As I persevered focusing on what I needed to accomplish, the process of satisfying customers' tastes was gradually revealed to me as a process of self-discovery.

My lor ark could not possibly please everyone. And it did not have to. As I slowly gained confidence in my culinary skills, their comments stopped chaining me up. I learnt to take them with a pinch of salt. I gradually derived at my very own special formula to braise ducks, one that contained my own judgments, and what I had learnt from others' comments. I only added changes to it only when I felt there was a need to.

I eventually felt proud of my own recipe. It became something I truly owned. Indeed, it was from my own blood and flesh. I felt like I had birthed it. It was magic. And finally, I began to understand Uncle Tham's words.

Thirty-Six

One evening, after a long day at work, I arrived home with a stiff body and worn-out mind. I slumped on the sofa and my gaze floated towards Hao.

Hao noticed me staring at him. He ran towards me and fished out a weird looking creature made of cardboard from his pocket.

'Papa, look at this!' Hao exclaimed excitedly, trying to get my attention by swinging his craftwork in front of my eyes.

I stared at him coldly and nodded slightly, trying to acknowledge his enthusiasm while calming my own tired mind. My heart, however, wished he could go away so I could rest.

Realizing I was not keen to talk to him at all, Hao screamed at the top of his voice, 'Look at this, Papa! Look here!'

I shut my eyes to avoid his craving for attention, but Hao's high-pitched screaming continued to irritate my ears.

I opened my eyes again.

Hao stared at me unblinkingly. His innocent stare hinted for some words from me.

Fits of anger tried to take over my sanity. My impulse was to grab and toss out his artwork on the ground. But I did not. I was too exhausted to react in a manner that required even the littlest ounce of my energy.

I pinched the ear of the weird looking creature and brought it to my eyes. I could see many hand-drawn crooked lines and patches of colouring done in pencil lead. The creature had upside-down ogling eyes and a huge nose that made its face look funny. I let out a slight smile and looked at Hao. He was giggling away.

'Did you make this?' I asked, raising my brows.

'Yes! Mama asked me to cheer you up.'

'So, you made this?'

'I saw a funny cartoon today so I drew the cartoon for you.'

'It does look funny. Can I keep it?'

Hao's face brightened up. 'Of course! Papa.' And he skipped to the kitchen, looking for Huey, and turning his head back and smiled at me.

My heavy mind was made lighter, perhaps, not by Hao's weird-looking creature, but interestingly, by my own willingness to listen to him.

If I had chosen to let anger take over, Hao's mouth would have been shut tight. In this case, I would never be able to know Huey's thoughtfulness and Hao's tender love for me. How could I then become the father to whom my son could speak his heart?

Looking at Hao's back view, I was reminded of my own childhood. Was I probably this little when I first came to Singapore? I recalled a moment when I was playing with something in our old apartment at the shophouse. Ah Mm was in the common kitchen while Ah Beh came home from work, exhausted. I wanted to approach him, to show him a paper plane I had folded. It was a trashy plane, one that could not slice through the air at all. But I was excited, and I needed someone to share that second of thrill with me.

I called, 'Ah Beh,' and I looked at him. He tossed his soiled capri blue collared shirt on the table and took a glance at me for the briefest jiff, not even a slight smile stretched across his face. Then he turned around and walked out of the house. I did not pursue my desire to show him that plane. I jilted the plane, abandoning it on the floor quietly. I also jilted my wish to get near to Ah Beh.

Was I becoming Ah Beh for the past few days? Or even, had I always been him all these while years ever since Hao was born? Heat rushed to my face, and for a while, I felt ashamed of myself, not because I was ashamed of Ah Beh, but rather, I was ashamed of myself for making my son accumulate neglect and hurt, bit by bit, in his own life because of my actions and words.

No, I will not let Hao become me.

I wanted to become a father who loved with my actions and words. Bit by bit, I would learn. Bit by bit, I would become better.

Bit by bit, my relationship with Hao would be different.

* * *

Stony but a little nervy.

I sat at the dining table with Huey and Hao, unable to focus. I was overcome by mental and physical exhaustion.

Rice, tofu seaweed soup, sweet and sour pork cubes, and stir-fried beansprouts with silverfish. Dishes were almost different every evening.

I was enthralled by Huey's ability to think of new recipes while taking care of a young child and elderly at home. Every evening, she seemed able to prepare dinner effortlessly.

I picked a small pork cube with my chopsticks and placed it into my mouth, sweeping a big mouthful of rice afterwards. Old habit dies hard. *Rice was more filling, Kuang. Eat more rice.* Ah Mm used to remind me.

I was starving and Huey could tell. She handed another bowl of white rice to me and commented, 'You must be tired and hungry.'

I looked up. My stony expression softened.

'How're you . . . I mean . . . how's your business?' Huey pursued with concern.

Huey and I had not been talking much with each other. A lack of communication could easily turn lovers into strangers. I could feel her words stumbling upon each other as they left her lips.

'Getting better,' I answered, stuffing another pork cube into my mouth.

'That's good. Are you coping with it well?'

Questions as such triggered anxiety.

'I don't know,' I replied. The stony expression returned to my face.

Hao stuck out his tongue and was licking sauce off his spoon. 'Mama, I want more rice,' he said.

'Yes, yes, ok.' Huey stood up to scoop more rice for him, occasionally turning her head around to look at me.

Huey returned to the dining table, blinking hard, and trying to find the right words to express her concern while making sure Hao was eating his dinner. 'What do you mean, Kuang? Is there anything . . . troubling you?'

'I'm trying. Trying very hard to survive.'

'Survive?'

The accumulated stress within surged through my being. 'It's nerve wrecking at times.' I sighed in frustration.

Upon seeing Huey's concerned expression, I started to blabber in dismay.

'Managing a long queue of customers every day, multi-tasking, constantly trying to lower my expectations I've of my employees and Ing, managing my frustrations over my own clumsiness. EVERYTHING. There's so much to manage. A hawker business is so much more than just making good food.' I shook my head and shrugged. My fingers slammed onto the tabletop and sent a chopstick flying towards the dishes and dropping onto the floor.

Hao gasped.

'I know.' Huey nodded. 'How could it be easy?' Huey stood up to pick up the chopsticks. 'What do you think you need?'

'I need more helping hands. Less arguments, less conflict . . . and less doubts. Harmonious relationship with co-workers. And more trust among us.'

'How about . . . getting more help?'

'No, Huey. That won't do.' I heaved another sigh. 'I'm still jittery about this business. I guess there's no way out for the time being, except to grit my teeth and pull through. I can't possibly hire more people. That would cost a lot.'

Huey shut her eyes and nodded slightly.

Hao remained quiet upon sensing an air of helplessness at the dining table.

My frustration was gradually extinguished.

Stony yet a little nervy, I continued to push another mouthful of rice into my mouth.

Huey remained silent for a while and stood up to wash the dishes. 'There'll be a way out for sure, Kuang,' Huey affirmed me in a firm but tender tone, with her back facing me.

'I'm sure everything will be fine.'

* * *

Still in bed after opening my eyes, I stared at the ceiling, stuck in my reluctance to get ready for work.

It was 5.10 a.m.

Huey walked without a sound. I knew she kept silent so as not to wake me up. Her concern comforted me. I shut my eyes, clinging onto darkness that felt like a sanctuary.

A few minutes later, Huey tried to wake me up.

'Kuang.' She touched my forehead gently.

'I'll be up in a while,' I assured her, exhaling a mouth of stale air, and covering myself with a blanket. After a few rounds of tossing in bed, I dragged myself out with an aching stomach and cold feet.

Another day of mixed feelings. Another day of being tugged in so many directions.

I started to believe lethargy was a kind of virus. It was always in the air. And whenever I had doubts about myself, lethargy would enter me through my nose and stay in my blood, making me limp.

With my bleary eyes, I stepped out of my room. I browsed the entire kitchen, including the bathroom.

Something was amiss.

Huey was not standing by the stove boiling water and preparing breakfast this morning. *Where did she go?*

Water was long boiled and was transferred into the hot flask before I woke. The kitchen was unusually quiet. Huey's patched up apron was left hanging at the windows and the house seemed to be thoroughly cleaned up.

'Huey?' I called out softly. 'Huey, where're you?'

There was no answer.

I inched to Hao's room. He was fast asleep, lying face down on the mattress on the floor. I switched on the small flickering orange light attached to the wall and found Huey squatting next to Hao.

'What're you doing, Huey?' I whispered.

'Shhh . . . !' Huey gestured with a finger on her lips. She stood up and tiptoed towards me. 'Kuang, I'm going to the kopitiam with you today.'

'What?' I was appalled by her sudden decision. It was not too long ago when she declined my offer to set up a hawker business together.

'Yes, let me help you. I'm going to give it a try today.' Huey smiled, touching my arm with her warm hands.

'But . . . but who is going to take care of Hao?'

'Ah Ma. Ah Beh too. He had been retrenched, remember? And starting from today, he'd be home for the time being till he finds another job.'

'Have you informed them?'

'Yes, of course.' Huey nodded confidently. 'Ah Beh agreed to it straightaway.'

'Did he . . . really agree to take care of Hao while you're away?'

'Yes, Kuang. He did.' Huey nodded hard. He encouraged me to go with you.'

The image of Ah Beh looking after Hao was beyond my imagination. He was always bad-tempered and impatient, especially when he was managing children. I doubted this could continue. But at the same time, I was baffled by Ah Beh's willingness to take care of Hao in order to support me in my business. My heart jumped a skip upon hearing Ah Beh's words from Huey. I did not know words could embrace. At this moment, I was wrapped up in warmth.

I stared into the darkness of the Hao's room, observing him as silence enveloped the room. My legs just could not move.

'Let's go, Kuang. Let's not hesitate too much.' Huey grabbed my arm and started shoving me to the main door.

'Doubts are like ropes. Think about them more, and they will wrap around us tighter. Eventually, they would tie us down.'

I could not figure out where Huey derived her courage from. It seemed to well forth from her, as if it had always been burrowed deep in her being. Sometimes, Huey still seemed like a distant figure even though we had been married for years.

Yesterday, she could be as meek as a mouse. And today, she could be a totally different person who was firm in her decision. Exactly like a captain who was all ready to lead others to safety. There was no way I could measure her.

We left house for the kopitiam together.

Thirty-Seven

The light of dawn slowly seeped into the kopitiam, warming up the rows of cooled round marble tops. The morning sky gradually illuminated with a pearly glow. Faded leaves rustled in the morning breeze, falling one by one on the roadside outside the shop.

Huey and I had just finished cleaning the ducks and were braising them over the hot stove. Beads of perspiration formed on Huey's forehead. Her face turned red and was gasping quietly for more air in the small kitchen. I wondered if she could bear with such steaming hot work environment for the days to come.

'What shall I do next?' Huey asked, like a child who was ready to spring into action.

I scanned the entire kitchen and was appalled by my sudden loss of direction for my new helper. It was my first time having my wife as my worker.

'Do you want to . . . peel the eggshells?'

'Let me do it.'

I stood next to Huey, keenly observing her actions.

She had not lifted her head for a long time. Her eyes were fixated on the tasks in front of her. Sweating through her clothes, after peeling the eggshells, she went on to separate the different kinds of duck innards and placed them neatly on the tray.

'Are you doing fine, Huey? Do you need a rest?' I asked, staring at the big drop of sweat that was about to fall from her forehead.

'Not at all. Let's finish all the necessary work before the stream of customers arrives,' Huey smiled and nudged. Her exhaustion sank into her skin, and was fully concealed.

Huey's unwavering determination quelled the fluttering butterflies in my stomach. Every single day, by this time, I would have been flustered, anticipating the truckload of customers and rushing through the preparation work. But I felt different today. When burden was shared, it surprisingly became lighter.

'Kuang.' Huey finally looked up. 'I have one request.'

'Yes?'

'Let me go home by two in the afternoon. Hao is still young. I don't wish to leave him for too long. You know, Ah Beh smoked non-stop. The thought of Hao being shrouded in smoke made me feel . . . very uneasy.' I could see Huey's eyeballs shaking slightly.

A mix of weird emotions filled my heart. Huey had never told me about this before. I wanted to say yes to Huey, but in the corner of my selfish heart, I hoped Huey could stay and help out at the stall.

I had an odd feeling as I pondered which area needed my wife more. My business or my family? I could not weigh them. They were both important to me. But knowing Huey, I knew I had to release her early.

'Go ahead, Huey.' I gave her the most assuring nod after a quick moment of hesitation.

Huey's tight lips loosened into a subtle smile. Her eyes rested and returned to the slices of cucumber on the chopping board.

* * *

Customers swarmed into the kopitiam for lunch like bees scouting for their new colony.

Most of them were smartly dressed in refined office wear. Ladies paced around the kopitiam hurriedly yet gracefully in their high-heeled shoes that gave them an appealing gait.

Times had changed. Women had become different. Economy was more developing at a faster pace; quality of life had improved. Now, women were taking significant strides in the Singapore workforce and across various sectors. I saw more women dressed in office wear walking along streets everywhere. They were more involved in wage work, rather than domestic work. Even their faces looked different as compared to the past. Nowadays, many of them were painted in make-up and glowing with more personal pride.

More and more *kiang*, I would say.

Conversations among diners were no longer only about mundane daily chores, children rearing, and stories of trading. They were about ideas and strategies to move companies forward, policy initiatives, and stories of individual successes. People's minds had changed with the times.

And so was their tolerance for slowness. They admired efficiency and almost belittled the opposite.

Huey stood next to me, dressed in a soiled loose t-shirt, a pair of black tight pants, and a pair of waterproof rubber boots. Her hair gave off a weird but familiar smell. The disappearing scent of yesterday's shampoo and an overpowering savoury smell of the herbs and spices we used to braise our ducks this morning. Droplets of perspiration formed on her forehead, rolling down her ears and neck, and soaking her t-shirt. The fabric in front of her chest turned darker, outlining the shape of her bra underneath.

Unlike the patched-up apron she wore at home all the time, the one she was wearing at the stall was covered with a sheet of transparent plastic. *Why?* I questioned her this morning. And when she replied, her face glowed with pride, like those ladies in high-heeled shoes talking about their successes.

'I don't want my cloth apron to be soiled with oil, Kuang.' Huey replied, holding up the plastic sheet and scanning its smooth surface.

'Clothes soaked with oil are hard to wash. Just like yours. Plastic sheets are easier to clean. I discovered it last night. Maybe you should wear a double-layered apron like this too.'

In Huey's world, the creative process was used to humbly cope with problems in life, not pursuits of success. She was glowing over her own innovations and I could not help but marvel at her capacity to feel joy in mundanity of life.

The queue of customers continued to lengthen after an hour.

Huey helped to pack rice with slices of ducks using brown papers for those who wished to take their lunches away. And on her first day of work, this very day, harsh glances were occasionally casted upon her, scrutinizing her every move. And whenever she was slow in getting the packed lunches ready, sounds of *'tsk'* mushroomed around her, hinting the customers' unhappiness upon waiting.

Impatience gnawed at our co-workers too. As the day got busier, out of exasperation, I caught them rolling their eyes at Huey.

Huey must have had a hard day, standing and working ceaselessly from morning till noon. Her hands were trembling at the end of the day and her face turned pale.

When she could finally sit down to rest, she swallowed water in big gulps as if she had not drunk any drop of liquid for days.

She took a quick glance at the clock hanging on the wall, every now and then, to check the time. When it was finally near two o'clock, Huey approached me and asked for my permission to leave for home.

'Go ahead, Huey . . . ,' I said, swallowing the rest of my words.

Quickly, Huey untied her soiled apron and stuffed it into a plastic bag and gulped the last mouth of water. She then took off her boots clumsily, her body swinging left and right, nearly falling.

'Hmm, will you . . . come tomorrow?' I asked, hoping her first day of work had not dampened her spirit.

'Why not?' Huey pressed her eyes hard and looked at me. 'Yes, I'm coming every day. Ok Kuang, *mai da liao*. I've got to go. I need to rush home to prepare dinner and take care of Hao. See you!' And she ran off.

My mind was blown by this woman. At this instant, I finally realized what I needed most. What was lacking previously and what had Huey given me?

Hope.

Her unwavering determination in supporting her loved ones had unleashed a powerful wave of hopes in me. And most crucially, through her determined actions, I was awakened to a new profound way of thinking that could sustain me. And that was, hope was a decision. When she decided to be hopeful, she was able to carry things through.

Uncle Tham was amazing. Not only because he was a hopeful man, but because he gave people hope—those he knew, and even those he did not know. Those who had spoken with him were able to bring hope back to their lives.

Hope is perhaps the most important decision we can make. It is perhaps the most important decision we need to make. It enables us to take action to make our dreams come true. We can achieve anything as long as we have hope.

It filled my heart with endless gratitude to think of Huey, who was likened to the sun of the family, emitting gentle rays yet powerfully sustaining lives.

I also had the distinct impression that Ah Mm was watching over me somewhere in another dimension, a parallel world where lives could touch each other without any physical contact.

'See you at home later.' I replied as I stretched my neck to make sure Huey crossed the road safely before she gradually disappeared from my sight.

Thirty-Eight

It was the year 1987, two years after I set up my braised duck rice stall.

Business had been good.

Every day, a long row of customers appeared before noon outside my kopitiam. Many of them were turned into fans of my braised ducks. Without fail, they arrived at every lunchtime. Many came in groups. Some came alone but bought braised duck rice for their families or colleagues. The word of mouth continued to bring in new customers.

I could still remember my envy for Uncle Tham's special recipe for galy poks when I was young. I wished to be like him—to create a dish that only I knew how to create. I was glad I made it. I created the kind of lor ark png Ah Mm would love. Not too salty. Not too oily. I could imagine Ah Mm savouring my flavourful lor ark and beaming with satisfaction. I knew she would be so proud of me.

Little Hao was no longer that little anymore.

Recently, we got him a new school bag. I chose it. It was his favourite Doraemon. When I gave the bag to him, he hugged

me. He was excited about going to primary school. His yearning
to learn was unquenchable. Looking at him donned in his new
school uniform reminded me of my first day of school after arriving
at Singapore. I was excited, just like him. All ready to learn to read
and write.

Our house got emptier. Dak and Ang moved out and started
their own families. But at the same time, it got noisier. Huey and
I welcomed the arrival of our daughter just a few months ago. Her
name was Jing. It meant capability. Huey had stopped working and
became a stay-at-home mother all over again. In exchange, Ah Beh
insisted to help out at the stall, even though I did not agree to it. I
rejected his suggestion straightaway when he told me how he felt.
But Ah Beh being Ah Beh, his loud voice defeated me, no matter
how hard I tried to persuade him not to. Ah Ma still lived with us
and her health was good. Not having many ailments at this age was
considered a blessing.

Ah Beh was getting on in age. I hope he would not have to struggle
to earn money the way he did when he was younger. However, I
could never defeat his obstinacy. To date, Ah Beh could not give up
working. Once in a few months, he would send some money back
to China. He was not just providing for his own family in China.
Instead, he was contributing money to the construction of an elderly
care center for the province. He said, whenever my hometown in
Shantou needed my help, I would always send help, no matter what.

From the letters sent to us from Shantou, we knew my two Ah
Gou had gotten married since years ago. Now, they had their own
children to look after them. My old Ah Ma was too, in the pink of
health. She was considering to visit us one day.

Uncle Tham had retired. Once in a while, he would come to my
kopitiam to pay me a visit. His humour and laughter never changed.
Contagious and comforting. This time, I was the one who insisted
on giving him free ducks for his family. He would shake his head and
say no, no, no, and drop notes at my counter sneakily. Before he left,
he would swing a bag of pastries like chocolate brownies, egg tarts,
or cookies towards my face, just like before. Even though he had
retired, he continued to make goodies at home at a leisurely pace.

He never stopped learning.

I must say, he was such an incredible man.

* * *

Morning spread out against the sky. The changing light of the sky tinted the kopitiam with the colours of sunrise. Orange rays soaked in deep yellow hues unfolded across and landed on the marbled tops in the shop, bending their shadows on the ground.

A row of braised ducks hung neatly in front of me. Some necks bent inward, revealing the duck heads, while others bent outward. They were perfectly braised. Their dark beaded skin gave off a shiny glamour. In the glass cabinet, freshly braised eggs, duck gizzards, heads, feet, livers, and tongues, pig head skin slices, pork belly, and fried bean curds lay categorized and neat.

Next to them, a big pot of cabbage with gluten was cooking slowly, bubbling gently. Boiled braised peanuts were left to shimmer in another pot, all ready to be served. At the front of the stall, two big bowls of chili sauces were placed side by side on the counter desk where customers collected their food. I loved both the chili-lime dipping sauce and stir-fried mixture of chili, garlic, and vinegar. One simply could not exist without the other.

A round thick wooden chopping board stood in front of me in the stall. It was old. Slightly deteriorated with some chipped edges that made it look vintage. I had been using it for the past two years. Occasionally, I would stare at it, recalling the days when I just started this business and was struggling to use the cleaver. I lowered my body to smell this good old friend of mine. Thousands of braised ducks had been piled on it, staining the top with the dark oily gravy that oozed out of them. It smelled awfully sweet and savoury at the same time.

I ran my right hand along the edge of the board to feel the rough ends and placed my left palm on the board, caressing its smoothness. I sprinkled some coarse salt on top of the board, rolled up my sleeves, and scoured it with half a lemon. The sour salty paste sat on the board for five minutes before it was scraped away. I then rinsed the board with warm water and dried it thoroughly.

I then looked up, holding my face upward to feel the warm light of the morning sun. The air smelt just right and I could see many birds, hopping up and down tables and chairs, waiting to pick up scraps.

I walked out of my stall, and sat down on one of the slender wooden chairs. Upon spotting the drink stall owner scrambling into the kopitiam, I roared, 'kopi-*o-kosong!*'

'*Lai liao!*'

The drink stall owner came over and placed my kopi-o-kosong on the table. Then, he sauntered to the grey cassette radio set placed at the counter of my stall and turned it on.

The sweet voice of the Taiwanese singer, Teresa Teng, weaved into the soft rays of the morning sun as her songs played in the background. Resting my mind and my body, I took a sip of the smooth black coffee that was placed in front of me. It was refreshing, with a lingering delicate bitterness.

A busy day was about to start. I remained seated, admiring the few rows of golden bell flowers that had blossomed along the roadside. Hope too, bloomed in my heart. I was all ready to be drenched in my own sweat. I was ready for my first customer to arrive.

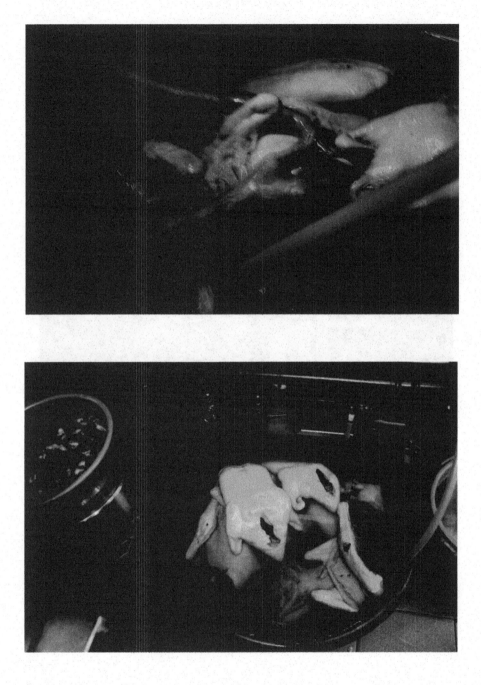

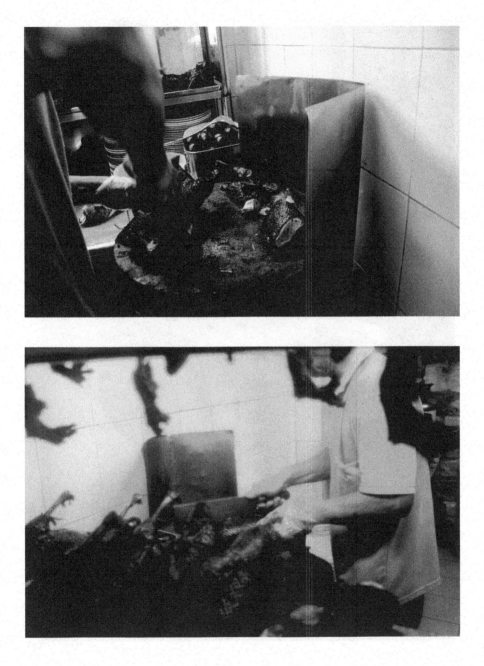

Glossary

Term	Definition
Ah Beh	father's older brother (Teochew)
Ah Chek	father's younger brother / a way to address older men (Teochew)
Ah Di	younger brother / a way to address a boy (Teochew)
Ah Gong	grandfather (Teochew)
Ah Gou	father's sister (Teochew)
Ah Hia	older brother (Teochew)
Ah Ma	grandmother (Teochew)
Ah Mm	father's older brother's wife (Teochew)
ah neh, jiak lo ke	swallow it this way (Teochew)
Ah Sim	father's younger brother's wife / a way to address older women (Teochew)
Ah So	older brother's wife (Teochew)
Ah Yi	mother's sister / a way to address stepmother (Teochew)
ai mai?	do you want it? (Teochew)

ang ku kueh	a Chinese traditional snack resembling a tortoise shell, traditionally prepared for joyous occasions such as a newborn child's first month birthday or an elderly's birthday
ang moh	a term used to refer to Caucasians in olden days Singapore It literally means red hair in Teochew and Hokkien
ang-pow	a red packet that contains money to represent good wishes
bak kut teh	pork bone soup
bak zhang	glutinous rice dumplings
bang sim	don't worry (Teochew)
bo si	not a big problem (Teochew)
bueh pai	not bad (Teochew)
bueh sai	no way (Teochew)
cai pou neng	fried egg with pickled radish
cao liu liang gia	smelly durian kid (Teochew)
charcoal-grilled satay	a Southeast Asian dish of seasoned, skewered and grilled meat, served with a sauce
char kway teow	a dish of flat rice noodles stir-fried in soy sauce and shrimp paste with whole prawns, cockles, and bean sprouts
cheng hu	government (Teochew)
cheongsam	a type of body-hugging mandarin gown
Chongyang Festival	a day for Chinese families to visit the graves of their ancestors to pay their respects
dum bai	retarded (Teochew)
diam	be silent (Malay)

de gor beh	old men who lust after women (Teochew)
di diang?	who's this? (Teochew)
di gu	national environment agency inspectors (local meaning) / an ancient Chinese name for earthquake (Hokkien)
dor mia gia	a lesser being who deserves early death (Teochew)
dua lao ya	big god (Teochew)
gaginang	my own people (Teochew)
galy poks	a deep-fried or baked, semi-circular pastry filled with curried fillings.
gam xia	thank you (Teochew)
ganggu-te	tea that is made with great skills and time, and is integrated into the everyday lives of people of all kinds of social backgrounds in Guangdong province
goreng pisang	fried banana fritters, a common dish across Southeast Asia and the Indian subcontinent
Guan Di Gong	a Chinese military general serving under the warlord Liu Bei during the late Eastern Han Dynasty of China who also turned into a deity worshipped in Chinese folk religion
hokkien mee	a dish of thick yellow noodles braised in thick dark soy sauce with pork, squid, fish cake and cabbage as the main ingredients and cubes of pork fat fried until crispy
ho ziah bo?	is it delicious? (Teochew)
ice kachang	a thirst-quenching concoction made of shaved ice, red beans, jelly (usually grass jelly or agar agar), and sweet syrup

jiak cao	eat grass (Teochew), which also means being poor
jialat	terrible / strength-draining (Teochew)
jin ho ziah	very delicious (Teochew)
jin kiang	very capable (Teochew)
jin mua huang	very troublesome (Teochew)
jin suay	very unlucky (Teochew)
jin ngia	very pretty (Teochew)
jin ziang	really look alike (Teochew)
kachang puteh	a delicious Indian snack that consists of an assorted mix of nuts.
ka chng dua, ho	good to have a big buttock (Teochew)
kah na cai	stir-fried Hongkong olive vegetable
kampong	village (Malay)
kay-poh	being a busybody, prying into the business of others (local meaning)
ki lai	wake up (Teochew)
kopi	black coffee with condensed milk, which is a thick and sweetened milk (local meaning)
kopitiam	a traditional breakfast and coffee shop found in Southeast Asia
ku chye kueh	Teochew chive dumplings
kueh	bite-sized snack or dessert foods commonly found in Southeast Asia and China
kuli	low-wage labourer
kwey teow	flat rice noodles
lai liao	I'm coming (local meaning)
lao gung	doctor (Teochew)
loh kai yik	braised chicken wings (Cantonese)

lok mei	skewers threaded with cooked food (Cantonese)
lor ark png	soy braised duck rice (Teochew)
lor sor	naggy (Teochew)
ma da	police (Malay)
mai da liao	don't say anything else (Teochew)
mai geh kiang	don't pretend to be more capable than you really are (Teochew)
mai kao	don't cry (Teochew)
mai keh ki	you're welcome (Teochew)
mai sng	don't joke / don't play (Teochew)
meh	fast (Teochew)
mue	plain porridge
murukku	a savoury, crunchy snack originating from the Indian subcontinent
paiseh	expressing a sense of shame (Hokkien)
pa niao tze	hitting rats (Teochew)
parangs	a machete used across the Malay Archipelago
png kueh	a peach-shaped savoury dumpling which contains glutinous rice, peanuts, mushrooms and dried shrimps
puay ko	street storytelling (Teochew)
pwa beh gia	sickly lesser being (Teochew)
Qingming Festival	a traditional Chinese festival—tomb sweeping day
siao	crazy (Hokkien)
si bo	is it (Teochew)
sinseh	a traditional Chinese doctor
si nya peh	death to your father (Teochew)
si nya bu	death to your mother (Teochew)

si zha bo	cursed woman (Teochew)
soon kueh	a Teochew steamed dumpling stuffed with bamboo shoots, jicama and dried shrimps
teh	tea (Teochew/local meaning)
Teochew-hee	street opera
tio bo	am I right? (Teochew)
toih	look (Teochew)
tok-tok mee	homemade noodles sold by hawkers who would attract customers by hitting a bamboo striker against a piece of split bamboo
Tor Ti Gong	Lord of the Soil and Ground / a tutelary deity in Chinese folk religion and Taoism
towkay	a business owner / boss
tze char	an economical food stall which provides a wide selection of common and affordable dishes which approximate home-cooked meals (Hokkien)
wa bo lui	I don't have money (Teochew)
yau siu gia	short life lesser being (Teochew)
youtiao	Chinese fried dough fritters
zao	run (Teochew)
zha bo peng you	girlfriend (Teochew)
zha si zha ho	the earlier you die, the better it is (Teochew)
欢迎	welcome (Mandarin Chinese)
丽的呼声	Rediffusion (Mandarin Chinese)
仙女下凡	celestial princess descending from heavens (Mandarin Chinese)

Acknowledgements

Foremost, my deepest gratitude to my parents for sharing their experiences with me unreservedly. Thank you, Papa and Mama, for your love and patience all these years, and allowing me to read to my heart's content at the library when I was a child. Papa, thank you for filling my heart with wonderful stories when I was growing up. And, Mama, thank you for all the Roald Dahl's books you once bought for me. They inspired and nourished me so much. And thank you, Roald Dahl, for your amazing inventions.

To women of the older generation who once shared their stories with me, your stories matter, and I am so touched to be able to represent you in my novel.

To my sister, Mei, for always believing in me. Thank you for freezing moments of Papa doing background work at his stall. I am always impressed by your eye for beauty. It is through your eyes that I see Papa's sweat come to life. I am sure your pictures will connect readers to the past and allow them to see the hawker culture from a different perspective.

To my beloved husband, who loves me and the family deeply. Your warmth and care have enriched my entire being. You're my best buddy, my cheerleader, my partner in life who has always regarded me as an equal. Thank you for your wisdom and bigheartedness.

To my two lovely boys, for teaching me about life—always live in the moment and be curious about learning. Life is indeed an exciting journey. May the both of you live life as earnestly as always.

To Jane, who always helps me with my children. Thank you for your kindness and dedication.

To Kor, Huang Ying, Jie, Roger, and Maurice, for showing me what a family means. Thank you for being my tribe.

To my husband's family, for showering me with so much love and care as always.

To Renna, whose friendship I can't live without. Because of you, my happiness is always doubled, sorrow is always halved, and my life, immeasurably enriched.

To Tammie, Karen, and Christina, for always listening to my stories and being my best sisters.

To my SGI family in Houston, for all the wonderful memories and warmth. I miss all of you.

To Jin Haw and all my wonderful SA sisters for your encouraging words, and never-ending belief in the potential of youth.

To all my ex-colleagues in school and students whom I once taught, I had all of you in mind when I wrote this novel.

I would also like to thank my primary school teachers who once gave me stickers for my compositions and my amazing professors at Rice University, Dr Matthias Henze, Dr David J. Schneider, and Dr Joseph Campana for broadening my world view and allowing me to believe in the beauty of my own voice, thoughts, and words. Thank you, Dr Newell D. Boyd, for guiding me to see history from a different angle. And thank you Rebecca for such a wonderful programme.

And to Nora Nazerene at Penguin Random House SEA, thank you for having faith in me and this book. To my editor, Amberdawn Manaois, for knowing and appreciating all the characters in my novel more than I do and allowing me to understand narratives at a deeper level. To Ishani Bhattacharya, Bhumika Popli, and the wonderful team at Penguin Random House who have helped make this book possible, thank you for all your support and ideas.

Thank you, Hanako Muraoka, for your unwavering dedication to translating great works of literature as well as advancing girls' educational opportunities in pre- and post-war Japan through writing more publications for the young people. I am deeply touched by your life.

Lastly, I would like to thank my mentor and my Buddhist practice. For without them, this book will not be possible.